8TH DAY

A Cassidy James Mystery

KATE
CALLOWAY

Ferndale, Michigan
2001

Bella Books, Inc.
P.O. Box 201007
Ferndale, MI 48220

Printed in the United States of America on acid-free paper.
First Edition

Editor: J. M. Redmann
Cover designer: Bonnie Liss (Phoenix Graphics)

ISBN 1-931513-04-X

For Carol, of course.

Acknowledgments

A heartfelt thanks to my friends (again!) for taking the time to read and critique a work in progress: Murrell, Linda, Carolyn, Deva, and especially Carol who keeps me honest! Thanks, too, to Jean Redmann and Kelly Smith for their input and encouragement, and to all my friends and family for their continued support.

Prologue — Madeline

On the night of April 1st, Maddie Boone was in her bed, almost asleep, when the door to her room opened a crack, admitting a thin sliver of yellow light that pierced the darkness. Her body stiffened and she held her breath, wondering if this time she'd have the courage to scream loud enough to bring someone to her rescue. Or maybe this would be one of the times the shaft of light would disappear again, the door would quietly click shut, and the footsteps would fade down the hallway, leaving her to struggle alone with her incessant nightmares. Her eyes were wide in the blackness, the only sound, the awful banging of her heart against her bony chest as she strained in the darkness to hear.

Suddenly, the door creaked open wider and a shadow filled

the doorway. It was not the shadow she'd expected. This time, there were two of them, and her heart hammered. Suddenly the room was ablaze with light.

"Don't be frightened, Madeline," one of the men said. He was huge, with those body-builder muscles bulging out of his white tee shirt. He wore a baseball cap and his blue eyes seemed to be laughing at her. She opened her mouth and screamed at the top of her lungs. It was a blood-curdling scream, deafening to her own ears, and instantly made her throat raw.

The other man stepped forward and sat down on the edge of the bed, gently putting his hand across her mouth. "Shhh," he said. "We're not here to hurt you. Your parents and grandparents are in the next room. They asked us to come here, okay? We're not the bad guys. We're the good guys. If you promise not to scream again, I'll take my hand away. Okay?"

Maddie nodded, eyes huge with terror.

"Promise?" He was as big as the first man, but softer as if his muscles had leisurely turned to pudge. His brown eyes seemed warm, but she knew from experience that eyes could lie. She nodded again, wishing she could sink her teeth into his stinking hand. He smelled like WD-40. He gently removed his hand and Maddie screamed again for all she was worth.

This time, it was the muscleman who stepped forward. His hand against her mouth was hard and mean.

"Big Ben here is real gentle with kids, Maddie. He's not gonna hurt you. That's not what he does. I don't want to do that either. You know why we're here, right? You've been screwing up lately. You've been stealing. Your grades have gone down. You don't listen to your grandparents. You're disrespectful to your father. Your mother had to get stitches after you assaulted her. You had to know this was coming, right?" He took his hand away so she could respond.

"She's not my mother and I just threw one of her stinking ashtrays. I didn't know it would cut her. Anyway, she was being mean!" Her words sounded tough, but she knew her voice was giving her away. It had that trembly, crybaby sound that threatened to break into sobs at any moment.

"Well, we're going to talk about all that a little later. Right now, we're going to take you to camp. Camp Turnaround. Your dad talked to you about this, right?"

Now she was terrified. He'd threatened to send her to reform school if she didn't shape up, but she'd never dreamed he'd actually do it. And now here they were in the middle of the night to take her away! This couldn't be happening. This was kidnapping!

"He never said anything like this!" she protested in a voice that sounded small and whiny to her. "Let me talk to him! Dad! Daddy!" Her cries were muffled by the muscle- man's hand once again.

"Shhh. He's not going to help you, Madeline. He's the one who asked us to come."

The realization that this could be true sank through her like molten lava and she felt her limbs grow heavy and useless. Seeming to sense the change, the big man removed his hand and this time Maddie didn't bother screaming.

"Why doesn't he just take me himself?" she asked, her voice barely audible.

"You're a runaway risk, for one thing. If your parents brought you up in their car, chances are, the first time they stopped for gas, you'd take off. Right?" This was the muscleman talking. Gentle Ben was taking a pair of handcuffs out of his briefcase.

"I would not!" she said, knowing that, in fact, that's exactly what she would do. "I want my dad. He wouldn't do this. You're lying!" But the doubt that had begun to seep in now took hold and her voice lacked conviction. If they hadn't planned this, why hadn't they come to her rescue?

Gentle Ben came up beside her and pulled one of her skinny wrists forward, snapping the cuff around it snugly.

"You can't do this!" she pleaded. "Daddy! Help! Please!

Don't let them hurt me!" But her words fell on deaf ears and in a moment of profound clarity she understood that this was as it always had been. Her daddy hadn't saved her before and he wasn't going to this time. With a sigh sounding far more grown up than it should have, she held out her other hand and let the big oaf cuff it.

As they led her out of the house, they passed her grandparents' room and she saw the telltale inch of light beneath the door. They were hiding in there! All four of them. She heard a muffled voice and then the unmistakable tone of her stepmother. "We agreed to this, Daniel. Now let her go." The ensuing silence told her all she needed to know.

Chapter One

A subtle shift in the wind altered the cadence of the rain against the window and I found myself suddenly awake, listening. Both cats were snugly burrowed beside me, oblivious to anything wrong in the night. So why did I feel uneasy? Maybe it was the dream. I'd had it before. The same dark, suffocating tunnel, the same feeling of doom that swept over me, causing panic to swell in my throat. This made the third time I'd had the dream. But what did it mean?

I punched my pillow a few times and settled back down, trying to ease my fears. And then it struck me. That's what it was! I was afraid! I sat up in bed and stared out at the black, moonless night, puzzling over the unaccustomed feeling. What was I suddenly afraid of? I closed my eyes, trying to rekindle the now murky images. Something was making the hairs on the back of my neck stand up, even now in the safety of my own bed. But the harder I tried, the more elusive the dream became.

I was about to give up. In fact, I lay back down and was nearly drifting off to sleep again when it came to me. The dream was about my own death. I was trapped somewhere in a dark, odious tunnel, and I was going to die.

I had known fear before. I'd been shot at and attacked, had scaled cliffs and raced down white water rapids, and through all of it, I had known some degree of fear. But the fear had always been overshadowed by a sense of duty, an urgent need, and sometimes, an exhilaration I couldn't quite explain. This time, the fear was nothing more than pure, naked dread.

I checked the clock. Four-thirty. Time for the night critters to start scurrying back into the woods. Soon the kingfishers and fat-bellied robins would be sounding the start of a new day. Even in the pouring rain, they never slept in. I stared across the blackened room at the rain-streaked window. I'd left the blinds up, as I often did, so that I could gaze out at the starry blanket of sky that hovered above the moonlit lake each night. But the pre-dawn sky was as black as obsidian. There would be no sun peeking through these clouds come morning. We were in for a long, wet day. I settled back against the pillow, still feeling uneasy, and stifled a yawn.

Then I heard a noise that had nothing to do with the wind and rain. This time I knew a board had creaked out on the front deck. It wasn't the wind. And it wasn't the skittering footfall of a raccoon or opossum. I sat up, then stealthily slipped out of bed and pulled on a pair of sweats. My cat, Panic, was awake now, her ears pointed toward the window, her yellow-green eyes wide in the dark. I moved across the bedroom to the closet, slid my hand inside the purse that hung from a hook on the wall, and pulled out my Colt .45.

Silently, I tiptoed down the hallway toward the front of the house, wishing for once that I had bothered to close the blinds. Almost every wall in the house was glass — either floor-to-ceiling windows or sliding glass doors. Easy to see out, equally easy to see in.

My back edging the wall, I moved into the entryway, my bare feet cold on the slate floor. Suddenly, I stood stock-still. I could hear someone on the other side of the sliding glass door, not two feet from where I stood.

I nudged Panic away with my foot, pulled back the hammer on my gun, and hit both outside light switches as I stepped in front of the sliding door, the gun pointed straight ahead. The hulking form on my porch had already started to turn away, but now froze in the sudden blaze of light. Slowly two hands rose in the air. No gun. At least not that I could see. I opened the sliding glass door a crack and stuck the barrel through it.

"Nice and slow. Turn around." My voice sounded much calmer than I felt and my gunhand was steady, but inside I was trembling.

"Easy. It's me, Cass. Grace Apodaca." The tall dark form did a slow turn, and I was suddenly staring into the dark, steady eyes of a six-foot tall, full-blooded Native American.

"Gracie?" I lowered the gun and shoved the glass door open. "What in the hell are you doing?"

"I'm sorry. I didn't think I'd wake you. We were going to wait on the dock until you got up. But it started really coming down and we thought we could wait it out under the eaves." She bent over and retrieved the paper that had fallen to the ground when I opened the door.

She'd said "we." I peered past the pool of light on the porch and saw nothing.

"My cousin Connie's with me." No sooner had she said it, than a wiry, dark-skinned woman draped in a yellow slicker appeared. She was shivering, and her jet-black eyes reminded me of a wounded animal's.

"Come in," I said. "Leave your coats and boots in the entryway."

I turned off the outside lights, switched on a couple of lamps in the living room, and began stacking kindling in the fireplace. Of all the people to show up on my front porch, I thought — Gracie-the-Wonder-Butch. Stifling a chuckle, I remembered our brief but thoroughly enjoyable adventure some time ago. We'd saved each other's asses. And we'd revealed secrets to each other that we hadn't shared with our own best friends. I'd always meant to keep in touch — she'd been someone I instinctively liked — but time had passed and somehow it hadn't happened. Now, out of the blue, here she was. By the time they'd shrugged out of their wet jackets and footwear, I had a decent blaze going and they both came to stand in front of the mantle.

"I'm really sorry to intrude on you like this, Cass. We didn't know what else to do." A striking woman, Gracie was tall and raw-boned with rippling biceps, long, muscled legs, short-cropped, jet-black hair going gray, and beautiful tawny skin that showed off her heritage. I knew she had a blackbelt in karate, was a trained Emergency Medical Technician, and had spent her youth fighting fires. She still had the body of an Amazon, though these days she spent her time working with hospice patients, doing something with holistic medicine. Her cousin was shorter and slighter, but there were plenty of similarities between them. They both had the same high cheek bones and classic Indian brow. They had smooth, flawless skin that models would kill for. Even their stance was similar. Standing in their stocking feet, they looked perfectly calm before the fire, though the cousin's clenched fists gave her away.

"You are still in the private investigation business? I mean, you're still for hire?" Gracie asked.

"I had a feeling this wasn't a social visit." I smiled to ease her cousin's obvious discomfort. "Tell you what. I'll make some coffee, then you can tell me what's on your mind, and we'll go from there." I moved into the kitchen and got the coffee going.

My living space is one great big open area divided more by change in flooring and furniture than walls. From the kitchen, I could see Grace inspecting my belongings in the living room while her cousin moved to the couch and pulled a knitted afghan onto her lap. Panic's sister, Gammon, who'd finally roused herself, came waddling out of the bedroom into the kitchen, rubbed against my ankle, sauntered into the living room to sniff Gracie's socks, then leaped onto the afghan and curled herself into Connie's lap. If Gammon liked her, I thought, the cousin couldn't be too bad. I had learned to trust a cat's instincts as much as my own.

"We didn't mean to get you out of bed," Connie said, stroking Gammon's luxurious back. I could hear the purring as I brought in the coffee.

"It's okay," I assured her. "Actually, I was already awake. Weird dream." I handed them their cups, then went back for my own. "So, what's up?"

Connie sighed. "It's hard to know where to start."

"We think Connie's daughter may be in danger," Gracie stated.

"What kind of danger?" I asked.

"You ever hear of a place called Camp Turnaround?" Gracie asked. "It's in Clackamas County, south of Portland. The nearest town is this dinky place called Portsmith Grove."

I shook my head.

"It's like a reform school. Supposed to get troubled youth back on track. They've got a good reputation. About eighty percent of the kids that graduate from the camp end up graduating high school. Most of these kids are real bad-asses — stoners, gang-bangers, juvenile delinquents."

Connie interrupted. "Not all of them. Some are low-achievers. Kids with low self-esteem. Some have been abused or abandoned."

"Yeah," Gracie said. "But mostly, the place handles bad-asses."

"And your daughter is there?" I asked, facing Connie.

"Yes." It was a simple statement, fraught with emotion. Anger, shame and guilt boiled beneath the surface of her dark eyes.

"You better start at the beginning," Gracie said, coming over to sit beside her cousin. She patted the younger woman's knee and winked. "Might as well start with the prison part, get it out of the way, eh?"

Connie nodded, took a sip of her coffee, and let out a long sigh. "Nine years ago I was sentenced to twenty-five years to life in the state penitentiary."

She'd said it so matter-of-factly, it took me a moment to notice that her eyes were threatening to spill over.

Gracie cut in. "It was a car accident. She was charged with vehicular manslaughter, which got upgraded to second degree murder with malice. Tell her what happened, Connie. Better start with that assbite you married."

Connie nodded and managed a small but bitter smile. "Fourteen years ago, I married a man named Daniel Boone. Honest. That's really his name. His father's, too. Anyway, my family warned me about marrying a white boy, but I didn't care. Daniel was every girl's dream, and he charmed the pants off of me. Literally." She allowed herself another small, sad smile.

"We'd barely been married a month when I got pregnant, and right away, things began to change. Daniel got a job as a truck driver and started staying away for long stretches. I knew he was cheating on me. He didn't even deny it. When Maddie was born, I thought he'd settle down, but if anything, he was gone even more. After awhile, I didn't care. It was nice and peaceful with him gone. And I had a beautiful daughter to raise. Who needed a husband?"

She took a sip of coffee and settled back against the sofa, seeming almost relieved to be talking about it.

"Tell her about that night," Gracie prompted.

"When Maddie was four, I enrolled her in preschool and got a part-time job as a groundskeeper for the local college. It was a great job because I got to work outside and meet people. With Daniel gone so much, we had almost no social life. Anyway, one night I was invited to a party and though I could hardly afford it, I left Maddie with a babysitter and went. I'd give anything to change that decision, to take back that whole night and just spend the evening at home with my little girl." She put down her mug and wiped at a tear that had started to slide down her cheek. I could tell the show of emotion angered her. She wanted to be tough, but she wasn't quite pulling it off.

"I had a couple of drinks at the party, nothing major, and I also took a few hits off of a joint. I wasn't a big partier, but it was a nice relaxed evening and I was really enjoying being with my new friends. Just that little bit of pot gave me the munchies, so when someone offered me a brownie, even though I was getting ready to leave, I wolfed it down. I had no idea that they were hash brownies. I'd never even heard of such a thing.

"The hash didn't hit me right away. In fact, I felt perfectly sober as I backed out of the driveway. It was about a twenty-minute drive back to my house, part of it on a windy mountain road. About halfway there, I saw a white convertible coming toward me. It's amazing how, in just a few seconds, I could see so much so clearly. The top was down and I could see four kids inside, all four of them with this blond hair blowing in the wind like they were on top of the world. I remember thinking that someday I'd like to have a sports car like that. I saw the driver lean over and kiss the girl in the front passenger's seat, and when he did, their car swerved into my lane.

"I laid on the horn and yanked the wheel to the right, but it was too late. My pickup fishtailed and the rear of the truck slammed into their car. I saw the car go straight up in the air like something in a cartoon, flipping over once as it sailed off the side of the mountain.

"By the time I managed to stop the truck and get out, the convertible was nowhere in sight. I didn't seem to be hurt, but I was shaken up pretty bad and could barely walk. I didn't know about the hash brownie. I thought I was probably in shock. I decided the best thing to do was drive to the closest phone and call for help. I got in my truck and went looking for a phone. Next thing I knew, I saw the police car behind me.

"Those four kids died in the crash that night. The girls were cheerleaders at the local high school. The driver was a big football star. I was an Indian with illegal drugs in her system. The prosecutor accused me of hit-and-run, and no one believed that I was looking for a phone or that I didn't know about the hash. Like Gracie said, vehicular manslaughter turned into second degree murder, and because I'd left the scene, they added on the charge of malice, which meant they could give me a life sentence."

Gracie unclenched her fists and stood up, taking over the story.

"Even that asshole husband of hers didn't believe her. No one went to bat for her. The people at the party stayed mum, probably afraid they'd be charged as accessories to murder. The locals would have lynched her if they could. The judge threw the book at her."

"The worst part," Connie said, "was losing Maddie. Daniel's parents petitioned the court for legal custody and were granted it. What could I do? Even if I got out in twenty-five years, my daughter would be almost thirty years old. It almost killed me to admit it, but I knew it was better all around if she just thought I was dead. Better that, than thinking her mother was a murderer and having to visit me in prison." Finally, Connie allowed herself to cry. Her fists were bunched at her cheeks as if to will the tears back where they came from, but the tears won out. I got up and brought her a box of Kleenex.

"So your daughter thinks you're dead?" I asked.

She made a sound that might have been a laugh, except I knew better. "They just told her that her mommy went away." She blew her nose and looked up, her dark eyes glistening with emotion. "Pretty soon, she quit asking, I guess."

"And then you were released early."

"A couple of things happened. In prison, I had a lot of time to read and I educated myself about the law. The court-appointed attorney they'd given me had screwed me over royally. I wrote letters to everyone I could think of, and finally someone responded. The next thing I know, I've got a real attorney working for me, pro bono. He did what the investigating officers and the first attorney should have done. The skid marks the officers had taken pictures of clearly showed that the convertible was on my side of the road. Then he tracked down people who'd been at the party and got their statements regarding the hash brownies. They admitted that I'd eaten one right before I left and that no one had told me what was in them. It turns out, it takes quite a while for drugs ingested orally to get into your system. After timing the drive from the house I'd left to the scene of the accident, they determined that the accident had probably occurred before the hash had even taken effect. Then they retraced the route I'd taken after the crash and determined that, had the cop not stopped me, I'd have reached the first pay phone along the way in less than a mile. I got a new trial with a new judge, who reduced the charge to vehicular manslaughter and reduced the sentence to time served. Just like that, I was free to go.

"It was like being given a second life. There are so many

things I want to do — go back to school, get a job where I can work outside everyday, breathing in the sunshine and fresh air. But mostly, more than anything else in the world, I want to get to know my daughter."

I sat back, regarding Connie with new respect. She'd survived an injustice. And now she wanted to take back what was hers. But things didn't always work out that neatly.

"How do your husband and his parents feel about that?"

"It's funny," she said. "I was so afraid that they'd resent my return, I put off calling until I could get myself squared away. I wanted to get a job and a place to live first. Daniel got remarried a few years ago, and, according to one of the few friends who kept in touch with me, he and his wife and Maddie were living with his parents in Portland. My friend thought the new wife wasn't too excited about motherhood and that she and Daniel were gone most of the time, which gave me some hope. If they didn't want her, maybe I could get her back. But, as much as I wanted her, I didn't want to do anything that would screw up Maddie's life. If she was settled and happy, I promised myself I wouldn't mess that up.

"But getting a job isn't easy when you're an ex-con. The best I've been able to do is hire myself out as a gardener. I'm renting a studio apartment I can barely afford. I realized that if I waited until I was financially stable, Maddie might be all grown up. When I finally got up the nerve to call, Daniel told me what was going on."

"Which was what?" I prompted, downing the remains of my coffee.

"He told me that Maddie had started acting out a couple of years ago. She was stealing stuff she didn't need from stores, beating kids up at school, that kind of stuff. Her grades, which had always been top notch, went in the tank. She started talking back to her grandparents, actually defying them, throwing stuff, causing scenes in public. He thought maybe she'd settle down once he married Suzette, but things just got worse. A couple of months ago, she actually threw an ashtray at Suzette, cutting her above the eye so bad she needed stitches. That was the final straw. They decided to send her to a reform school."

I got up to refill our mugs as she continued.

"I guess Daniel did some research and decided that Camp Turnaround was the best of the lot. Not only was it the cheapest of those he found acceptable, but he liked the idea of a working ranch. Plus, it's fairly close by. Some of these places are out in Utah and Colorado. This one's only a few hours away from where they live. Not that they're allowed to visit."

"What?" I asked, handing her a steaming mug. "What kind of school doesn't let the parents visit?"

"I guess the kind you pay for six months in advance," Connie said, finally cracking a genuine smile. "Actually, it made sense when Daniel explained it. The kids all want to leave at first. They're supposed to hate it. But they have to earn the right for visitations. In fact, everything they do either earns them points or takes them away. Reward and punishment. The hope is that pretty soon the kids will actually want to see the parents that they couldn't stand before."

"Okay," I said. "So Daniel sent Madeline to this Camp Turnaround. What makes you think she's in trouble?"

"After Daniel told me about the camp, I asked if I could come see him, at least see some pictures of Madeline. He was against the idea at first, but after a while, he gave in. He said it couldn't do any harm, since Maddie wouldn't even be there. So, I drove up to Portland." She took a deep breath. "Talk about awkward! His new wife is looking at me like I'm a leper, Daniel's folks won't look me in the eye, and Daniel's so nervous he's about to pee his pants. Finally, I just asked Daniel's mother if she would show me Maddie's room and she led me up the stairs.

"Oh, God, I was so proud to see how beautiful my baby had become. She looks just like Gracie did as a kid! So strong and healthy. And smart as a whip, too. Her grandmother showed me report cards and certificates of merit. She won the spelling contest two years in a row." She beamed, a mother's pride undeniable, though her grief at having missed all these events was evident.

"But that all seemed to end around the fifth grade. Her last report cards were awful. So were some of the drawings in her notebook. I'm no shrink, but Maddie's definitely troubled. You can tell that by the letters. It breaks my heart to think about it." Her eyes threatened to well up again.

"What letters?" I asked.

"From the camp. They let the kids use e-mail. Her first letter was just like they told Daniel to expect. Daniel's wife let me make copies. Here." She dug a rubber-banded stack of folded sheets from her purse and handed me the top one.

> *Dad. If you care about me at all, get me out of here! This place is a prison! I thought the gestapo was outlawed! I hope you're not paying for this torture. Please, please, please! I promise to be nice again. I'll try! Love, Maddie*

"She's thirteen?"

Connie nodded. "It tore Daniel up. He called the place and demanded a visit. The woman in charge said he shouldn't worry — that all the kids' letters sounded like that the first few months. Said a visit at that point would only undo all the good that had been accomplished. She reminded him that he'd signed an agreement and that the rules were clearly stated. No visits the first six months, and then only if earned by the student. Inmate is more like it. He said the only thing that kept him from driving up there and kidnapping her was the calls from the shrink."

"Madeline sees a therapist there?"

"He calls once a week. According to him, Maddie is progressing nicely."

"What's his name?" I asked. I hadn't agreed to take the case, whatever the case actually was, but I'd started taking notes out of habit.

"Dr. Biscane. Daniel thinks he really cares about Maddie. He's the only real contact Daniel has with the camp."

"Show her the other letters," Gracie prompted.

Connie sighed and handed me another folded page.

Dear Dad, What? Did you think that by sending me here I'd suddenly turn into a girl scout? What a laugh! If you want to know the truth, I hate this. But then I hate just about everything. You probably don't know that though. What do you know? You spend all your time with Suzette. The whole world could burn down, for all you'd care. So don't worry about me. If you even still remember who I am. Maddie.

"Sounds like a good thing the kid's seeing a shrink up there," I said.

"Wait till you see the next one. Show her, Connie."

Connie handed me the last printout.

Dear Dad, Things are not so bad but it's still cold. I have no CLUE when summer will finally arrive. I did something dumb yesterday and tried to run away. It was a stupid thing to do but it made me realize how lucky I am to have a roof over my head. THEY work me hard but I'm learning quite a bit. I hate to admit it, but sometimes this place isn't quite so bad. Say hi to DREMUR for me. I really MISS him. I hope he's being a good dog. Tell my SISter to put my room back the way I left it because I'll be home SON! Your daughter, Maddie. p.s., when I'm out of here, I'd really like to go to the GRANDE canyon!

"Hmm," I said. "She runs away one day and the next day everything is suddenly rosy?"

"That's not the half of it," Gracie said. "First of all, Maddie doesn't have a dog named Dremur. She never had a dog in her life. Second, she doesn't have a sister. "

"Oh," I said.

"Exactly," Gracie said.

"And Maddie won the spelling contest two years in a row," Connie reminded me. "No way she'd misspell 'Grand Canyon,' let alone soon. She's obviously trying to tell us something." She looked at Gracie, then me, daring us to challenge her on this. Her black eyes were fierce.

"What's Daniel think?"

"He said Maddie's always had a vivid imagination and that she's probably pretending to have a dog and sister to impress someone at the camp. The shrink told Daniel that at first some of the kids invent fantasies about their lives back home and that it's nothing to worry about. I couldn't believe they were willing to just let it go that easily. That's why I asked for copies. It took me a while to figure it out but I finally got it. See the words she wrote in all caps? She didn't do that in the other letters. If you just take the capitalized words by themselves, she's sending us a message."

I noticed Connie had begun thinking of the letters as addressed to her, but didn't point this out. I read the capitalized words aloud. CLUE THEY DREMUR MISS SIS SON GRANDE. I read it again. "This make sense to you?" I asked.

"Not at first," Gracie said. "But play with the letters a little, Cass. What do you call it when someone rearranges the letters to make a different word?"

"An anagram?"

"Right. I think DREMUR's supposed to be an anagram for MURDER."

"They MURDER MISS SIS SON GRANDE!?"

"Miss Sisson. She's one of the teachers. And I think GRANDE is an anagram for danger. Connie, show her the brochure."

Connie handed me a tri-folded pamphlet featuring wholesome looking teens riding horseback with a beautiful forest as backdrop. Inside, the main features of the camp were highlighted, punctuated by a few candid snapshots of staff and students. I scanned the photos. In one, a robust blonde in her thirties stood by a computer while a student worked the keyboard. The caption read, "Miss Sisson, one of our highly-trained staff, gives one-on-one instruction in the classroom. 80% of Camp Turnaround graduates go on to graduate high school."

I refolded the brochure and sat back in the swivel chair.

"What makes you think Madeline isn't just yanking her father's chain?" I asked.

"That's what I said at first," Gracie said. "But what if she isn't?"

"I called the camp," Connie said. "Pretended to be an old friend looking up Miss Sisson. They told me she's no longer an employee. I asked when she'd left, and they said she had some sort of family emergency a week ago, and that they weren't sure if she'd be back. The lady asked me for my name so she could give Miss Sisson the message if she did return, and I made one up."

"And Daniel isn't concerned about a possible hidden message?"

"First off, he thinks I'm seeing things that aren't there. He says now he knows where Maddie gets her imagination. Plus, he thinks the place is working miracles. Not just him, but his parents and new wife, too. They couldn't be more thrilled with Maddie's progress. Even if it didn't mean losing all that money, I'd never be able to convince Daniel to take Maddie out of there. And I don't really have a say in it. I gave up my right to Maddie when I signed the custody papers." She sighed and her voice wavered. "I never would've done it if I'd known I was going to get out."

"I'd like to help, but I'm not sure what you want me to do," I said at last. This was met with utter silence. Gracie raised an eyebrow.

"What?" I asked.

"You used to be a teacher," she said.

"Uh, huh?"

She grinned. It was that conspiratorial look I remembered, the one that made you feel like a complete whimp if you weren't up to the challenge.

"They're looking for a sub for Miss Sisson."

"And how would you know that?" I asked.

"Because I drove out there yesterday," she said, grinning. "You're looking at the new stable-hand."

"Stable-hand?"

"They breed and raise horses. After Connie left Daniel's, she came to see me and showed me Maddie's letters. I checked the place out on the internet. It just so happens they post an employment page listing the various openings, and one of them was for a stable-hand during the spring foaling. I drove up to see if there was any way to get a feel for the place. I figured, a few days on the inside, I could see for myself what was going on. I didn't really expect to get hired, but apparently, there aren't that many people anxious to move all the way out into the boonies for mediocre pay. Anyway, I start tomorrow and figured two heads might be better than one. With me working the stables and you in the camp, together we ought to find out if anything funny's going on."

"So you want me to try and get a job at this camp? As a teacher?"

"There is an opening. They've got it posted on the employment page, complete with application. Boot up your computer and I'll show you." Gracie looked as stoic as any Native American I'd ever seen in a western. Strong, penetrating eyes, firm line separating lips, slight crease between the brows. Even though I sensed she could do this look for effect, it was nonetheless daunting.

"I just want to make sure my daughter's okay," Connie cut in. "After thinking I'd never lay eyes on her again, and then coming so close, only to find out she's locked away in some camp, and now to think that there might be some danger there, it's more than I can take!"

I sipped cool coffee and thought about it. "Just because Miss Sisson left doesn't mean necessarily Maddie's in danger. But I guess it couldn't hurt to make sure. If everything checks out okay, you plan to leave her there?"

"I have no choice, I guess. Daniel seems to think it's doing her some good. Maybe the shrink there can get to the bottom of her problems. I just want her to be happy."

"Tell you what," Gracie said, winking at her cousin. "If it turns out she's just playing a prank, I'll kick her little butt from that camp to China and back. It's high time she got to know her Aunt Gracie anyway."

"You sure she won't recognize you?" I asked.

Gracie frowned. "I was up in Canada from the time she was born right through Connie's accident. When Connie got sent up, I tried to see the kid, but Daniel thought my resemblance to Connie might confuse her and make things worse. I'm ashamed to admit it, but she wouldn't know me from Adam."

"You realize that there's a possibility they may not hire me," I said.

"I kinda doubt people are beating down the doors to apply, Cass. Wait 'til you see the application. And I'm telling you, this place is out in the middle of nowhere. I think they'll take what they can get."

I gave Gracie a look and she shrugged sheepishly. "That didn't come out exactly right," she said, "So, you up for it?"

I owed Gracie. But for some reason I felt tentative. Then

it hit me. It was that damned dream. For the first time since becoming a P.I., I was afraid to take a case. I was losing my nerve. Furious, I forced a smile and nodded. "I'll need directions," I said.

Connie smiled, and it changed her whole appearance. The last nine years had taken their toll on her, but underneath the pain and suffering, she was a beautiful woman.

"We made a pretty good team before, Cass." Gracie said, getting up and moving to look out the window. The sky was beginning to lighten, but the rain continued unabated. She turned, settling those deep, dark eyes on me. "Think we can do it again?"

I thought about it. I looked from Connie to Gracie and nodded.

"Yeah. If there's something going on down there, we'll find it. And if there isn't, I'll help you kick Maddie's little butt myself."

Chapter Two

After Gracie and Connie left, I called a friend of mine, Sheriff Tom Booker. Aside from his job as sheriff, Booker ran a horse ranch on his property, which sprawled along the very edge of Rainbow Lake, about fifteen minutes from my place by boat. He'd been threatening to retire for years so he could expand his stock and work the ranch full-time, but so far I hadn't noticed him slowing down much.

"Think you could use a hired hand around the ranch?" I asked. I told him about Gracie's cousin and the trouble she was having landing a decent job.

"She know anything about horses?"

"I think she's a fast learner, Tom. I'm sure she's a hard worker."

Booker hesitated, and I could just picture him twirling the ever-present toothpick between his teeth while he thought it over. It was a lot to ask, I knew. But Booker knew I wouldn't ask if it weren't important. Finally, he sighed. "I've got that old cottage out back that's not much more than a shack. I suppose she could stay there if she's willing to fix it up. There's plenty of work, that's for sure. I lost old Pete a few months ago and haven't hired a replacement yet. I want someone I can trust."

I knew what he was asking. "I'm pretty sure she's good people, Tom. And she could use a break."

"I guess it can't hurt to give her a try, then."

"I owe you one," I said.

"Oh, hell, Cass. You owe me so many already, what's one more?" We both laughed, knowing it was true.

"In that case, can you run a name for me?"

There was only a brief pause before I heard his familiar sigh. "What are you looking for?"

"Missing person. It's probably nothing, but, before I go chasing shadows, it'd be good to know if she's already been found. All I have at the moment is a name and last known address."

"Let me grab a pen."

I gave him what little info I had on Annie Sisson.

"How soon you going to want this?" he asked.

"Couple of hours?" I said, knowing how this would go over.

"Cass! I'm up to my ass in horse manure right now!"

"I'll make it up to you," I said. He didn't say anything. He was waiting.

"How about pan-fried filets with a tarragon-cognac cream sauce?"

"Go on," he said gruffly, like he wasn't really sold yet.

"And sauteed chanterelles with lemon-buttered artichokes."

"I like those garlic mashed potatoes you make," he said, getting into the spirit.

"Well, we could do that."

"What about dessert?"

I sighed. "Raspberry topped chocolate mousse?"

"Done!" he said. "I'll hold you to this, Cass."

I laughed and hung up before he had time to change his mind, then went to work on what I could find out about Annie Sisson myself. Booker would be able to tell me if she'd landed in the morgue or jail. But assuming that wasn't the case, there were a number of things I could learn on my own.

I booted up my Mac and logged onto the Web, accessing my favorite detection link called Little Brother. Relatively new and considerably more expensive than other subscriber links that probed into the personal lives of private citizens, Little Brother was quick, user-friendly, and well worth the monthly fee. In less than an hour I knew Annie Sisson's social security and driver's license numbers, her age, DOB, parents' names, address and phone number, her last two places of employment, the name of her bank, account numbers, and her credit history. Using these bits of information, I was able to access more personal background and, by filling in the blanks, I began to visualize the person behind the smiling face in the Camp Turnaround brochure.

Annie Sisson had grown up an only child in Wheatland, Wyoming and left home at seventeen to put herself through college at Colorado State University before transferring out west to Fresno State and then San Diego State. She was still paying off her student loans. Though armed with a teaching credential, rather than pursuing that career, after college she'd joined the Peace Corp. Apparently her stint with the Corp had been cut short, because two years later she was working at an Institute for the Blind in Seattle, Washington. A year after that, she'd hired on at Camp Turnaround, where she'd been for just over two years. A call to her parents' number yielded a recorded message revealing that Harold and Irma Sissons still lived in the house Annie Sisson had grown up in. I'd been hoping to actually talk to them, to find out if she'd come home for a visit, but that would have to wait. I hung up, not leaving a message, and thought about what I knew.

Annie would be twenty-seven now. Still unmarried, still apparently searching for a niche. Had she left Camp Turnaround as abruptly as she had the Peace Corp and the Institute for the Blind? She seemed to change jobs and towns as readily as underwear. Was she running from something? Or had something happened to her at Camp Turnaround, as Maddie Boone insisted? One thing I did know, she hadn't used her Visa or Mastercard or even a gas card since she left. But I knew I was no closer to knowing the truth than before, and when Booker called back to say he'd come up with a big fat zero, I wasn't surprised. If something sinister had happened to Annie Sisson, no one, except maybe Maddie Boone, knew about it.

I switched gears and spent the rest of the day researching Camp Turnaround, learning what I could about its history, philosophy, track record, and general layout. I also researched other reform-type schools for comparison.

One of the things that struck me during my initial fact gathering was that Camp Turnaround was not an accredited institution. They claimed that 80% of their kids graduated from high school and that their teachers were highly trained, but nowhere in their literature did they use the word licensed, credentialed, or accredited. Maybe that's why they could afford to be a thousand dollars a month cheaper than some of the others I read about.

That was another thing. I couldn't believe the amount of money people paid to ship their kids off to these places. Five to six thousand dollars a month wasn't unheard of, and that wasn't including expenses, which could cover anything from clothing and medical needs to property damages, which were mentioned frequently. Gracie was right, I thought. These kids were bad-asses.

But, aside from the fact that they didn't actually cite specific accreditation, Camp Turnaround sounded pretty good. Situated in an old mining camp, it was both picturesque and isolated. The photographs in the brochure showed heavily treed forests nestled beside wide-open pastures complete with running streams and grazing horses. In addition to offering a competitive curriculum, the place boasted a working horse ranch, computer-driven machine shop, technology training, physical fitness program, group and individual therapy sessions, small class sizes, one-on-one counseling, and an intensive behavior modification program. With only eighty students and over a dozen staff members, the student-adult ratio was ideal. Actually, I could see how parents of a troubled teen might see the place as the miracle they'd been waiting for. And there were plenty of parental testimonies to that effect.

Once I'd satisfied myself that I knew as much as I could about Camp Turnaround, I completed the online application. Based on what I'd read, I had a pretty good idea what they were looking for, and I concocted a story that I felt would satisfy their needs. I was a currently unemployed, loner-type who had teaching experience and a slightly jaded past. I didn't say all this, of course, but I painted the picture just enough to provide the image. Less than two hours after I'd sent the application, I received a phone call from Camp Turnaround.

"Miss James? This is Ida Evans, Administrative Director of Camp Turnaround? We received your application for the substitute teaching position. Would you be available for an interview tomorrow?" She had a slightly southern twang and sounded a little breathless.

"So soon?" I was trying not to sound too anxious.

"The position is to be filled immediately. You did say you were available?"

"Oh, yes, of course."

"And you have previous teaching experience in the language arts?"

Before I could answer, she gushed on. "That's terrific. It says you've worked with troubled teens before. In what capacity, if I might ask?"

I had used a little creative license there, figuring all teens were pretty much troubled to some extent. "Teaching assertive discipline, mostly. In junior high school." Which basically meant that when a kid screwed up in my classroom, I gave them the teacher look and they quit screwing around. Classroom discipline had never been a problem for me, but I didn't elaborate.

"Wonderful. We use a behavior modification program here ourselves, with components not unlike assertive discipline. So, you can make it tomorrow?"

"I'll be there. What should I bring?"

"Well, in the event you are selected, I suppose you should be prepared to stay. We're a long way from the nearest convenience store, if you know what I mean. But, really, all you need is your clothing and personal necessities. Food and lodging are provided, of course, as are conveniences such as laundry, entertainment, and healthcare services. You saw on the application what kind of clothing to bring? We do have a dress code here. And the evenings can be quite chilly."

"Yes, I saw that. It shouldn't be a problem. Anything else I need to know?"

"You saw the directions and the map? Be prepared for a bit of a drive. We are in a rather isolated locale."

"I can probably be there by noon," I said.

"Wonderful. We are so looking forward to the interview, Miss James. Call if you get lost."

With that, she hung up, leaving me with the feeling that Gracie had been right. People probably weren't beating down the door for interviews. I suspected that anyone who bothered to drive all the way out there would be hired on the spot.

Packing was a challenge, because the cats decided to leap into the suitcase and duffel bag respectively, roll onto their backs, showing spotted bellies, waiting expectantly for me to tell them that it was all a big mistake — that I wasn't going anywhere. I can lie to people, but cats are another story. I did my best to explain while packing around them. I slipped my .45 between a pair of Levis and a hooded sweatshirt, tucked my cell phone inside a rolled up pair of socks, and wrapped my PowerBook inside a down jacket. I zipped my lock picks in one inside jacket pocket and a roll of duct tape inside the other. I wasn't sure how I was going to hide these items, or if I'd even need to, and there was a good chance I wouldn't use any of them; but nonetheless, I felt better taking them with me.

Once I managed to zip my bags closed, I called my best friend, Martha Harper, in Kings Harbor.

"Oh, ho," she crooned. "So the great martyr is alive after all." This was, of course, in reference to my estrangement from Erica Trinidad, which Martha thought was exaggerated sainthood on my part. That I hadn't felt much like socializing since the breakup had Martha worried.

I laughed. "Alive and even starting to kick a little," I said.

"Good! It's about time. Tell me you're calling to invite us out for a weekend of great food and wine."

"Actually, I was wondering if you could look after the cats for a few days. I know it means a drive and a boat ride, but Rick and Towne are in Hawaii, and, well, I hate to ask anyone else." Meaning Erica. Martha knew exactly who I meant.

"Are you kidding? I'd be happy to. Maybe Tina and I can spend a couple of nights out there. It's been a while since she's been to the lake. Where you going?"

"Remember Gracie Apodaca?"

"How could I forget? Gracie-the-Wonder-Butch. Isn't that what you called her?"

"Not to her face."

Martha chuckled. "So what's up?'

I told her.

"Sounds kinda hinky, Cass. But maybe it'll be good for you to get away." Meaning away from Erica, who was presently living two coves away in her lakefront home. She'd been there off and on since we'd broken it off, and even though we'd managed to avoid each other, living in a tiny resort town made it impossible not to be aware of each other's presence. I knew when she was at the library, the hardware store, or a restaurant. When her car wasn't parked at the marina, I couldn't help wondering where she was. As much as I wanted to disagree with Martha, I knew she was right. Erica's presence on the lake was stifling me, even if we never saw each other. Last night's dream was new proof of that.

Somewhere I'd read that to give yourself to someone once and get burned was a learning experience. To give yourself to the same person a second time, and get burned again, was stupidity. I wasn't sure what doing it a third time would count as, but I wasn't about to find out.

"You still there?" Martha asked, sounding a little worried.

"Yeah. But you're absolutely right. I'd do this for Gracie anyway, but part of this is for me."

"Jeez, Cass. You may actually be going smart on me." Martha laughed that deep, throaty baritone that always reminded me of pancakes with warm syrup, and I found myself relaxing a little.

"So tell me what the little beasts need, aside from the usual."

"Just lots of hugs, Mart. I may only be gone a day or two; I'm not sure. I've got to get hired first."

"Oh, you'll get hired. Knowing you, you'll be running the place in a couple of days. Just promise to be careful."

I promised and hung up, beginning to look forward to a

little adventure, even though that familiar tingle I sometimes got at the base of my spine had suddenly flared up out of nowhere and a brief flicker of the tunnel dream resurfaced, making me uneasy.

Chapter Three

Sunday morning, the May rain had turned to drizzle and I was more than a little wet by the time I pulled my boat into its slip at the marina. There were a lot of nice things about living on a lake without road access, but there were times when I'd have welcomed a big dry garage attached to my house instead of a boathouse down on the dock. Still, I wouldn't change the way I lived, I reminded myself as I toted my bags from the boat to my Jeep Cherokee in the marina parking lot. I couldn't help notice that Erica's Miata was gone from its usual space and wondered if she'd left for good, or was just off on some adventure of her own. I willed the thought from my head and tossed my stuff into the back of the Jeep. I shook off the rain and climbed into the Jeep, settling in for the long drive. The sky had begun to lighten, with pinkish orange hues shouldering in on the clouds to the east, but no one in town was out and about yet, as far as I could tell. Just as well, I thought. For some reason, I felt like a bandit making a clean getaway.

Maybe it was because I was the one leaving town this time. Good ol' stay-put Cassidy who kept falling for the same woman, who kept pulling the same disappearing act every time things got too good. I shook my head, still angry at myself for being such a fool. How could I keep making the same mistake? There was no question that Erica was still as beautiful as the day I'd met her. She was easily the sexiest woman I'd ever known. Strong and sensual, sharp-witted, yet seductively alluring, she kept me on my toes. But it was as if Erica Trinidad felt compelled to sabotage her own well-being. Just when we had reached that point of intimacy when ecstasy blends with contentment, Erica found another reason to bolt. There was always a different reason, but in truth, it was always the same thing. Erica was scared shitless of commitment. Just because I understood it, didn't mean I had to put up with it. Erica was going to have to grow up on her own time. Or someone else's. I'd already given her way too much of mine.

I gunned the Cherokee and headed north, then east, then followed the road north again, willing my thoughts away from Erica, making myself think over what I knew about Maddie Boone. No matter how much of a bad-ass she'd become, I thought, no kid deserved to be whisked away by strangers in the middle of the night. No wonder she was ticked off! But had she really seen someone murder Miss Sisson? Or was this just a prank to get attention?

I turned up the volume and listened to Annie Lennox's almost perfect voice. The windows down, I sang along with the CD, letting the miles race past along with the cedar and fir that lined the highway and the wild blackberry bushes that crowded the asphalt wherever the sun managed to break through the evergreens. The farther northeast I traveled, the better the weather seemed to get.

By the time I reached Portsmith Grove, a tiny, now defunct logging town midway between Portland and Salem, I was feeling decidedly better. The town, or what was left of it, reminded me of dozens like it scattered across the Pacific Northwest. The once thriving timber industry had left a string of dilapidated ghost towns in its dying wake. Once the mills closed, people of working age moved on, leaving the towns to those too old or feeble to work. From the number of now closed bars, diners, and poolhalls along Main Street, I could tell that Portsmith Grove had once thrived. There had been a schoolhouse, a post office, a general store, and two hotels. One of the hotels was still operating, though I doubted the No Vacancy sign was needed much. Surprisingly, two of the town's bars had also survived the exodus, and one of them was already open for business, a couple of rusted pickups parked outside.

At the edge of town, I slowed, checked the map, turned east on a dubiously marked county road, and began to climb. The road snaked upward through a forest thick with fir and cedar. I crested a hill and hit the brakes. For miles, on either side of the road, the beautiful trees had been clear-cut. Ugly patches of stripped land where the loggers had decimated the forest lay before me. I'd seen clear-cut land before, but never so much of it, so suddenly. New growth had poked through the rubble and debris along the forest floor, and I knew that, in another fifty years or so, the trees would be big enough to cut down again. Not much consolation for the deer and bear who'd inhabited the forest, I thought glumly.

I continued my slow trek, dodging potholes the size of possums every twenty feet or so. The road had not been maintained in years, making driving a challenge. But there was no traffic at all — in fact I hadn't seen another vehicle since leaving Portsmith Grove — and I began to think that there was a fine line between peacefully remote and eerily deserted.

According to Gracie's directions, Camp Turnaround was fifty miles northeast of Portsmith Grove, away from anything resembling civilization. According to my odometer, I'd gone about half that when the ravaged land was blessedly replaced by healthy forest again, leaving the ugly scars of logging behind. After another fifteen miles of picturesque wilderness, I reached a patch of the old two-lane road that had been recently graded and tarred, a sure sign that I was getting closer.

Patience is not usually one of my virtues, but this time I didn't mind the slower pace. It gave me time to work on my cover and to work out a plan. If something had happened to Miss Sisson, someone besides Maddie Boone had to know it. Which meant Maddie might be in real danger. If someone was watching Maddie, I'd have to be careful when I talked to her. Either way, I'd find out soon enough. At the top of the next rise, not fifty feet away, I could see a brightly painted wooden sign arched over the road announcing the entrance to Camp Turnaround.

I'm not sure exactly what I'd expected — perhaps a barbed-wire-enclosed compound with militaristic gendarmes guarding the entrance. Instead I was taken by the unexpected beauty as I rounded the last bend and descended into one of the lushest, greenest valleys I'd ever seen. I slowed to a halt and sat gaping down at the vista. Camp Turnaround lay sprawled before me, nestled in what seemed miles of pristine meadows surrounded by woodlands on three sides, a steep rocky mountainside on the other. No wonder they don't escape, I thought. Who in their right mind would want to leave?

But, besides the beauty, there was another obvious advantage to the locale. Anyone leaving would have to have transportation or wings. Even if a kid managed to traverse the length of the valley before being spotted, he'd never get through the forest surrounding it. And where would he go? The closest, and as far as I could tell by looking at the map, only civilization, was back the way I'd come, in Portsmith Grove.

I eased the Jeep down the steepening path toward the camp. As I neared, I studied the layout. Some of the buildings were rustic — probably the original miners' lodges — while others were much more modern. I stopped the Jeep and, using the binoculars on the seat beside me, studied them more closely. The brochure had listed the amenities, and it wasn't too difficult to sort the buildings out. I counted what appeared to be four large dormitories, an infirmary, a mess hall, a shiny modern factory, a small chapel, and an administration building, all set in a semi-circle around the large, well-manicured parade grounds. Behind these buildings were a smattering of small cabins, which I assumed were staff housing. A good quarter mile to the west were the stables, more outbuildings, cabins, and rows of corrals. Beyond the corrals was the lush meadow I'd seen from the ridge, with dozens of grazing horses. To the west side of the meadow was a pond, fed by a brook that snaked out of the mountain on the east, across the meadow, and into the woodlands on the west. Whatever else it might be, Camp Turnaround was indeed a hidden paradise.

At the base of the long drive into camp was an electronic gate, which opened automatically as I neared. Apparently, someone was watching for me. Before I could find a place to park in front of the administration building, I was greeted by a bustling, silver-haired woman wearing a starched white blouse tucked into a denim skirt that didn't quite reach the top of her calf-high cowboy boots. Her skirt was the wrap-around kind and billowed out each time a gust of wind caught it. She held the skirt in place with one hand, extending the other through my Jeep window in greeting.

"Ida Evans. You must be Cassidy James," she said. "Glad you could make it!" Her accent had even more Texas in it than over the phone, I thought. Her grip was enthusiastic enough to whiten my knuckles, and from the calloused palms, I knew she did more at the camp than answer phones and shuffle paperwork. She waved me over toward another electronic gate that surrounded a parking lot and punched in a code that caused the metal gate to slide open. I parked in the spot she indicated.

"This place is beautiful," I said, climbing out. I wasn't kidding.

"Oh, you're going to love it here. Heaven on Earth is what I call it. And once you get to know the kids and see how they blossom, well, you won't want to leave."

Which made me wonder why Miss Sisson had left so suddenly. If in fact she had.

"I'm surprised you have an opening. I can't imagine anyone wanting to leave here."

Ida glanced at me, then led me toward the cedar-sided building in front of us. The electronic gate slid shut behind us and locked itself. "Surprised all of us, to tell the truth. Miss Sisson was so well liked here. But she had some kind of family emergency, I understand. Anyway, here we are. If you want to freshen up, there's a lady's room first door on the right. The morning sessions won't be over for another half-hour, so, if you want, I can give you a brief tour before we get started."

"I'd like that. It'll be good to stretch my legs."

I stepped into the administration building and took a quick peek around. Ida's desk and filing cabinets took up most of the main office. There were other rooms off of the main office, the placards on their doors denoting their use. One read Testing, another Video Room. Another read Orientation. I slipped into the restroom, because I really did need to use it, then met Ida back outside.

"Classes are held over there," she said, pointing her chin at one of the newer looking buildings. "Besides the basics of math, science, and humanities, we offer intensive training in technology and practical arts."

"Practical arts?" I asked, raising an eyebrow.

"Manual labor, actually," she said, gracing me with a wink. "Practical Arts sounds better in the brochure. We do extensive aptitude assessments here, and for those kids who show an inkling of ability or interest, we provide pretty advanced technology training, giving them hands-on experience as machinists in our computer-assisted machine shop. Even those who aren't technologically minded can learn to be machine operators, and all the kids participate in both the shop and the ranch operations."

"So, kids provide the labor and you provide the training?"

"Exactly. We have a wonderful work experience program, where, in addition to the machining skills, they learn animal husbandry, ranching, a bit of farming, you name it. They learn to build fences, dig trenches, install irrigation pipes, tend the gardens, feed and care for the horses, and so on. They also work shifts in the mess hall and laundry. They leave with more than their self-worth intact. They leave here with employable skills. Most of these kids, when they first get here, have never done a lick of work in their lives. When they graduate from here, they not only go on to graduate high school, but most of them get good jobs." Ida was getting wound up, her enthusiasm bubbling over.

"Sounds almost too good to be true," I said, wishing I could take it back the second I said it. Ida looked as if I'd spit on her.

"Well, I'm sure it does to an outsider. And don't get me wrong. It's not all a bed of roses. These kids come in hard and angry. Most of them want to run away at first, and quite a few of them try. We're not talking overnight success here. It takes a lot of work and a lot of love. Tough love. We teach them respect. First they learn to respect us, then they learn to respect themselves. Most of them, anyway. We can't save them all, but we come pretty darn close."

"What happens to the ones who run away? I can't imagine they get very far in these woods."

"We let them go. We keep an eye on them, of course. Coach

could track a snake through a swamp if he had to. City kids in the forest aren't much of a challenge. Of course, he's on horseback. Sometimes, one of them gets brave enough to steal a horse, too, even though they all know the consequences. Doesn't matter though. Coach always brings 'em back before they're eaten alive out there. Not before they're scared witless, however. They usually don't try it twice."

"What are the consequences?" I asked.

Ida shot me a funny look. "Everything at Camp Turnaround has consequences," she explained. "Good behavior earns privileges; bad behavior takes privileges away. The severity of the bad behavior determines the severity of the loss of privileges. Dinner, for example is a privilege. Social interaction is a privilege. Showers, a good night's sleep, bathroom breaks, these are all privileges. It doesn't take kids long to begin to appreciate these little privileges. And to want to keep them."

She seemed both proud and slightly defensive on this topic, so I changed tack.

"Coach is one of the teachers here?"

"His official title is Physical Fitness Training Instructor, but he does a lot more than get these kids physically fit. He teaches discipline. He shows kids how to channel their anger into productive energy. He teaches team building, group responsibility, and self-worth. He's got a knack for working with the real problem-kids. They all call him 'Coach' behind his back. To his face, they call him 'Coach, Sir.' "

"I can't wait to meet him," I said.

"Oh, you won't have to wait long. He's on the Interview Committee. In fact, if we hurry, we might be able to catch the last few minutes of drill."

Ida marched me past the other buildings, pointing out the massive machine shop, where I could hear the buzz and hum of work in progress, the mess hall, where staff ate three squares a day, right along with the kids, the infirmary, which employed a certified RN, who also taught the science classes, and the bunkhouses where the kids slept. "Your cabin is back there," she explained, pointing toward the smattering of rustic cabins nestled in the trees behind the dormitories. "That is, if you take the job."

I noticed she didn't say get the job. Apparently, it was mine if I wanted it.

As we rounded the bend, we came upon the parade grounds where a group of twenty or so blue-shirted teenagers were engaged in push-ups to the steady cadence of a deep throated teen belting out the commands, "Down, up! Again, down, up! Again, down, up!" As the acne-scarred exercise leader drove the sweating teens, a well-built, deeply tanned man in his thirties paced the rows, occasionally placing his foot on a youth's buttocks to encourage better form. He briefly removed a sweat-stained ball cap to run stubby fingers through his sandy brown crew cut, then replaced the cap and fingered the whistle that hung around his neck. His white T-shirt bulged with muscles. He held a two-foot-long prod in his right hand, which he tapped against his leg, sometimes tapping a kid's shoulder or butt, mumbling something too low for me to hear. Suddenly, he held his left hand up, gave three short blasts on the whistle, and the exercise leader brought the boys to their feet with a sharply shouted, "Atten-tion!" As a unit, the boys sprang to their feet.

One overweight kid in the back wobbled awkwardly to a semi-standing position. Gasping for breath, he stumbled and muttered, "Shit!" It was just loud enough for almost everyone to hear. He looked to be about fifteen, with a recently shaved head that was pink from sunburn. None of the boys dared to glance at him, but it seemed they were all aware that an infraction had occurred. The exercise leader's voice sounded an octave higher than during the push-ups. "On your feet, Toad."

"I'll take care of this, Dobberteen. You can lead the unit to the showers."

"Yes, sir, Coach, sir. About face!" The boys pivoted in

unison, then on command, began jogging toward the dormitory. The man they called Coach glanced in our direction, but if he was curious about my presence, he didn't show it. He stepped toward the chubby, bald kid who was now standing fully erect, though his knees were visibly wobbling. Coach said something softly to the kid, then raised the prod in his right hand and lifted the kid's chin with it so that the boy was looking him in the eye. His voice was low, but certainly not soothing, because whatever he said made the boy start to cry. The prod was no longer lifting the kid's chin, but was pressing into his Adam's apple, and I could tell the boy wanted to step away but didn't dare. Suddenly, Coach's voice rose and I could hear his words clearly.

"You want to hit me, don't you, Toad? But you're a chickenshit. A fat-ass, mama's boy, chickenshit. Otherwise, you'd do it!"

The boy's face was red, but not from the sun or the exertion. Rage was building inside him, and I felt Ida tense beside me.

"You got something on your mind, fat boy? You got something you wanna say?" The rod in Coach's hand was still pressed against the boy's throat.

"Fuck you," the boy finally spat, pushing the prod away with surprising strength. His face was mottled with fury. "Fuck you!" he shouted again. As swiftly and as calmly as a snake strikes its prey, Coach jabbed the prod into the boy's gut, sending an electrical jolt that lifted the kid off his feet and sent him sprawling backwards onto the asphalt.

Without thinking, I started toward him but Ida held me back, her nails digging into my wrist, her grip startlingly fierce. The boy lay motionless for a second, then his feet jerked a few times and a wet stain spread from his crotch down his pants leg.

Coach walked over to him and nudged him with his tennis shoe. "Did you want to say that again, Toad?"

The boy turned his tear-streaked face away.

"I know you're angry at me, boy. But I ain't the enemy. Not unless you want to make it that way. Up to you. Now I know you've never done no exercise like you did today and every muscle in your body's on fire. I understand that. But no matter how tired you get, when your House Leader says 'attention,' you gotta stand at attention. You understand?"

The boy nodded, though his face was still turned from Coach.

"Maybe what you need is a couple days to let them muscles loosen up a bit, give you a chance to get things clear in your head. Your House Leader tell you about Isolation?"

The kid nodded again, his lower lip trembling.

"Don't be afraid to look at me, son. What did he tell you?"

The kid turned his face toward Coach, and I could almost see the anger turn to fear.

"Speak up, son."

"He said it was something to be avoided at . . . at all costs. Please, sir. Don't make me go. I'll try harder."

Suddenly Coach laughed. "Yeah, I imagine you will. Tell you what. I'm gonna go easy on you this time." He twirled the prod in his right hand and deftly slipped it into a loop on the side of his belt. "Hell, boy. When I was your age, I was fatter than you are now. And twice as pissed off. I know you don't believe me right now, but someday you're going to look back on this moment as a turning point. Now, come on, I'll give you a lift to the showers myself. You could use some cleaning up." The Coach extended a hand, which the boy rejected. He rolled away and pushed himself off the ground, seeming to notice for the first time that he'd soiled himself.

"Ah, fuck," he said.

"Don't worry, kid. Everyone pisses himself sooner or later."

Coach led the boy toward a four-wheel ATV that was parked on the edge of the parade grounds. Attached to the back of the ATV was a rectangular metal wagon, which the boy climbed into awkwardly. I saw Coach shoot Ida a quick wink as he mounted the ATV and pulled away. The boy's pudgy white fingers gripped the sides of the wagon as it bounced along behind the ATV, his eyes looking mortally wounded.

"Like I told you," Ida said, "it ain't all a bed of roses. Come on. We don't want you to be late for your interview."

Chapter Four — Madeline

Six Weeks Earlier

Three days in this place and Maddie was ready to tear her hair out. Not that there was much left of it after that nurse from hell had hacked it all off. Right away she could tell which kids had been here the longest by the length of their hair. Her House Leader, a red-headed witch named Belinda Pitt, had a ponytail halfway down her back and wore it like a badge of honor. She was always tugging at it, wrapping it around her index finger, showing it off like it was some damn mink stole or something. And she had a way of smirking like Mother Superior, which just made Maddie want to punch her lights out. But Belinda was sixteen, and even if she hadn't been twice as big as Maddie, there was something in her blue eyes that made Maddie cringe a little whenever their eyes met. At the moment, Belinda was lecturing her on the quality of Maddie's bed-making.

"What part of hospital corners don't you get?" she said, tugging the top blanket off Maddie's upper bunk.

"I guess what I don't get," Maddie said, "is the point of them at all. I'm just going to get back in it tonight. It's not like someone else is going to sleep in my bed. I like the covers loose on the bottom." This was treading on dangerous ground, she knew. You weren't supposed to talk back to your House Leader. A couple of the girls making up nearby bunks stopped to listen.

"The point is, you were told to do it the right way. Not your way. No one gives a rat's ass how you prefer your covers. Get it? No one cares. I personally took the time to explain how you were to make the bunk, and you defied my authority. That's a loss of privileges, Toad. You don't put the blankets on right, you don't get the blankets." She tugged the next blanket off the top bunk, leaving only a thin white sheet on top. "Fold these properly and bring them to my bunk immediately." She dropped the second wool blanket on the floor next to the first and strode away, her long red ponytail swinging haughtily behind her.

Maddie swallowed hard, willing herself not to cry as she folded the scratchy blankets into neat square piles. She'd been cold the last three nights as it was. Now she'd probably freeze to death. Well, she thought. That's one way to get out of this place. She could feel eyes on her as she carried the blankets down the corridor toward Belinda's bunk. She didn't know if they were looking at her with compassion or glee, because she didn't look back. Eyes straight ahead, chin held high, she marched alone to the end of the bunkhouse and dropped the bundle on Belinda's bed. Belinda had already left, so at least she didn't have to endure another snotty remark.

Outside, a clanging bell announced morning roll call, and

the girls inside the bunkhouse began to scramble into their exercise uniforms, racing each other for the door. To be late was not the way anyone wanted to start their day. Maddie hurriedly tucked her sheets using the correct method, then pulled on the yellow sweats she'd been issued, glad at least that they weren't forced to wear skirts or something. The sweats were too big for her, but at least they were comfortable. After morning workouts, they'd shower, then change into their yellow T-shirts and blue jeans, eat breakfast, and begin the long workday. The classes seemed like they were going to be okay, although so far she'd spent most of her time taking diagnostic-type tests and going through Orientation, a program designed, she decided, to scare the shit out of the inmates. You weren't supposed to call them inmates, of course, but, as far as she was concerned, that's exactly what they were. Mostly, she'd kept her mouth shut and her eyes open, trying to figure out the best way to make her break. Not that she had any intention of going home, but she damned well didn't intend to remain a prisoner in the camp either.

The last one out of the bunkhouse, she raced toward the parade grounds, where the others were already on their numbers, standing at attention. A few boys from the other houses were also straggling, so at least she wasn't the only one in danger of being late. Even so, Coach noticed her tardy arrival and headed straight for her, that idiotic prod thing tapping against his massive thigh. She hadn't seen the prod in action, but she knew instinctively that it wasn't something with which she wanted first-hand experience.

"Having a bad morning, Toad?" he muttered under his breath, so only a few people closest to her could hear. She hated the way they all insisted on calling her "Toad." It had taken her two days to realize it was because she was new and not because they thought she resembled a frog with her new haircut.

"No, sir," she mumbled back. She knew she was supposed to speak clearly, look him directly in the eye, and call him

Coach, Sir. The orientation video was clear on that. But she was still seething over the midnight kidnapping, could still feel his cold, hard hand against her mouth, and she could barely bring herself to look at him at all.

"That's not what I hear. I hear you're having problems following your House Leader's instructions. That's not going to do at all." He was tapping the silly prod against his thigh, his chilly blue eyes boring into her. "You do understand that's not acceptable." It wasn't a question.

"Yes." Her dark eyes glared back at him, all the anger she felt at the world focused on his tan, handsome features. If she were bigger and stronger, she'd slug the son of a bitch and run.

"Fine. Let's don't have any more incidents, shall we? After morning exercises, while everyone else is at breakfast, you'll do the mile. Give you time to think about your attitude."

He turned on his heel and strode to the front of the troops, now fully assembled. He stood with his hands on his hips and studied each row in turn, his close-set eyes searching for dress code violations, slouched shoulders, unkempt hair, and God-knew what else. It was almost a relief when, at last, he nodded to the Blue House Leader to begin the exercises.

Maddie didn't mind exercising, and she really wasn't upset about having to skip breakfast and run the mile. Running had always been exhilarating to her. Sometimes she ran in her dreams, sprinting like a wild colt over fields of green, leaping gracefully over fences, her long dark hair flowing in the wind behind her.

But her hair wasn't long anymore and, by the time exercises were over, it was plastered against her scalp with sweat. Most of the kids, even the older ones, were panting and some were holding their sides as they trudged off to the showers. Maddie stood on her number and waited for Coach to give her instructions.

"I'm gonna give you a choice, Madeline." Now that no one was within earshot, he'd dropped the Toad business, like he was trying to win her over, though she couldn't figure out why. "You can take the longer, scenic route, or stay right here and run the parade grounds." He raised an eyebrow, expecting an answer.

"Scenic route," she said, still trying to catch her breath. He smiled, like he knew that would be her answer.

"Know where the stables are?" he asked. She nodded. "You follow the road there, turn right, head for the old mine. You'll see an old boxcar. You know what a boxcar is?" She nodded again, getting excited. This might be her chance to get out of here.

"Soon as you reach the boxcar, turn around and come back the way you went. It's actually longer than a mile, all told. If you prefer, you can circle the parade grounds seven times instead."

She shook her head. Even if it were double, she'd take the scenic route. Coach smiled at her like he knew what she was thinking.

"You know you can't run far enough or fast enough that I won't catch you, right?"

She looked at him like it had never even crossed her mind.

"Good." He lifted the walkie-talkie from his belt loop and spoke into it. "Tell Clutch we got a miler coming your way. Should be there shortly. Keep an eye on her, will you?"

"Ten-four," came the reply.

Coach pointed his finger as if it were a gun, pulled the imaginary trigger, and Maddie shot off like a cannon.

The road to the stables had been built wide enough to accommodate a large truck and horse trailer, and it was easy to run along. Maddie settled into a comfortable trot, her mind racing ahead of her. Coach might be expecting her to make a run for it, but even so, she was tempted to try. On the other hand, she wasn't really prepared for travel. She had no food. She had no compass. No jacket for the cold nights. Worse, she didn't really know where she was or where she'd go. The road in had been long and bumpy, and it had been too dark to see much. As much as she wanted to get out of there, she knew she'd have to bide her time and make a workable plan. The best thing she could do for now was take everything in. You never knew what knowledge would come in handy later.

Before she knew it, she'd reached the stables and she slowed down, partly to ease the cramp in her side, but mostly to gawk at the horses. There were dozens of them grazing in the open pasture behind the stables. Yellow ones, chestnuts with white nose blazes, and jet black ones with long silky tails. Scattered among them were spindly legged colts, some of them nursing, others frolicking in the spring sunshine. In the distance, she could see other clusters of horses grazing along the creek. A few yards away, a handful of cowhands were sitting on top of a fence watching the man they called Clutch work a magnificent, shiny black colt with a lead rope and switch. The horse's nostrils flared as it pranced around the corral, snorting and pawing as it went. Clutch was talking softly to the horse, calling him a pretty boy, a fine young colt, all sorts of flattering things that made the horse's dark eyes slide sideways like he was checking to see if Clutch was poking fun at him or not. In the same voice he was using on the colt, Clutch said, "Ain't you supposed to be running?"

Suddenly, Maddie realized he was talking to her. She'd come to a complete halt, watching the beautiful horse in the arena.

"What's his name?" she asked.

"Haven't picked one yet. Waiting for an inspiration." The colt kicked up his heels, and Clutch shushed him, pulling down on the lead just enough to settle the horse down. "This fella's spooked by his own shadow," he chuckled. "You got any ideas? On his name, I mean?"

She couldn't believe he was asking her. It was the first nice thing that had happened to her in so long, she almost cried.

"Well, you think on it. Hey, I think he's taken a fancy to you. Look at him showing off, now." Clutch had eased up on the lead, and the colt, given a little leeway, turned toward

Maddie and reared. The cowhands on the fence laughed, making Maddie's cheeks color. "You better get going, now. Coach finds out you been lollygagging around the horses, he's liable to give you worse than a mile run."

Maddie turned toward the boxcar in the distance, smiling for the first time in ages. She forgot, for the time being, about running away. She forgot her sore legs and some of her anger. She kept her mind on the most beautiful colt she'd ever seen and racked her brain, thinking of a name that would do him justice.

Chapter Five

The interview took place in a small room off the mess hall, and, in the interest of killing two birds with one stone, Ida explained, they'd hold the interview while we ate lunch.

We carried trays of food back to a round table, and Ida shut the door to drown out the noise of the kids inside before introducing me to the interview committee. There were five of them including Ida, and, despite myself, I felt nervous. I knew that my performance would not only determine whether or not I got the job, but would set the stage for any subsequent interaction I'd need to have with the staff. To my relief, the atmosphere was relaxed, and they seemed as interested in the meatloaf as they did in my answers, so I began to relax as they took turns talking about themselves and asking questions.

The first to introduce himself was Dr. Biscane, the psychologist and co-founder of Camp Turnaround. He was a tall, angular man in his fifties, with deep brown eyes beneath a prominent forehead. His black hair was thinning, combed straight back to cover the bald spot on the top of his head. He wore neatly trimmed sideburns and a goatee, which only served to make his equestrian face seem longer. When he spoke, his voice was a deep baritone, and gently commanding. "How did you learn of Camp Turnaround, dear?" he asked, just as I pushed a forkful of mashed potatoes into my mouth. They were surprisingly good.

"On the internet," I said, trying to swallow. "I've been looking around for a while now, interested in alternative settings of education."

"Disenchanted, I take it, with the public school system?" he asked, smoothing his goatee.

"A little. Been there, done that, I guess. I wasn't going to go back at all, but then, after a while, I missed teaching. I missed the kids. It was the other stuff I could live without."

"Ah, yes. The bureaucratic bullshit." Dr. Biscane smiled and the others laughed. Coach leaned forward, his elbows on the table. His rippling biceps bunched beneath his white T-shirt.

"Not that it matters that much, but I'm curious. You're too young to have retired. Did you just up and quit? Or did they fire you?"

Ida, who was sitting next to him, slapped his elbows off the table. "Don't mind him, Miss James. Coach always assumes the worst. It doesn't matter why you left the Santa Bonita District. We only care about why you want to work with us."

Nowhere in my application had I mentioned what district I'd worked for. Obviously, they'd done some homework. Luckily, I'd mixed enough truth into my application to make my story plausible. I had, in fact, quit teaching years ago, but not for the reasons I was about to explain. I had quit when my first lover, Diane, had died of cancer. I'd left my job, the house we'd shared, and everything else I'd ever loved. Somehow, I knew instinctively that the only way I was going to survive her death was to make a clean break of everything, and I had. But they didn't need to know this. I swallowed a mouthful of meatloaf and tried to look earnest.

"No, that's okay," I said. "It's a fair question. The truth is, they could've fired me, but they didn't. Out of courtesy mostly. The kids liked me. The parents even liked me. But I blew it, big time, and the administration couldn't just ignore it, so they let me take a leave of absence with the understanding that I wouldn't return. Nothing went on my record. It was a verbal agreement. I just disappeared, free to start up somewhere else if I wanted."

"But you never did," said Dr. Biscane. "Why not?"

"Because I wasn't a hundred percent sure that what happened then wouldn't happen again."

"And what did happen?" Coach asked, ignoring Ida's glance that told him to lay off. "You have a fling with one of the students?" His cool blue eyes appraised me, letting me know he wouldn't blame a kid for finding me attractive. I ignored the look, as well as my sudden desire to sling mashed potatoes in his face.

"I hit a kid," I said, looking Coach squarely in the eye.

"In the classroom?" Lacy Godfrey, who was sitting next to Dr. Biscane, asked. She was in her late twenties, a plump and wide-eyed version of Dolly Parton. She wore a frilly white blouse that accentuated an ample bosom. She taught math and the beginning computer classes, but looked like she could break into a country western tune at a moment's notice.

"Yes," I nodded. "What happened, was, my ninth grade English class was in the middle of this really good discussion on the theme of good versus evil in literature when this new kid, who'd only been in class a few days, came sauntering in late and disrupted the lesson. He was a transfer from another school and looked at least two years older than the rest of the kids. He was just trying to win approval from his new peers. I should've understood that, but the truth was, he ticked me off.

"Anyway, I asked him to sit down and let the rest of us get back to learning, and he made some rude remark that to this day I can't remember. I do remember that a few of the kids laughed, which made me even madder. I should've just let it go, but I said something ridiculously adolescent like, 'If your brain was half as big as your mouth, you could probably contribute to this discussion. But since that obviously isn't the case, I'd appreciate it if you'd sit down and shut up so the rest of us can engage in an intelligent conversation.' "

"Good for you!" Lacy said, clapping her hands. Even Dr. Biscane looked amused. Nurse Beckett, however, gave me a disapproving glance. She was a tall, bony woman with a no-nonsense haircut she wore like a helmet surrounding her stern face. She'd eschewed the mashed potatoes and meatloaf, opting for the salad and vegetable medley, a plain glass of water on the side. She was the only one who seemed to be taking the interview seriously.

"What happened?" Ida asked.

I paused. "He said, 'Make me.' "

"And?" Coach prompted.

"He was still standing near his seat. He was a good two inches taller than I, but not all that big, really. Anyway, I'm not exactly sure how I did it, but I crossed the room in about three strides, grabbed the collar of his shirt, and threw him against the door."

Nurse Beckett's lips were pursed as if she were about to get up and leave, and I quickly glanced at the others. Coach and Ida were nodding. Dr. Biscane stroked his goatee. Lacy's eyes were huge. I went on. "I guess I should've left it at that."

"There's more?" Ida asked.

"Well, the kid tried to throw a punch at me. It was a pathetic swing, really. Before I knew what I was doing, I decked him. Got him square in the nose, which was awful because blood spurted everywhere. Then, to make matters worse, when he saw all the blood, he fainted."

"All right!" Lacy said, starting to clap again.

"It's not something I'm proud of," I said, glancing first at the nurse, then Dr. Biscane. "It scared me to death." Nurse Beckett seemed to thaw, but just a little.

"What scared you most?" Dr. Biscane asked, leaning forward. "That he was badly hurt? That you'd lose your job?" His brown eyes penetrated mine, and I wondered briefly if he knew I was making the whole thing up.

"Those things crossed my mind, of course. But I think what really scared me was that I kind of liked hitting him. I know he was just a juvenile, and that made it doubly wrong. But he was . . . may I speak plainly here?"

"You already have," Dr. Biscane said, smiling. "Please continue." The others nodded. Nurse Beckett seemed as riveted to my story as appalled by it.

I cleared my throat. "He was an asshole. I've never been much for abiding assholes."

Dr. Biscane leveled his gaze on mine. "This place, I'm afraid, is full of them. At least that's how they come to us."

"I realize that," I said. "I think that's why I'm here. I need to get past this incident. I need to prove to myself that there are better ways of dealing with jerks than punching their lights out."

Finally, a nod of approval from Nurse Beckett.

"Sometimes you have to do that first to get their attention," Coach said, stuffing most of a biscuit into his mouth.

"The way you got that kid's attention with the cattle prod?" I asked.

Coach's cool blue eyes met mine, and he quit chewing. The table fell silent.

"You have a problem with that?"

"I didn't like watching it," I said.

"I didn't like doing it," he answered. He managed to say this with his mouth half-full. He swallowed half a glass of milk and went on. "But I got his attention, didn't I? And, in a few months, that kid's going to be looking at the world in a way he never has before. By the time he earns his first parental visit, they won't even recognize him."

I didn't answer, and the group seemed to take my silence as acceptance.

"What did the other kids do?" Lacy asked. "I mean, when you decked the, uh, jerk?" She giggled when she said this.

I managed to blush, getting caught up in my own act. "They applauded," I said. "If I hadn't told on myself, I'm not sure the administration would've ever found out. The students were on my side, and the new kid was too embarrassed to tell." Again, the table fell silent.

"Well, that satisfies everything I need to know," Dr. Biscane said, buttering a biscuit. "Anyone else have any more questions?"

The staff exchanged glances, silently confirming my status as a new employee. Even the nurse seemed mollified by my willingness to admit my wrongdoings, though it was obvious she disapproved of my past behavior.

Ida was beaming. "I had a feeling you were going to fit in here. Why don't you let Lacy show you your cabin and help you get settled in. Then you can come back up to the office and we'll fill out the dreaded paper work. Even here at Camp Turnaround, we have a bit of the old bureaucratic bullshit." The others laughed, then stood and shook my hand, each in turn offering their congratulations. Part of me felt sheepish for lying to these people so blatantly, but mostly I was relieved that the story had had the desired effect. If someone had murdered Miss Sisson, it was possible that he or she was in that room. It was important that they regard me as both harmless and trustworthy.

The kids were still eating when we filed back through the mess hall, as were some of the staff members. I made a quick scan for Gracie, but she wasn't among those lunching. There were about eighty kids in all, seated at long tables and grouped, as far as I could tell, by gender and the color of their T-shirts. One long table had nothing but boys in orange shirts; another one boys in green; a third table, boys in blue; and the fourth group was full of yellow-shirted girls. Each group contained about twenty adolescents of varying ages and ethnicities. Despite their differences, though, there was a sameness about them. Something in their demeanor or their posture, I thought. And then it hit me. No one was slouching. In fact, when we walked into the mess hall, it seemed the whole group sort of came to attention, although no one had asked them to sit up straighter. The kids continued their conversations, ignoring the adults, yet seemingly aware of our presence. Perhaps wary was a better word. Like the deer who grazed in my front yard — seemingly relaxed, yet ready to bolt at the first hint of danger.

I scanned the girls' table and spotted the skinny, long-legged Madeline almost immediately. With the same jet black hair and inky eyes as her mother, she was a miniature version of Connie. She looked like a spindly colt, all knees and elbows. The silky black hair I'd seen in the photograph had been chopped to just below the ear, but there was no denying that, in a few years, the kid would be a beauty — even with the determined frown she wore. Thinking back to the reports her mother had found, I wondered what had happened in the fifth grade to make that frown appear out of nowhere. I wondered if Dr. Biscane was helping her work it out.

Trying not to stare at Maddie, I looked around at the other kids. At the head of the blue table sat Dobberteen, the acne-scarred exercise leader I'd seen earlier. He was watching over his charges like a nervous Mother Goose. I noticed each of the tables had an older kid sitting in a similar fashion.

"Who are the kids at the head of the tables?" I asked Lacy as she walked me toward the door.

"House Leaders. It's a pretty big honor. Takes a long time to earn the rank. They're kind of like peer police, though I think the term *conflict managers* is preferred. A lot of the discipline problems are handled by them. They're in charge of making sure everything in their house is in order."

"What if it isn't?" I asked. We'd stopped at the door and were looking back over the whole group.

"They report infractions to Coach," she whispered. "Coach takes it from there."

"What if they don't report an infraction?"

She looked at me like I was nuts. "If they don't, and someone else does, they get punished, too."

"What if no one else tells?"

She took my elbow and led me outside, talking to me like I was a slow learner. "Let's say a couple of boys in the orange house start talking after lights out. If Dillinger, the House Leader, doesn't stop the problem immediately, and/or if he doesn't report it at morning roll call, then not only will the two kids get double what the punishment would have been, but Dillinger gets punished too. Because there's always the possibility that someone else will tell, see? And Dillinger can't take the risk of not telling. If it happens a second time, Dillinger loses his status as House Leader. Just knowing that someone might tell is enough to motivate a kid like Dillinger to report everything. House Leaders do not want to lose their status or privileges."

Lacy steered me toward the parking lot, and, when we neared the electronic gate, it swung open as if on command. I glanced around and saw Coach, not fifteen feet behind us, aiming a hand-held remote control in our direction. I waved my thanks, though, in truth, his presence made me uneasy. It was like being guarded by a Doberman you couldn't quite trust. I retrieved my bags from the dusty Jeep and handed Lacy the lighter of the two. Lacy led the way past the administration building toward the staff cabins I'd seen earlier.

I noticed that, behind us, students had begun to file out of the mess hall, heading toward their afternoon sessions. They did not seem to be color-coordinated in their destinations, and I pointed this out to Lacy.

"Oh, no. Doc groups them by compatibility for their houses, but by interests and capabilities for their classes. This way, boys and girls get a chance to interact, which Doc thinks is healthy."

Some of the kids were headed for their work stations while others went in the direction of the classrooms. Maddie, I noticed, was headed for the machine shop.

"Yours is the last one on the end," Lacy said, leading the way up the dirt path past dozens of small cabins nestled in the pines. Each little cabin was separated from the next by a stand of trees, giving them all a sense of privacy. The last cabin was indeed off by itself, nearly hidden by the evergreens that shaded the front porch. Lacy flung open the creaky door and ushered me inside like a bellhop showing me to my suite. I was tempted to tip her.

"Pretty cool, huh?" She set the duffel bag on the wood floor with a gargantuan sigh.

"Not bad," I agreed. The cabin was rustic but tidy with a nice picture window looking out onto the lush meadow behind it. Sun streamed in through the lacy curtained window, catching dust motes floating lazily in the air. The center of the main room was filled by a patchwork quilt-covered double bed that looked inviting enough to crawl right into. In fact, Lacy walked over and plopped herself on top of it, letting her legs swing over the side. She acted like she'd done the same thing a hundred times before.

"Not the Hilton, but it's got everything you need," Lacy

said, getting up to show me the miniscule closet. The far right side of the room was divided between a tiny kitchenette and a half-bath. "You can even cook meals, if you want, but, with Pat cooking over at the mess hall, why bother? She's a great cook. You should meet her pretty soon. She's in the next cabin over. You want me to help you unpack?"

"No, thanks," I said hastily. "To tell you the truth, what I'd really like to do is grab a quick nap and a shower before I go sign the paperwork, then maybe walk the grounds. The drive up here wore me out." What I really wanted to do was find a place to stash the stuff I didn't want someone else to stumble upon, namely my gun.

Lacy looked a bit crestfallen, like she'd been looking forward to hanging up my clothes, going through my stuff. It occurred to me that she might have been friends with Miss Sisson. If so, she was probably missing her.

"Did this cabin belong to the teacher who left?" I asked nonchalantly.

"It sure did," she said, sighing again. "Annie had a real knack for making things homey. She had bright pictures on the walls and always had a vase with wild flowers on that little table. Even her grandmother's old quilt makes the place feel homey, doesn't it?"

"It sure does. Why'd she leave it?"

"That's what I wondered, too. I mean she cleared out of here in the middle of the night with not so much as a goodbye to anyone. Maybe she was just in too much of a hurry to take it. It was hanging out back on the clothesline, so I guess she could've overlooked it, but it had belonged to her grandmother. I thought about taking it myself, but, I don't know, it just didn't seem right. Besides, I keep thinking she might change her mind and come back. I'd feel funny having her grandmother's quilt on my bed if she did come back."

"I see what you mean. Maybe I should fold it up and save it for her."

"Nah, Annie wouldn't mind you using it. She's real

generous that way. Too generous sometimes. She's one of the easiest going people you'd ever want to meet. The kind people tend to take advantage of sometimes."

"Really? How so?" I didn't want to sound too interested, but I wanted to keep her talking.

"Oh, I don't know. Like everyone knew she'd cover a class if they asked her, 'cause she just never liked to say no. So, naturally, people were always asking her, and she ended up working right through her days off. Stuff like that."

"Any idea why she left?" I asked, pushing my luck.

"Oh, I've got my suspicions," she said, folding her arms over her ample chest. Her pink lips had become pursed.

"Really?" Trying not to push. Trying to coax gently.

"It's a long story," she said, "and not really mine to tell. Anyway, if I don't see you sooner, I'll catch you at dinner. I'm just four cabins over. Holler if you need anything." With that, she flounced out the door, letting it bang closed behind her, leaving a hint of Chantilly in her wake.

Wondering how I was going to get Lacy Godfrey to tell me the long story that wasn't hers to tell, I began unpacking. It only took a few minutes to hang my clothes and put away my toiletries, but quite a bit longer to find good hiding places for my cell phone and gun. There was no rule as far as I knew against having a cell phone at the camp, but I'd learned in the past that it was good to keep a few surprises in reserve. Having immediate access to the outside world might come in handy in an emergency. I flipped open the cell phone and punched in my security code, waiting for the computerized voice to tell me I could make a call. Instead, the image of a flashing antennae filled the tiny screen, alerting me that I was not in calling range. So much for emergencies. Maybe the phone would work once I got out of the shadow of the mountain. In the meantime, I'd just need to stash it someplace safe. Not that anyone was likely to come looking through my stuff, I thought. Still, out of habit, I felt the need to play it safe.

The problem was, there weren't too many hideyholes in

the cabin. There was a large wicker basket, which I supposed was for use as a laundry hamper, but that would be too obvious. I could always stash the gun and phone under the mattress, but that was probably the first place someone would look if they were searching the cabin. I finally settled on using the duct tape I'd brought to secure both the gun and cell phone behind the drawers in the small chest beside the bed. Not as easy to get to, I knew, but less likely to be discovered by a nosy neighbor.

I slid the top drawer out and turned it over on the bed, then stopped, my mouth open with surprise. Someone had beaten me to the punch. Something was already taped to the bottom of the top drawer. My heart raced as I peeled the masking tape back and pulled three small pink plastic packets free. They were lightweight in my palm and harmless looking. I slid a hard plastic card the size of a credit card from one of the packets and stared down at twenty-one green tablets half the size of an aspirin. I turned the packet over and read the prescription made out to Annie Sisson for Low-Esterin. It appeared that Annie was taking birth control pills and for some reason had felt compelled to hide them.

Quickly I checked the rest of the drawers, but found nothing else out of place. I taped my holstered gun behind the bottom drawer and my cell phone behind the second drawer, making sure the tape would hold their weight and that the drawers would close normally. Once I had them right, I put Annie's pills back beneath the top drawer as well. If Lacy was right and Annie decided to come back out of the blue, I didn't want her stumbling upon the gun when she went to retrieve her pills.

Then I sat back on the bed and wondered why someone who decided to leave in the middle of the night would leave her grandmother's quilt and three months' supply of birth control pills. Maybe someone else had cleaned out the place, not realizing the quilt was hanging out back, not knowing there were pills hidden beneath the drawer.

Well, I wasn't going to get any closer to the truth sitting there brooding about it. I gave one last look around the cabin, knowing I'd done the best I could, then looked at my watch. It was time for a quick shower, another session with Ida Evans, and then, if I could wing it, a self-guided tour of the camp, giving me a chance to catch up with my friend, Gracie Apodaca.

Chapter Six

The session with Ida turned out to be a much more involved ordeal than I'd anticipated, and it was nearly dinnertime by the time we'd finished. The paperwork, as she called it, took almost no time at all. But my orientation was intense. First, I got to watch a videotape about Camp Turnaround. It was the same video shown to parents of prospective enrollees. Then I got to watch the staff video, which had a lot of the same information but with a different slant. First and foremost in both tapes was the emphasis on behavior modification. Taking unacceptable behavior and turning it into desirable behavior was the goal of Camp Turnaround. The parent video focused more on the work and education programs, while the staff video stressed the active use of consequences for appropriate and inappropriate behaviors. Inappropriate behavior was to be confronted, consequented, and redirected, while appropriate behavior was to be reinforced and rewarded. I kept waiting for a shot of Coach zapping another kid with the cattle prod, but somehow they'd decided not to include that particular behavior mod method in the tape.

Yet a third video turned out to be the most interesting. With Ida serving as commentator, the video consisted of personal testimonials by camp graduates and their parents, teachers, ministers, and even employers. One after another sang the praises of Camp Turnaround. It seemed all of the graduates had gone on to be successful in life and credited the camp with getting them back on track. Nobody mentioned the cattle prod, and there was no reference to Isolation, though a number of the grads did talk about learning to be accountable for their actions and about how self-discipline led to self-worth. By the time I'd finished the video series, I was fairly convinced that all kids should be sent for at least a summer to Camp Turnaround, and that most adults could use a month or two there themselves.

After the videos, Ida showed me a map of the facilities and a daily student schedule that began with roll call and morning calisthenics at six, included four hours of classes, four hours of work, an hour for physical training, an hour for group or individual counseling and/or therapy sessions, an hour for leisure, an hour for planned social activities, an hour for team building, and of course, the three squares a day. Lights Out was at ten o'clock, which left very little time for homework or reading, but I doubted too many of them put up much of a fight over it. By the end of the day, they were probably exhausted. There were no televisions, no computer games, and no telephones at Camp Turnaround. The only phone calls home, like the e-mail, were closely monitored. There were no weekend passes or home visits, and the only parent visitations were on planned parent days such as Camp Graduation.

"Everything's so organized," I told Ida when I'd finished my reading assignment.

"Has to be. When Doc and Clutchie and I started, we had no idea what we were getting ourselves into. We learned to get organized quick or we'd sink."

"Who's Clutchie?"

"That's Clutch to you." She gave me a schoolgirl laugh. "Got his nickname from his platoon leader in Nam, who said there was no one better in a clutch situation. In fact, I'm the only one who gets away with 'Clutchie.' " She winked. "He's my husband. He's also the finest horse trainer and breeder this side of Kentucky. He'll tell you so himself. Just ask him!" Her eyes beamed, and it was clear that she thought Clutchie hung the moon. It was also clear that Ida loved nothing more than talking about Camp Turnaround.

"Clutch and I started out with a dream of running a summer horse camp for kids. His uncle owned this land along with the old worthless gold mine on it that he spent his younger years trying to make pay off. It took Uncle Joe half a lifetime to realize the land was more valuable than the mine, and that's when he started raising horses. Anyway, he practically raised Clutch on the ranch, teaching him what he knew, and when he died, he left the land to him.

"While I was in school training to be a high school guidance counselor, Clutch got called off to Vietnam. When he came back, all he wanted was to work with horses on this land; I couldn't get him anywhere near a city. It was either give up my dream of working with kids, or give up on Clutch. The camp idea just seemed a natural compromise. He could work with horses, I could work with kids, and we could stay right here in paradise. Am I boring you?"

"No. Not at all. Really."

"Well, after that first summer, which was something of a

nightmare, it was Doc who approached us about turning the camp into a ranch for troubled teens. He and Clutch served in Nam together and had kept in touch. After Nam, he'd finished med school, but he knew he wasn't cut out for the sterile environment of a hospital clinic. He wanted to work with adolescents and do therapeutic interventions. He just needed the right location, the right setup. What Clutch and I needed was capital, and that's where Doc's little brother Ben came in. He was already doing pretty well as a machinist. He wanted to start his own machine shop and needed the space to build. One thing we've got here is plenty of space. So Ben built his machine shop, and the kids get valuable hands-on skills they can take with them while Ben gets cheap labor. Clutch gets the help he needs during the peak seasons of horse breeding, and the kids get hands-on experience in ranching. It's a win-win situation. And Doc and I get to work with kids. Sometimes things really do work out the way they're supposed to." She was brimming with pride.

"You've come a long way from a summer horse camp," I acknowledged.

"Boy, if that ain't the truth. After the first few years, we just kept growing and growing, taking on more staff as the enrollment grew. Pretty soon, we were running the camp year-round. We finally had to start turning kids away. Now the camp has a waiting list a mile long. Soon as someone leaves, we open a spot for someone else. You sure I'm not boring you?"

"Please. I find this fascinating."

"The hardest part is knowing that some of these kids could revert to their old ways once they're back in the old environment. We've got seminars for the parents now, giving them some parenting tools. But, of course, some of the parents were part of the kids' problem in the first place.

"Still, I imagine it's hard for most parents to give up their kid," I said, thinking about how difficult it must've been for

Connie to let Maddie go. But that was different, I knew. Connie didn't know she'd be getting out of prison.

"Oh, sweetie. These parents are so darn grateful that someone will take their kid, they'd pay us double if they could afford it. By the time they come to Camp Turnaround, they've all but lost hope. They've already given up on the kid. Giving him up is a lot easier than you'd think. We get stories all the time about how, for the first time in years, their household is sane again, just because they've got the bad kid out of the house."

I thought about Maddie. She hadn't started out a bad kid.

"Don't you wonder sometimes what makes these kids bad in the first place?"

She laughed. "There's more answers to that one than you'd believe. Some of the kids are into drugs. Some of their parents were into drugs, and the kids are so-called 'drug babies.' Those are the ones we have the most difficulty with, because they seem to lack the natural sense of right and wrong the good Lord gave the rest of us. Some of the kids were abandoned as children; some were abused. The list goes on and on. That's what Doc does so well. He gets to the root of their anger. Clutchie and Ben teach them the value of a hard day's work, how to care about something other than themselves. Doc reaches right down inside them and tugs on the things that make them tick."

"And what does Coach do?" I asked.

She frowned for a second, shaking her head. "You can't be too quick to judge Coach, Cassidy. There's more to him than meets the eye. Like he told you, he gets their attention. But he does much more than that. Sure, he has to tear them down a little. That's so Clutchie and the rest of us can build them back up. That's so Doc can work his magic. Someone has to play the bad cop. And Coach knows the value of the role he plays. He's a big reason our success rate is so high."

"You've convinced me," I said, and she laughed again.

"I do go on sometimes, don't I? Clutchie calls me a motor-mouth when I get wound up. Just tell me to shut up the next time I start waxing philosophical about the merits of Camp Turnaround. You think this is bad, you should hear me with the parents!"

I laughed, but I was beginning to wonder if Ida weren't a little too wound up, like maybe she was getting a little pharmaceutical help. Diet pills could do that, sometimes, and her eyes did have a glassy brightness to them; but Ida hadn't appeared to be dieting at lunch and some people were naturally effervescent, I thought. Either way, I imagined Clutchie rarely got a word in edgewise.

Just when I thought I was finally going to get out of there, Ida spent another half-hour going over my teaching schedule and class rosters and loaded me down with a pile of books to peruse before the next day's lessons. So much for getting to see Gracie. If I was going to pull off my role as substitute teacher, I was going to have to hit those books and make some lesson plans. Besides, I'd seen Ida put my newly created file in an unlocked metal filing cabinet marked Personnel. I knew that before I did another thing, I needed to find out what else I could about Annie Sisson, and where better to start than her personnel file? Which meant I'd need to come back as soon as Ida Evans was gone. Watching the way she'd scarfed down her lunch, I had little doubt that she'd be on time for dinner.

Ida walked me to the door and opened it for me, asking if I'd like a lift in one of the camp ATVs. I pictured the poor fat boy being carted off like a wounded animal to the showers, pathetically relieved to have avoided Isolation. I started to ask her just exactly where Isolation was, but thought better of it. She'd likely launch into another lecture, and I really wasn't up to it.

I declined the ride and was halfway up the path toward the staff cabins when a noise startled me. I stopped in my tracks and listened, straining to hear what had sounded like someone humming. Then I heard it again, coming from the woods to my right. Someone was definitely humming under their breath. Had some of the students managed to ditch class? What were they doing in the woods? Carefully, I set down the pile of books and inched toward the noise, trying not to step on twigs. The humming had stopped again, but I heard the rattle of paper, and, then, in a few seconds, the humming resumed.

Hoping I wasn't about to stumble on someone relieving themselves in the woods, I crept forward and pushed back a bough of pines, then had to stop myself from laughing aloud. There, sitting on a rock not fifteen feet away, was Nurse Beckett, eating a Hershey's candy bar. Her eyes were nearly glazed over with contentment as she folded the paper down an inch at a time and savored the chocolate. Oblivious to all around her, she seemed a far cry from the uptight woman I'd seen at lunch. Her body seemed more relaxed, her shoulders were slumped forward, and her expression was that of a cat having its belly rubbed.

As quietly as I could, I backed away, leaving her to hum in private, her secret intact. For some reason I liked Nurse Beckett better now that I knew she was a closet junk-food junkie. And it served to remind me that things weren't always as they seemed.

It turned out I was right about Ida. As soon as the bell clanged announcing the start of dinner, Ida left the administration building and headed straight for the mess hall. There was already a line of cowboys, Clutch included, standing outside, and Ida joined them. I watched from behind a stand of trees as they filed in, then, making sure no one was watching, set out for the administration building.

Naturally, the door was locked. I examined it closely before selecting a pick from the set of lock picks my old mentor, Jake, had bestowed upon me during my internship with him. Over the years, I'd become pretty handy with the picks, and it didn't take me long to work the dead bolt free. I slid the picks back in my pocket, and, giving one last glance around to make sure no one was watching, slipped into the building.

I checked my watch, then hurried to the filing cabinet I'd seen earlier. It only took a minute to locate Annie Sisson's file, and I quickly scanned the pages, noting that the home address and phone number matched those I'd found earlier. But the last entry in her file gave me pause. It was a one word and a date scrawled across the bottom of the page: Departed. May 7, 2000. Strange choice of words, I thought, given the potential situation.

The file itself was not particularly illuminating as I already knew much of it. Annie had worked at the camp for two years. She had taught in a private school for the blind in Seattle before being hired at Camp Turnaround. She'd been voted Outstanding Teacher of the Year two years in a row by the camp students. Even on a small staff, I figured that was still quite an honor. From what I could tell, she'd elected to stay at the camp right through her vacations, hiring on for extra pay at the ranch instead of traveling or visiting friends and family.

I closed the file and reached for the phone on Ida's desk, punching in the parents' number one more time, thinking that a second call might be worth the trouble. This time, the phone was answered on the second ring. The man's voice was gravelly, like I'd awakened him from a nap.

"Harold Sisson," he said.

"Yes, Mr. Sisson. This is a friend of Annie's from school. I'm helping organize the class reunion and wondered if you knew where I might find Annie. It's been ages since I've seen her." While I talked, I opened Ida's desk drawers and sifted through her belongings.

"Same here," he said. He coughed into the receiver and his voice cleared somewhat. "She's probably off doing one of her goody-two-shoe deeds. Repenting is what I call it. First all that college malarkey, then the Peace Corp, then a private school for the blind, and now some reform camp out in Oregon. I imagine she'll try a convent next."

"So, you haven't heard from her at all?"

"Oh, her mother gets letters now and then. But, after what she done to us, up and leaving that boy at the altar, embar- rassing us in front of the whole town, why her mother don't have much to do with her. Can't say as I blame her. Were you there? At the wedding?"

"No, sir. I was already off at college. So, the last you heard, she was still at the reform camp in Oregon?" In Ida's top left-hand drawer I found two half-empty prescription bottles. One was for Lithium carbonate. The other for something called fluoxetine. The prescribing physician for both was Dr. Biscane. Interesting, I thought. I wondered what they were for.

"Last I heard," he said. "Like I said, she moves around every few years. God knows what she'll think up next. But you can forget about the reunion. Don't even waste your time. Annie don't come back to Wheatland. She knows she's not welcome here."

"Is there another family member she might be visiting?" I asked.

His laugh was more of a bark. "We're all that's left. She shoulda thought of that before she humiliated us."

So much for the family emergency theory. I thanked him for his time and hung up, then dialed my own home number and hung up once my answering machine clicked on. If for some reason Ida hit redial, at least she wouldn't get Annie Sisson's number. I knew that the call would eventually turn up on her monthly bill, but by then I planned to be long gone.

Maybe Annie really had left Camp Turnaround on her own and headed off for another adventure, I thought, checking my watch. I slipped Annie's file back into the cabinet just as the front door opened. The file drawer was still wide open.

"Cassidy. What are you doing here?" Ida Evans stood with her hand still on the knob, her brow furrowed.

I wheeled around, my back to the file drawer, blocking her view of it as I leaned against it, slowly easing it shut. "Oh, sorry. I guess I should've asked first. I came to borrow your phone. The door was unlocked and I didn't figure you'd mind. I called collect, so there won't be any charges." My heart was thudding as I inched the metal drawer closed.

"This door was unlocked?"

"Yes. That's why I thought you were here. But I called your name, and, when I realized you were gone, I started to leave, but, the thing is, I forgot to leave the key for the guy renting my house while I'm gone, and I thought I better tell him where to find it before he breaks the door down or something."

"This door was unlocked?" she asked again, examining it like the concept was completely foreign to her. "I remember locking it myself."

"Honest." While she peered at the door, I pushed the drawer completely in and stepped away from the file cabinet. "I just came in a minute ago and it was unlocked. Sorry if I'm intruding. I just wanted to use the phone."

"No, that's all right, dear. You can come use the phone any time. I'm just a little addled about leaving this door unlocked. They say the mind's the second thing to go, you know." She gave me a semi-lewd wink and chuckled. "So, did you get everything settled, then?"

"I sure did. And it was a good thing I called when I did. He was just about to head over there, and I know he would've broken a window or something. The guy's not real bright."

"So many of them aren't," she said.

I let myself out, feeling Ida's eyes follow me as I walked toward the mess hall. That had been a little too close for comfort, I thought. But it had been worth it. At least I knew it wasn't any family emergency that had sent Annie running, and so far, the only people who didn't seem to like her were her parents. The more I learned about Annie Sisson, the more I found myself hoping that Maddie's cryptic letter was just a hoax.

Chapter Seven — Madeline

Four weeks earlier

Shadow Dancer! she thought, sitting up in bed. Finally! The perfect name! She could hardly wait to tell Clutch. A smile crept across her face, a rare occurrence, though no one was there to appreciate it. It was pitch black in the bunk house, and from the cacophony of snoring, she knew everyone else was sound asleep. She hugged the scratchy wool blankets around her, glad to have them back, and gazed out at the black night. The worst part about her bunk was also the best — she was right next to a window. It was permanently closed to prevent escape attempts, although with a screwdriver, one could make short work of the four screws holding the hinges in place. So far, she hadn't been able to find one, but she was on the lookout. Even if she did find one, it would be quite a jump to the ground below. The dormitory, though single story, like the other buildings in camp, was built on stilts. She supposed this was to prevent flooding during the rainy season when the creeks overflowed, but to her, all it meant was a more difficult escape. She had survived fifteen days in the camp, and she'd spent most of that time thinking up escape plans. Now, snuggled into the blanket, she stared out her window, thinking.

Despite being sealed, the window was drafty, making Maddie's bed one of the coldest in the bunkhouse, and, thus, the least desirable. But having her own private window was a luxury she relished. At first light, before even the obnoxious clanging of the roll call bell, she could look out through the trees to the meadow where some of the horses were already grazing in the distance. It was too far to tell, really, but she liked to pretend that she could see Shadow Dancer out among them, his beautiful black tail swishing in the breeze. Right now, it was impossible to see anything but shadows in the moonless night, so she lay back down and thought about her plan.

She'd need fire, which meant matches or at least a lighter, both prohibited items at the camp. But she'd noticed wooden stick matches in the kitchen yesterday and knew she could swipe a couple, maybe two a day, when Pat, the cook, wasn't looking. She'd been assigned as kitchen helper for her first work shift, which gave her plenty of time to scavenge.

Her biggest brainstorm thus far was taking the zip-lock baggie out of the trash. She'd found a safety pin the week before, which she'd pinned to the inside of her pants, and now she could pin the baggie to that, thus giving her a hidden purse in which to cart her goods. So far, she had two pieces of beef jerky that she'd lifted from an open cellophane package lying on a bench when she'd last visited the stables. She felt bad stealing from Clutch, but she'd been careful not to take too much. Hopefully, he hadn't even noticed.

She also had a handful of Kleenex tissues, which she'd carefully folded into a flat package. There'd be no toilet paper in the woods. If nothing else, they could help her start a fire. Her most prized possession, though, was a can of tuna. Most of the canned products in the kitchen pantry were jumbo-sized, but she'd found a whole row of regular-sized tuna cans and had helped herself to one right away. Not only would the tuna sustain her, but the can could be used as a cup for water and the top would be sharp enough to use as a knife. On the other hand, she had no can opener yet, so, for the time being, the tuna was useless.

It had, however, given her an idea, and yesterday she'd liberated the discarded lid from a large can of stewed tomatoes. She'd managed to fold the lid in half so that one side had a safe edge to grasp onto and the other two sharp edges for cutting. Last night, in the darkness, she'd used the lid to slice open the side of her mattress — the side against the wall — just enough to slide her hidden loot, the can lid included, inside. She'd been living dangerously, stashing things under the mattress, but she knew Belinda made spontaneous bed checks and was bound to find her cache sooner or later. Now, with the goods hidden inside the mattress, Maddie stood a much better chance.

As she lay in bed, silently making her shopping list, she thought about what Dr. Biscane had said during their last therapy session. He asked her if she thought she'd been stealing to get attention. At first, her heart pounded, thinking that somehow he was onto her plan. Had someone seen her? It took her a minute to realize he was talking about before her incarceration in the camp. She'd begun to view her life in terms of whether something happened B.C. (Before Camp) or A.I. (After Incarceration). Doc was dealing with B.C. issues — something she preferred not to think about.

"Think about it, Maddie. We'll talk about it next time. Why do you think you're trying to get attention? Maybe when we talk next time, you'll have some ideas. Hmm?"

He tended to end his sentences with that little "hmm?" like he knew she was perfectly aware of the answer and was just being coy with him. This made her feel kind of bad, because it was partly true. But she didn't always feel like being probed. She'd learned a long time ago how to put unpleasant memories in boxes and store them in places she didn't have to look at. She'd heard the term used on a talk show once — selective amnesia. That's how Maddie thought of it, when she allowed herself to think of it at all. And she figured she had every right to forget whatever she wanted.

She rolled over on her slightly lumpy mattress and turned away from the drafty window, forcing her mind away from Dr. Biscane and everything connected to her life B.C. She pictured the black colt instead, snorting and pawing the ground, a beautiful, untamed beast just waiting for her to join him. She imagined herself on his back, flying across the meadows, the two of them racing off into the forest together.

Chapter Eight

Monday morning I was jolted out of bed by the same bell that seemed to announce every change of events at Camp Turnaround. I knew I wasn't expected to attend roll call or morning calisthenics, but I leaped out of bed just the same and jumped into the shower. By the time the water heated up enough to be deemed lukewarm, I was out of the shower and shivering on the postage stamp-sized bath mat, rubbing a stiff white terry cloth towel over my goosebumps. I dressed hurriedly and made a cup of instant coffee, glad for the meager supplies left in Annie's kitchen. There was definitely a spring mountain chill in the air, I decided. I sat at the kitchenette table, my hands wrapped around the steaming mug, and sorted through what I knew about Annie Sisson.

Now that I knew it wasn't a family emergency that had sent her packing, it changed things. Whether she had left by force or by her own volition, she hadn't gone running home to her mother and father. Why had Ida said it was a family emergency? Is that what Annie had told her? Or had someone else passed that lie on to her? But who would consider Annie Sisson an enemy? No sooner had the thought crossed my mind than I chastised myself. Lots of really good, decent people had enemies. It's not just beauty that's in the eye of the beholder. Jealousy, rage, resentment, fear, envy, unrequited love — the list went on and on. It only took one sicko psycho to make a perfectly good person the object of a hate-fantasy. If Annie had fallen victim to someone like that, it would be a lot more difficult than I'd initially thought to sort this out.

I took a sip of the steaming coffee and concentrated on what I did know. Annie had been on the pill, which presumably meant she was having sex with someone at the camp, and that for some reason she'd wanted to keep it a secret. I also knew that she'd disappeared in the middle of the night. She hadn't taken her pills or her grandmother's blanket, which meant she was either in such a hurry that she'd forgotten them, which I found unlikely, or that someone else had packed her things and hadn't known about the blanket out back or the pills under the drawer. If someone else had packed her things, then it was safe to say that that person knew where she went. Had she left on her own? Or had she been whisked away in the night? Or, as Maddie might be saying, had she been murdered right there at camp? Someone could have killed her, then tried to make it look like she'd left in a hurry. But why would someone murder Annie Sisson? According to both Lacy Godfrey and Ida Evans, Annie was well liked and generous to a fault. Which brought me right back to my sicko-psycho theory. Anything was possible.

Lacy thought she had an idea about why Annie left in such a hurry, but she seemed reticent to share her hunch. I knew I'd need to get her talking again. Maybe she knew who Annie was sleeping with, if nothing else. But who I really wanted to talk to was Maddie Boone. The problem was, if something untoward was going on at the camp, I couldn't afford to blow my cover just yet. Which meant I couldn't just walk up to Maddie in broad daylight and ask her what she meant by her cryptic e-mail. If someone were watching her, any suspicious behavior could put her or both of us in danger. Until I figured out a way to talk with her in private, I'd just have to reconstruct the events leading up to Annie's disappearance on my own.

Since my first class didn't start until ten, I had several hours to kill — plenty of time to talk to Gracie, explore the camp on my own, and still catch breakfast, so I rinsed my cup in the sink and headed for the stables.

The sun was just starting to blaze an orange trail over the eastern mountain, and a breeze rustled the air enough to make me glad I'd brought a jacket. Morning calisthenics were due to end any minute, giving students an hour to shower, dress, and do as they wished — a rare pocket of freedom before breakfast. I knew that sometimes the best way to find out what people were really like was to watch them when they didn't know you were watching. So far, every time I'd seen the kids in camp, their collective guard had been way up. As anxious as I was to talk to Gracie, I wanted to see what these students were like when no one was around. I stepped off the path and concealed myself behind a stand of trees, waiting for the morning workout to end.

I could tell when calisthenics ended by the sound of pounding feet on pavement, and I could also tell the moment they were out of Coach's line of vision by the way the steady cadence gave way to undisciplined chaos. From my vantage point behind a fir tree, I saw a handful of sweaty, blue-shirted boys running back toward their house. They were racing each other, laughing and carefree, quite unlike the way they'd acted during their exercises yesterday under the careful eye of Coach. The House Leader was nowhere in sight, so maybe that explained their lightheartedness. Or maybe it was the prospect of a whole hour to themselves.

Several orange-shirted boys ambled by, in less of a hurry than the first group, intent on making fun of the kid in front — perfectly normal adolescent behavior, I thought. I heard more voices coming down the path and stepped farther into the shadows as I watched. The kids came by in twos and threes, in large batches, and, occasionally, alone. The fat boy who'd been carted off in Coach's wagon walked by himself, his head down, his fists clenched at his side. He was struggling to catch his breath and his shirt was soaked through with sweat. Finally, I spotted Maddie toward the end of the processional, walking beside a spiky-haired, anorexic blonde who seemed barely able to keep up, though she was several years older than Maddie. As badly as I wanted to talk to Maddie, I knew it would be safer if I could catch her alone. Suddenly, she glanced up and looked in my direction, her dark glassy eyes wide and alert. Then she glanced behind her and quickened her pace. She hadn't seen me, but she seemed to sense my presence, or someone else's, I thought. She had the look of someone afraid she was being followed.

Just when I thought they'd all passed and I was about to step out of the forest, I heard a pair of stragglers. I recognized the couple strolling toward me as house leaders. One was the gangly, acne-scarred kid named Dobberteen who'd led the exercises yesterday, and the other was the Girls' House Leader, Belinda Pitt. Belinda was shaking her long red hair free of its ponytail, a sensuous move that seemed to fascinate Dobberteen. She had pale, almost translucent skin with a smattering of freckles across the bridge of her pert nose; full, pouty lips; and melon-sized breasts that had Dobberteen nearly tripping over himself.

"It wouldn't have to be like all the way or anything," he stammered, turning to walk backwards in front of her.

"Forget it, Deano. You're too young, too dumb, and too, um, how should I put this? Too provincial."

"I am not dumb! What's that mean? 'Provincial?' " He'd stopped in front of her, forcing her to stop, too.

She laughed, throwing her head back. Suddenly, he lunged forward, wrapped his arms around her, and pulled her toward him. His lips covered hers, and, for a brief moment, it appeared that she'd succumbed to his dubious charms, because her white freckled fingers circled his neck, pulling him closer. Suddenly, Dobberteen jumped back, emitting a terrible shriek.

"You fucking bitch!" he screamed, dabbing at his lip. A wet, red bubble of blood formed as quickly as he rubbed it away.

Belinda pushed past him, then turned to face him when she was a few safe feet away. "Practice on some of the younger ones first, Deano, then come see me in a month or two. And do learn to do something more interesting with that tongue." She flipped her red, wavy hair back over her shoulder and strutted down the path, leaving Dean Dobberteen to staunch the bleeding of his lip, not to mention his pride, in private.

Except that I was six feet away, hidden behind a fir tree, watching the whole sorry exchange. It was what Deano muttered under his breath after she was well out of earshot, however, that I found most interesting. What he said was, "Bet you never bit Coach, you fucking bitch."

I waited until he was well down the path himself before resuming my trek toward the stables. When I reached the outermost corrals, I leaned against a wood post and took in the view. This was what I'd seen from the road coming in. Beyond the stables and pastures stretched acres of pristine meadows surrounded by plush forest, and, along the east side, a steep, rocky-faced mountain that tapered off to the north, before plunging into a deep gorge. I could hear a distant waterfall and spotted a handful of trickling streams crossing the meadows. I tore my eyes from the beauty and scanned the stables and pastures until I spotted Gracie. She was standing beside a dun-colored mare in the next corral, cinching up a saddle. A weathered, wiry middle-aged man wearing faded Levis, a black T-shirt, and a wheat-colored cowboy hat was saddling up beside her. When Gracie saw me, she broke into a grin, then quickly glanced at the man to make sure he hadn't noticed.

"Howdy," the man said when I approached.

"Hi. I'm Cassidy James. Just hired on yesterday and thought I'd check out the horses before my first class."

"Welcome, Cassidy. I'm Clutch Evans. This here's Gracie. You the one taking over for Miss Sisson?"

"That's me. You must be Ida's husband."

"Guilty as charged," he said, showing me a tobacco-stained grin. His face was ruggedly handsome, with crows feet around the eyes from perpetually squinting. "You a rider?" he asked, patting his horse on the rear.

"Used to be. It's been a while, but part of what attracted me to this job was the horse ranch. I was hoping to work out a way to get a ride in now and then."

"Hell, girl. You can ride every day if you want to. This time of year, we can use all the help we can get. Gracie, why don't you take Miss James here with you to help you get that gate. It'll save me the trouble." He winked at me. "You reckon you can handle this gelding?"

I took the proffered reins and set my left foot in the stirrup, pulling myself up onto the saddle. Clutch wasn't a tall man, but even so, the stirrups were a bit long.

"I appreciate this, Clutch," I said as he adjusted the stirrups. I leaned back, taking in the beauty of the meadow and surrounding forest. "Boy, I sure don't know why anyone would want to leave a place like this. That Miss Sisson must've been crazy."

"Well, it was a surprise to me, her leaving like that. She

always seemed to like it, much as I could tell. Still, a woman's prerogative, I guess, changing her mind."

"Did she ride?" I asked, trying not too sound too interested. Gracie rolled her eyes at me like I was pushing it.

"Oh, yes. She loved to ride. Always took that little Appaloosa, said it fit her just right. I believe she even went for a ride the night she left. Probably wanted one last turn before she skedaddled."

"I wonder, why she did go?" I asked idly, leaning over to pat the chestnut gelding's neck.

Clutch looked at me with narrowed eyes. "Like I said, it pretty near surprised us all. Reckon we'll never know." With that, he slapped my horse's rear, causing him to bolt forward until I gathered the reins and brought him back under control. Gracie was laughing.

"You are a little rusty," she said. "Come on, I'll show you around."

As soon as we were past the corral, Gracie leaned over and whispered. "I knew you'd get the job! Whaddaya think, so far?"

"First impressions?" I said, coaxing my horse into a trot beside her. "I think Coach likes his job a little too much. I think Camp Turnaround probably breaks a few child labor laws, and I think, if this place is half as good as Ida Evans says it is, then all kids should spend some time here, and half the adults I know, as well." Gracie laughed. "What I don't think is that Annie Sisson left voluntarily." I told her about the birth control pills and blanket.

"I'll tell you something interesting," Gracie said, leading me across the pasture toward a gathering of grazing horses. "The night Annie Sisson disappeared, all sorts of stuff was going on around here. I've been snooping around a bit myself. After we open the gate, there's someone I think we should talk to."

She kicked her horse, breaking into a lope, and I followed

suit. As soon as Gracie could tell that I was handling it, she coaxed the bay mare into a gallop, and the gelding shot forward, his red mane flying in the breeze as we kept pace. My own short hair was blowing behind me as we raced across the meadow, easily jumping the stream that meandered across our path. By the time Gracie pulled up at the end of a fenced pasture, I was grinning from ear to ear.

"I'd forgotten how much I missed this," I admitted, leaning forward to pat the gelding.

"You ride pretty good for a white girl," she said, sliding off her horse. "Come on. This gate takes two of us."

I climbed down and dropped the gelding's reins so that he could munch a little grass, then helped Gracie with the huge iron mesh gate that spanned a good hundred feet. It swung on a hinge and took both of us to push it open.

"They do this every day?" I asked.

"After sunup and before sundown. Mountain lions," she explained. "Used to be grizzlies, too, but Clutch says they haven't been around in years. Still, there's plenty of other dangers. The tops and bottoms of the fences are hot-wired each night to discourage adventurous predators, and in some spots there's even barbed wire. Even so, every year they lose a few horses."

"No wonder the kids don't run away," I said, looking out at the dark forest surrounding the meadows.

"Speaking of which, remember Maddie's remark about running away? Turns out that happened the night before Sisson disappeared. And she was still out there somewhere the night Annie left."

"Really." It was hard to picture that little black-haired waif venturing out into the perilous forest on her own at all, let alone, lasting two nights.

"Unfortunately, that's all I know. Except the one to ask is a horse trainer named Joe Bell. Best horse handler I've ever seen. Makes old Clutch look like an amateur. You know what a horse whisperer is?"

"I saw the movie. Didn't know they really existed."

"Well, this kid's as close to one as I've ever seen. Takes a wild-eyed pony and talks magic to it, makes it as gentle as a lamb. I've been trying to catch him alone, but I'm not having much luck. Maybe we can try this morning. He seems to ride the perimeter every morning, checking the fences. If we can't catch him, I know where his cabin is."

She swung back onto her horse, looking every bit the television Indian, and we galloped toward the east side of the meadow.

"What's that?" I asked, slowing to point at a boxcar incongruously perched on a rail track that seemed to run straight out of a gaping hole in the mountain along the east side. Gracie pulled her horse to a stop.

"Clutch told me it's the entrance to an old gold mine. They still use the boxcar to dump junk from the machine shop into the sludge heap down that ravine." She pointed back the way we'd come, where the meadow ended in an abrupt drop-off. The rusty steel tracks ran north along the edge of the mountain, ending at the ravine. "According to Clutch, it's about the only thing that old mine is good for. It never did produce much gold."

"So, this mine connects to the machine shop?" I tried to picture it. The machine shop was a good half-mile east of the stables on the far east end of the compound, abutting the mountain that ran north and south along the entire valley. The road to the stables followed a thick stand of trees separating most of the compound from the meadows, making for a pretty long hike from one end of the camp to the other using the road. But now that I thought about it, as a crow flies, the distance from the main compound to where we were riding would be much shorter. I could see how a tunnel through the mountain, running mostly north and south, would allow for quite a shortcut.

Suddenly, I felt a paralyzing fear rise up in my gut, as I recalled the dream I'd had the night Connie and Gracie had come to hire me. Without any warning, my throat felt as if it were clamping shut and my palms began to sweat.

"You okay?" Gracie asked.

"Yeah," I lied as the panic slowly abated. But the sense of dread was nearly overwhelming. What I really wanted to do was turn my horse around and ride straight out of camp. How could one lousy recurring dream about dying make me lose my nerve, I wondered. Furious at my cowardice, I forced myself to sound casual.

"You ever been inside the mine?"

"Me? No way. Scared to death of anything underground."

For some reason, this admission made me laugh and I instantly felt better.

"Gracie, you ever dream about dying?"

She looked at me for a minute and I felt her eyes probing me, searching.

"Uh huh," she intoned. "But I ain't dead yet."

I laughed again and this time she joined me. "There something you want to talk about?" she asked.

There was, actually. But I wasn't sure where to start. How could I tell her that I had just discovered, despite years of false bravery, that deep down I was a coward? That the thought of my own death paralyzed me? What kind of private eye did that make me? One thing I'd always relied on was my ability to think fast and move quickly in a crisis. Suddenly, I was overwhelmed with the possibility that the next time, I might not rise to the occasion. I might stand stock still and do nothing. I might die.

"So," I said, ignoring her question, "you afraid of heights, too?"

"Nah. Just depths. Probably buried alive in a past life. Just the thought of going underground makes me nervous."

Me, too, I thought, but I didn't share this. I changed the subject.

"Speaking of nervous, Ida Evans seems a little wired to me. And she's taking Lithium carbonate and something called Fluoxetine. You ever run across those in your med-tech days? Could they be making her a little hyper?"

Gracie narrowed her eyes. "Not likely. How'd you find out all that?"

I told her about my sneaking into the office to check Annie's file and going through Ida's desk drawers.

"Hmm. The only time I've seen something similar to that combo was to treat bipolar disease."

"You mean as in manic-depressive?"

"Exactly. If Ida seems wired, I doubt it's the drugs' doing. More likely, she's taking them to keep herself on an even keel. Come on, maybe that's him up there."

She pointed her chin at a distant figure leaning beside a horse. As we drew nearer, it became clear that a young filly had become entangled in the barbed wire fencing along the east side of the pasture, and Joe Bell was trying to free her. Gracie motioned for me to pull up, and we both dismounted quietly, dropping the reins so our horses could graze as we walked closer.

The filly was wide-eyed and terrified, several nasty gashes still oozing onto her dark, sticky, matted coat. It was clear that the horse had been trapped for some time. Her ears were torn and bright red blood ran down to mingle with the black ooze already coagulated on the crooked white blaze of her nose. We inched closer, hearing Joe's gentle voice soothing the colt. " 'Atta girl. You can do it, now. Come on, baby."

Flies buzzed around the horse's wounds, and, every time the horse tried to swish its tail to clear them, the tail became more entwined in the barbs. Though the horse was clearly panicked, Joe's words seemed to calm her.

"Careful, girl. Just let me get this one leg free and then we'll be good as new. Watch your tail, there, that's right. I know this hurts, I wish I didn't have to do this. That's right, good girl." As he spoke, the kid pried the two twisted, tangled wires apart as far as he could, ripping open his own flesh in an attempt to free the trapped hoof. His black hat came off in the process, revealing blond hair combed straight back off the forehead, and surprisingly fine features.

Gracie spoke so quietly I barely heard her myself.

"Would it help if I came over and pulled those for you, or would that frighten her even more?"

Joe didn't even turn. His gentle, soothing voice stayed the same, though his hands were covered with blood, some of it his own.

"Don't want to spook her even more than she already is. I just about got it. Thatta girl, one more time now. Okay. Yes! That's it, sweetheart. You can do it, let me just get the tail."

The filly's leg had finally come free, though her tail was still hopelessly entangled in the barbed wire. Feeling her battered hoof touch ground, however, caused the horse to bolt forward. When she realized her tail was still trapped, she laid her ears back, rolled her eyes, squealed a horrifying cry, and kicked back with both hind legs, ripping her tail free from the fence.

Joe took the brunt of the kick to his hip, sending him sprawling straight into the barbed wire. The filly raced away, and Gracie and I dashed toward the writhing form entangled in the fence.

"Shit! Hold still. You're cut pretty bad." Gracie pried the barbed wires apart, and I tried to rip the torn flannel shirt free in the dozens of places where it had caught on the fence. The shirt was practically shredded and blood streamed freely down Joe's arms.

"Hold on, I've almost got it," I said. With one final tug, Joe suddenly came tumbling free of the fence, toppling both Gracie and me in the process. I heard the flannel shirt rip apart, rendering Joe's chest completely bare, but my brain didn't quite process what my eyes beheld.

"Oh, my," Gracie said, sitting up on her heels. We looked at each other, and then again at Joe, who lay sprawled before us. Ribbons of blood criss-crossed Joe's fine, tawny skin, but that's not what had Gracie and I gaping. Joe Bell, despite outward appearances to the contrary, wasn't a man at all. She was, in fact, a very striking woman.

Chapter Nine — Madeline

Three and a half-weeks earlier

On her twentieth day of incarceration, during kitchen duty, Maddie had scored! Her plastic baggie was dangerously close to bulging and tugged at her pants, but she could barely suppress the grin that threatened to break the surface of her practiced stoic expression. Ten wooden matches, a box of birthday candles, and, miracle of miracles, an honest to goodness Swiss Army knife! This was an unbelievable find, though theft was probably a more accurate description. It was one thing to swipe stuff from the kitchen drawers. It was something else entirely to go through the cook's purse that was hanging in the coat closet. It had been a risky endeavor, one that could easily have landed her in Isolation, had she been caught. But she'd been very careful not to touch any money or personal belongings that the cook was likely to notice missing. She even bypassed the car keys, though it was tempting to take them. But she knew the parking lot was locked, and that, without the code to the gate, the car would be useless, even if she had known how to drive, which she didn't.

She was about to give up on the purse, her heart racing so fast that her palms were sweaty, when she felt a hard bulge in the bottom of one of the zippered compartments. Hurrying, she unzipped the pocket and plunged her hand into it, pulling out the cherry red knife. She could hardly believe her luck! She quickly stashed the knife in her baggie, causing her waist band to sag, and put the purse back the way she'd found it. Just as she was closing the closet, a door banged open, and Pat, the cook, came bustling around the corner.

"Maddie! There you are. What in the world are you doing back here? You're supposed to be helping set up."

"I thought I heard a cat," she said, thinking this was the lamest excuse she'd ever come up with in her life. To her surprise, it had the desired effect.

"Really? Out back or in here?"

"Out back, I guess. I only heard it once."

"One of the barn cats, probably. Must be hungry." She opened the door and looked outside. "Here kitty, kitty. Here kitty, kitty."

Maddie followed right behind her. "Here kitty, kitty," she called.

"Oh, well," Pat said, patting Maddie's head in a way that wasn't completely awful, Maddie thought. "He'll be back if he's hungry enough. We better see what's happening out front, eh?"

"Okay," Maddie said, heading off toward the serving lines. Her heart was practically in her throat by now, but she'd pulled it off. She couldn't wait until dark when she could stash the new loot in her mattress and explore the hidden parts of the knife in private. She wondered if it had a screw driver, like some of them. If so, the latches on her window were history.

Heart still thudding, she took her place at the end of the assembly line and went to work. Today she was in charge of spooning out strawberry Jello. Rebecca Patterson, who was even newer to the camp than Maddie, though two years older, was at the very end, squirting a dollop of whipped cream onto each blob of Jello that Maddie passed to her. It was the better job of the two, and Maddie had let Rebecca have it because Rebecca looked like she could use a little fun.

Since Rebecca's arrival, Maddie had not been called Toad as much. Now Rebecca was the official Toad. She was an emaciated, strung-out-looking blonde with wispy hair cut so short before she arrived that the nurse from hell had been denied her ritual hack job. It was clear from the number of holes in the girl's earlobes and nostrils that she'd once sported an impressive collection of hoops and studs. Since jewelry was not allowed at Camp Turnaround, the holes went unadorned. She had an aqua-colored tattoo on her left shoulder and another on her ankle, which Maddie had seen in the shower. Despite these colorful enhancements, the girl looked washed out. Maddie guessed she'd been into drugs and that that had led to her troubles with the law. Whatever her past, however, the girl seemed to be wilting before their very eyes at Camp Turnaround. She hardly spoke to anyone, went through her daily exercises listlessly, shuffled from class to class with the enthusiasm of a slug, and in general wore an expression of extreme indifference. Even Coach had been unable to scare her into line. She wasn't defiant. She wasn't rude. She just plain didn't seem to care if she lived or died.

Maddie waited for Rebecca to finish topping the Jello with whipped cream, then handed her another plate. Rebecca was holding up the assembly line with her listlessness, but Maddie felt so sorry for her she didn't complain. She looked up and saw Belinda Pitt scowling down at them, waiting for her dessert.

"Speed it up, Toad. You're holding up everyone's lunch. We haven't got all day."

Rebecca was momentarily startled out of her trance and accidentally dropped Belinda's plate, sending the Jello and whipped cream crashing to the floor. She looked down at the mess, then bent over to pick up the fallen plate.

"Don't even think about giving me that plate back, you idiot. Go get me a clean one!"

"Now, you're holding up the line," Maddie said quietly to Belinda. "Why don't you go get your own plate. If you hadn't yelled at her, she wouldn't have dropped it in the first place."

Belinda's pale face turned crimson. "What did you say?"

"Which part didn't you get?" Maddie asked. She knew what she was doing was suicidal, but right then she didn't care. She was sick of Belinda Pitt.

The line behind Belinda had definitely started to queue up. The girls that always seemed to hover around Belinda like moths to a flame, crowded in, not wanting to miss the unfolding scene.

"You're asking for it, Toad," she spat. Now Maddie was back to Toad status. Unexpectedly, this made Rebecca Patterson smile.

"What are you smiling at?" Belinda said, leaning across the counter to jab her pointed nail into Rebecca's chest.

Rebecca stepped back, saying in a thin, flutie voice, "I thought I was the toad. Now she's the toad. Just confused, I guess. Or maybe you're the one who's confused."

Belinda leaned farther over the counter, snarling. She looked ready to attack. "No, assbite. That would be you. Obviously you've forgotten who's in charge here. Or is your brain so fucked up with meth you can't think straight?"

"Leave her alone, Belinda," Maddie said. "You really don't need the Jello, anyway. Correct me if I'm wrong, but you seem to have put on a few unwanted pounds lately. Maybe you should lay off the desserts for awhile."

This drew a few giggles from Belinda's faithful followers until she turned and leveled them with a seething glare. Then she turned her wrath on Maddie.

"You're dead meat, you fucking nigger-skinned Indian."

Maddie was stunned, but she hid her fear. She turned to Rebecca, her voice rising so the girls behind Belinda could hear. "Apparently, not only is she a fat-assed bully, but she's racist, too. Hey, Dee," she called to the black girl standing a few feet away. "You hear what your friend just called me?"

"Shut up!" Belinda screeched. She lunged across the counter and grabbed Maddie by the hair, yanking her face-down into the Jello bin and holding her under with both hands. Maddie choked, trying to breathe, and panicked. In desperation, she reached up and swung with all her might, slugging Belinda Pitt in the face. Suddenly, Belinda's grip loosened, and Maddie stood up, gasping, her face dripping strawberry Jello. Belinda was sprawled backwards on the floor, her nose bleeding profusely.

The next few minutes were chaos. Nurse Beckett was summoned, and Belinda was carted off like a fallen hero, with her gaggle of sidekicks crowding around her in a pathetic display of devotion. Coach, who had just entered the cafeteria and saw the tail end of the action, grabbed Maddie by the elbow and marched her out of the mess hall, his prod pressed into her rib cage, his voice menacing in her ear.

"Don't even think about putting up a fuss, Madeline. You're in so much trouble as it is, you can't afford to piss me off on top of it. Now climb in!"

They'd reached the ATV with the little metal wagon hitched to the back, and Maddie crawled into it, starting to shiver. The last time she'd seen someone hauled off in the wagon, they'd done two days in Isolation. When the boy had come back, he'd been as meek as a mouse.

As mortified as she'd been to have her face and hair covered with slimy Jello, and as exhilarated as she'd felt decking Belinda, the only real emotion she could summon at the moment was abject terror.

Chapter Ten

As Gracie and I helped her back to her cabin, I was burning with curiosity. Why, I wondered, had Jo Bell pretended to be Joe Bell? Her cabin was perched on a bluff at the edge of the meadow and once we got her inside, I looked through her medicine cabinet for hydrogen peroxide and Neosporin. While Gracie worked on Jo's wounds, I surreptitiously checked out the rest of her belongings — you wouldn't know she was a woman by the clothing in the closet — but there were signs here and there. For one thing, her small library of books included a copy of *Patience and Sarah* and several volumes of Emily Dickenson. There was a box of tampons under the bathroom sink. Though small, her arsenal of cookware included a fancy copper saucepan and skillet that most cowboys wouldn't be likely to own. There were jars of spices and herbs she'd apparently grown in the little garden out back. There was a case of wine, the bottles stored properly on their sides in a hand-carved rack next to the table. Half a dozen watercolors depicting wild horses in varying degrees of colorful motion adorned the walls. A guitar was propped against the corner of the room.

But what really gave her away, I decided, were the fine, delicate features. How anyone could've mistaken her for a boy was beyond me. She had incredibly graceful hands with long, fine fingers, delicate wrists, and strong, well-toned, muscled arms. Her cheek-bones were high, her brow strong, and her eyes were bluish-gray, the color of a calm sea. She caught me staring and a puzzled frown clouded her lovely face. I glanced at Gracie who was looking at me with utter bemusement. I felt myself blush and looked away.

"I've got to check on the filly," Jo said, resisting Gracie's attempt to treat her wounds.

"These aren't deep but they could get infected if we don't treat them," Gracie said. "Hold still."

Jo looked down at the tangle of welts and cuts on her chest and arms, her pale cheeks coloring. I knew I should look away, but my eyes were drawn to her. How could I not have noticed her breasts? They were small, but round and firm and I was suddenly envious of Gracie who was gently soothing the lacerated skin. Jo brushed a wisp of blond hair from her forehead where it had fallen loose, seemingly mortified at the attention and the exposure. "Thanks for doing this," she managed, though her cheeks were still blushing. "I guess it's a good thing you two came along when you did." The second Gracie finished with the chest wounds, Jo grabbed a towel and held it in front of her while Gracie went to work on the arms.

"We haven't officially met, but I've seen you around," Gracie said. "I'm Grace Apodaca. This is my friend, Cassidy James."

"I've noticed you, too," Jo said, her blue-gray eyes smiling first at Gracie, then landing on me. Again, I felt my cheeks grow warm. "You, I haven't noticed. You must be new."

"Yesterday," I said, knowing if I didn't leave in the next few minutes, I'd be late for my first class, but somehow not wanting to budge. I checked my watch. "Uh, I'm supposed to be teaching in about fifteen minutes and I left all my books and stuff in my cabin. Can I come by and see how you're doing later?"

This sounded ridiculously like I was asking her out on a date. Gracie was grinning but I ignored her. Jo smiled, too.

"I'd like that, Cassidy James."

By now, Gracie was barely suppressing laughter. "I'll walk you to the door, Champ. Don't worry about the horse, I'll take him back for you. You sure you remember how to get back to camp?"

I rolled my eyes at her but my color gave me away. I hadn't felt this giddy since, well, since I'd first laid eyes on Erica Trinidad. Which was all the reminder I needed to stuff the feelings back where they came from and make sure they stayed there. But when I stepped out into the bright spring sunshine, I found myself smiling, and I jogged all the way back to my cabin. Actually, I may have skipped once or twice, but I was pretty sure no one was watching.

I had butterflies in my stomach and I didn't know if it was the prospect of standing in front of a class again, or of seeing Jo Bell later that afternoon. I didn't have much time to dwell on it. As it was, I was a few minutes late for my first class.

There were twenty kids in all, a mix of boys and girls from the various houses. Maddie wasn't in the first group. I knew from the roster that I'd be seeing her after lunch in my second class. But Belinda Pitt and Dean Dobberteen were sitting right across from each other and I noticed Dean reach up and gingerly dab at his lip from time to time, refusing to even glance in Belinda's direction.

It's amazing how things come back to you, I thought.

Camp Turnaround kids weren't that much different from those I'd taught years earlier. I'd once had a class where they'd lumped all the discipline problems together. Camp Turnaround was like that, only ten-fold. But underneath the bad-ass attitudes, these kids were still kids, and they were as curious about me as I was them. A few of them tried to test me right off the bat, which I expected. I gave them the old teacher-look and slung a few well-aimed barbs that seemed to convince them that I knew my stuff. That settled everyone down and by the end of the first hour they were writing their first assignment for me.

But what really came back to me was how much I enjoyed teaching. I loved the give and take, the raw need in kids' eyes, their vulnerability and the power it gave me to do right by them. I'd forgotten about some of that, and it was a humbling reminder, standing in front of the kids at Camp Turnaround whose needs were so much more than those I'd taught before.

Wanting to find out as much as I could about them, I gave them the choice of writing a poem, a rap-song, an essay or a short story on their personal strengths and weaknesses. I told them to do their best work so I could assess their writing abilities and interests. The truth was, I was more interested in assessing their personality traits than looking at their writing. If it was a possibility that Miss Sisson had been murdered, it was not out of the realm of possibility that it might have been by a student, or even a group of students. One thing about people — regardless of whether they were hard-core criminals or budding adolescents — they revealed things about themselves on paper that they would never dream of saying aloud. I'd be happy if something jumped out at me, but I wasn't holding my breath.

The first two-hour block flew by and by the time the bell clanged for lunch, I had a stack of papers to read and a growling stomach. Before I joined the kids in the mess hall, I skimmed the papers. I separated them by type; six rap songs, eight poems, three short-stories and three essays. It only took a glance to know that the rappers weren't very talented, most of them choosing the medium because it sounded like fun, not because they were particularly adept at rhythm or rhyme. Some of the poems were pretty bad too, but setting talent aside, there was a lot of emotion in both piles. Anger and resentment ruled the day and depression was a close third.

The essays tended to be more detached, but no less revealing. Belinda Pitt, for example, wrote in big loopy letters about her strengths; she was organized, neat, responsible, hard-working, mature and ambitious. Best yet, she was humble, never getting a big head even if she was the most popular girl, whether it was in school or camp. Her only real fault, she conceded, was that she resented her parents for dumping her in this camp so they could justify traipsing all over Europe. All because of a little incident with some boys on the football team! Like she was the only high-school girl who ever flirted! She'd be free of them soon, however, and then she wouldn't have to resent them any longer. Thus leaving her faultless, I presumed, suppressing a grimace.

What little I'd seen of Belinda Pitt in action, I knew she'd left a few faults out. People who thought that highly of themselves worried me. And the statement about being free of her parents soon was equally troubling. Maybe she just meant that once she reached eighteen, she'd be legally free of them. Or maybe she'd meant something more sinister.

I saved the rest of the papers for later and hurried over to the mess hall for lunch. The aromas of good, home-cooking greeted me before I even entered. They were right, the food at Camp Turnaround was something to look forward to.

Pat, the cook and kitchen manager, was standing behind the aluminum serving bins, supervising the student-workers. She was a round, pleasant woman with kind brown eyes and a hearty laugh. She had a streak of flour on her cheek that she swiped at, but missed, only adding another smear of white dust. "You must be the new gal, taking over for Annie. I wondered when I'd get to meet you. I'm Pat Mayberry. You're in the cabin next to mine."

"Cassidy James," I said. "Boy something sure smells good." I eyed the bins, searching for the source of the heavenly aromas.

Pat grinned. "Chicken-fried steak, fresh green beans, mashed potatoes and sausage gravy, buttermilk biscuits and chocolate cream pie for dessert. Or there's the salad bar," she said, rolling her eyes. Pat looked like someone who didn't waste a lot of time at the salad bar. I had a feeling she and Nurse Beckett weren't bosom buddies.

"Let's go with the works," I said, holding out my plate.

"Woman after my own heart. Load her up, kids."

The student workers each stood behind a separate bin, scooping out mountainous portions onto my plate before passing it on. I was surprised to see Maddie in line in front of me and tried to catch her eye. She graced me with a brief glance, then looked away again quickly. She had the same dark expressive eyes as her mother, I thought. But whereas her mother's eyes had looked wounded, Maddie's seemed both frightened and defiant.

Pat met me at the end of the line. "Come by some time," she said. "I'm usually through here and back in my cabin by eight. If you'd like to swap war stories over a little vino some time, stop by."

"Thanks, I'd like that," I said.

Lacy Godfrey was waving me over to the table she shared with Nurse Beckett and Ida Evans. I brought my food-laden tray and joined them, though they were nearly finished eating. Nurse Beckett eyed my plate with obvious disdain.

"I don't know why she insists on serving those ridiculous portions," she said, taking a dainty bite of her salad.

"Looks good to me," I said. I took a bite of the potatoes. "Tastes good, too. I hope I'll have room for that chocolate cream pie."

I'd deliberately set the pie right in front of Nurse Beckett.

I saw her sneak a quick glance at it, then force her gaze away. The closet junk-food junkie in her was crying out for a bite of that pie.

"Well, how'd it go?" Ida asked. "Kids give you a hard time?"

"Not after the first few minutes or so. They tested the water a little, then settled right down. I was a little nervous," I admitted. "But once we got going, I really enjoyed it. I'm looking forward to my afternoon class."

"Good. I knew you'd like it here. I understand you ride, too."

Obviously, not much went unnoticed at the camp. I'd have to be careful. I nodded and swallowed some green beans. Pat had cooked them in chicken broth with bacon and onions, just the way I liked them. "I got to meet Clutch," I said. "He let me ride this morning. I'd forgotten how much I like riding. Can hardly walk, though. My thighs aren't used to it."

Ida laughed. "So he told me. You just missed the stable crew. They're always first in line for meals. Surprised they leave anything for the rest of us." She looked at Nurse Beckett and patted her hand. "Oh, go on and get a piece. It ain't gonna kill you."

Nurse Beckett colored and stood up, gathering her tray. "I don't know what you're talking about," she said, carrying her tray to the counter. Ida pushed herself up from the table and followed, chuckling the whole way.

Lacy used her fork to skim a little of the whipped cream off the top of my pie and daintily licked at it with the tip of her tongue.

"Nurse Beckett's a little paranoid about cholesterol and fat," she said. "But she's not as uptight as she comes off. She got drunk as a skunk at the Christmas party last year. You shoulda seen her. The way she was hanging all over Coach, it was hilarious. She even got Doc to dance."

"Sounds like fun," I said, slowing down on my lunch. "So,

does she have a thing for Coach? He doesn't really seem her type."

She laughed. "In case you haven't noticed, there's not a whole lot of eligible bachelors around here. Even Coach probably looks pretty good after enough Christmas punch."

"Doesn't sound like you're too enamored, though."

"Me? No way. Not after the way he treated Annie." As soon as she said it, I could tell she regretted it. She put down her fork and dabbed at her mouth with her napkin, looking chagrinned.

"Coach and Annie Sisson were an item?"

"Shhh," she whispered, glancing around. She took a sip of her Pepsi. "It wasn't exactly common knowledge. But yeah, they were dating."

"But why would they have to hide that? I mean, they're both adults, right?"

"I guess it's because Coach is kind of like one of the bosses here. Doc, Ida, Clutch, Ben and Coach are like the administrators. The other teachers and counselors might think Annie was getting special privileges or something if they knew she was dating Coach. So they kept it quiet."

"But you knew," I said, pushing my pie toward Lacy who thought for several seconds before she retrieved her fork and dug in.

"Annie was my friend," she said between mouthfuls. "I found her crying one day and knew something was wrong. Once she started talking, it just all came out. The way Coach treated her one way in private, then was cold to her in public. The way he made promises that he kept breaking. And then the last straw was — Annie thought he might be seeing someone else. She wouldn't say who, but I knew she was really upset about it. I think that's why she left, if you want to know the truth. I think Coach gave her the cold shoulder and she just packed up and left before he broke her heart any more."

"Makes sense," I said. "Maybe she caught him with whoever else he was seeing."

"Exactly! That's what I think must have happened. If I knew who it was, I'd sure like to give them a piece of my mind!"

"No ideas?" I probed.

"Not really. Not that I haven't thought about it, but I keep drawing blanks."

"Any chance it was a student?" I asked.

"A student?" she echoed, looking genuinely taken aback. "Not even Coach would go that far," she said. "It's one thing to date a teacher. You know how fast Doc and Clutch would kick him out of here if they even thought he was screwing around with a student? Coach may be selfish, but he's not stupid."

With that, the bell clanged, signaling the beginning of the afternoon sessions and both Lacy and I rushed toward our classrooms.

The highlight of my second two-hour class, a repeat more or less of the first one, was that Maddie Boone was in it. I was eager to see which writing assignment she'd choose and what she'd say about herself. I was surprised to discover that though among the youngest at the camp, she was nonetheless one of the brightest. She also seemed to be studying me as carefully as I was her. Was it because I'd replaced her teacher and she resented me for it? Or had I somehow telegraphed my curiosity about her, rousing her own curiosity in turn?

She chose to write a poem, and though brief, it was, if not exactly illuminating, at least intriguing.

my strengths, in case you want to hear
are truly weaknesses I fear
the things I think I do the best
are secretly what I detest
the parts that others want to change
those are among my favorite things

so who's to say what weakness is
or which ones we should just forgive
and who's to say what makes us strong
for all we know, they could be wrong!

by Maddie Boone

She may not have revealed many details, I thought, but I was impressed by a thirteen year-old who understood that her weaknesses were also her strengths, and vice versa. I knew a lot of adults who had never conquered that concept, myself included, at times. She could also use rhyme better than all of the rappers in both classes put together. Knowing her penchant for hidden messages, I read the poem several times, looking for something that might help me unravel the mystery of Miss Sisson. In the end, I decided to just appreciate the poem for what it revealed about Maddie.

When the bell rang to end class, I asked Maddie to stay after for a minute.

"Why?" she asked, looking troubled.

A few of the other kids were still loitering near the door.

"Just wanted to go over your poem with you. No big deal."

"I'm supposed to meet Dr. Biscane," she said, backing toward the door. "He doesn't like us to be late for appointments."

"Maybe later, then," I said, trying to put her at ease. She definitely seemed spooked about something. I watched her walk away, wondering if I should just go ahead and tell her who I was and why I was there. That is, if I ever got the chance to talk to her alone.

Chapter Eleven

After the afternoon class, I spent some time reading the kids' papers and sorted them into three piles. Those who bragged, those who showed shame or guilt and those who did neither. Maddie's was an example of the latter. She wasn't particularly proud of herself, but she wasn't sold on anyone else either. Some of the kids degraded themselves to the point of being pitiful. A few of them listed faults and weaknesses until they ran out of room, never getting to their strengths at all. On the other hand, there were some like Belinda Pitt who were so taken with themselves they wouldn't recognize a weakness if it hit them over the head. I decided to start with that group — partly because it was the smallest pile — partly because of the sociopaths and criminals I'd run up against, most were braggarts. If Miss Sisson really had been murdered and it was a student who did it, I was putting my money on the sociopaths. Of course, so far I'd only seen half the kids in camp. Tomorrow, I'd give the same assignment to the other half.

I swung by the cabin and decided to spruce up a bit, meaning I showered for a second time that day and changed into my favorite blue pullover that Erica Trinidad always said matched my eyes. With a start, I realized that I'd scarcely thought about Erica all day. This was definitely progress, I thought, taking a little extra time with my hair.

Without really meaning to, I made a mental comparison between Erica and Jo Bell. One was dark and sensually feminine, the other fair and, what? Masculine? Not really. But she'd passed as a boy, hadn't she? Why was that? With her short blonde hair brushed back off her forehead like that, and the cowboy hat and the jeans and flannel, she looked just like the other cowboys on the ranch. Yet you couldn't say she wasn't sensual. You couldn't say she wasn't graceful. At first glance, Jo Bell and Erica Trinidad might seem opposites. But there were similarities as well — riveting eyes and graceful hands, high cheek bones and great smiles. This was ridiculous, I chastised myself.

Still, there was no denying the attraction. Maybe it had been the shock of seeing her breasts when I'd been expecting a boy. Maybe it was the way her eyes acknowledged the look on my face when our eyes met. Hell, I thought. Maybe I was just plain lonely.

I shook the thought from my head. I didn't have time to think about Jo, let alone Erica Trinidad, or any other woman. I hurried down the now-familiar path to the stables, passing kids along the way who were enjoying the free hour before the late afternoon team activities.

When I got to the stables, I practically ran smack into Maddie Boone who was just coming out of one of the tack rooms, something concealed in her right hand.

"Hey, nice poem," I said.

She glanced up, surprised.

"You really read it?"

"Of course I read it. I thought you showed a lot of insights. I believe my strengths are my weaknesses, too."

"Yeah? Like what?" she asked. She graced me with a dark, challenging look and strode off toward one of the corrals where a black colt was charging back and forth, frolicking in the afternoon sunshine. I followed behind her.

"Like, I tend to be pretty quick to catch onto things. That's a strength, right?"

She looked at me and shrugged, opened her fist and held out a sugar cube in an open palm and whispered to the colt. "Come on, Shadow Dancer. Come on, boy."

"But, it also makes me kind of impatient when others aren't as quick. That's a weakness. See?"

She looked at me again, this time acknowledging that what I said made sense.

"What else?" she said, clearly testing me.

"I'm a good talker. Some people might see that as a strength. On the other hand, people who are good talkers are often lousy listeners. I have to work on it."

She snuck another sideways glance at me. "That's a good one." She nodded her head like she'd run into lots of lousy listeners in her time.

The colt pretended not to be interested in her outstretched hand, though it managed to mosey in her direction just the same. Maddie was showing a considerable amount of patience.

"You like horses?" she asked.

"Yeah. You?"

"Some. I like this one. I named him Shadow Dancer."

I studied the colt. "It suits him. He's quite a horse."

"Thank you," she said solemnly. Like she'd given birth to the horse herself. It occurred to me that Maddie was lonely. This horse was probably her closest companion at the camp. Probably the only one she trusted, too. Shadow Dancer had finally worked his way within nudging distance but still pretended to be more interested in pawing the ground than sniffing the sugar.

"I know you want this, boy. You know you want this. Quit playing games."

As if he'd heard her, the colt straightened up and arched his neck toward her open palm, nostrils flaring. He curled his lip, showing large yellow teeth and he made a soft nickering sound before gently pursing his lips onto her palm and slurping up the proffered lump of sugar.

"Good boy," she said, gingerly running her fingers down the bridge of his nose before he backed away. "That's the second time he's let me touch him," she said excitedly, her eyes shining.

"He obviously likes you," I said. "Maddie, there's something I need to talk to you about."

She glanced at me, her eyes suddenly clouded. Then she jumped down off the fence just as the bell announcing the end of free time chimed in the distance.

"Gotta go. See you tomorrow!" she said, loping off down the path. I wasn't sure if she was talking to me or Shadow Dancer.

"Maddie!" I called after her, but she didn't turn around.

"She's quite a kid, isn't she?" Gracie's voice startled me and I wheeled around.

"She sure is. Kinda reminds me of this colt. Wild-eyed, ready to bolt, but full of promise, too. She's smart as a whip, Gracie. You should read the poem she wrote today."

"You find out anything about Annie Sisson?"

"Not from Maddie. She won't let me talk to her. I've got to find a way to get her to trust me. I do know Annie was seeing Coach on the sly."

"Really? Hmmm. I wonder if Jo knows that. I told her who we are and what we're up to. She's anxious to talk to you."

"You sure we can trust her?"

"We gotta trust someone, Cass. I'll put my money on the

horse whisperer every time. Besides, I got the feeling you were kinda taken with her yourself."

I ignored her probing look. "Just took me by surprise, that's all. I wasn't expecting her to be a woman." But I knew as I said it that there was more to my reaction to Jo than surprise. I was pretty sure Gracie knew it, too.

"Yeah. Kinda threw me, too. When I heard the name, I just assumed it was Joe. But the way she moves . . . I don't know, Cass. I must be losing my touch."

I laughed. "Come on, let's go find out what she knows."

I kept pace with Gracie's long strides up the hill toward the edge of the pasture where Jo's cabin sat off by itself. It was a nice sunny spot with an herb garden in back and a porch swing out front. From the porch, you could see the stables back to the south, most of the meadows as far north as the distant gorge and the rich forestland to the west. Most of the other ranch hand's cabins were hidden in the trees along the stream, giving Jo's place a sense of privacy.

When we got there, Jo was outside, looking much stronger than she had earlier.

"Feeling better?" I asked.

"Pretty good, actually. They're mostly just scratches. Got a pretty good bruise on my backside, though. Nurse Beckett checked me over. Said Gracie did a good job. Clutch gave me the day off, too, so it's not all bad." She grinned and I was struck again by how attractive I found her. She was definitely boyish, but there was a supple grace about her that was undoubtedly feminine.

"You all want a cup of tea? Or a glass of wine? I've got a bottle of Pinot Noir open that's pretty nice."

Gracie looked at me, then shrugged. "I'm through working for the day," she said.

"How about you, Cassidy?" Jo asked.

"A glass of wine would be nice."

Gracie and I settled into a pair of adirondack chairs on the porch while Jo went to fetch the wine. When she came out, she handed me a short juice glass half-filled with the berry-colored wine, and her fingers grazed my hand. It lasted less than a second, but the effect was electric. Her gaze locked with mine and I knew she felt it, too. Once again, I felt heat rush to my cheeks. Jo seemed as startled as I was by the exchange and turned away to give Gracie a glass, then sat back in the porch swing, taking a sip from her own.

"Sorry I can't offer you something fancier. My wine glasses are packed away in storage."

"This is fine," I assured her, taking a sip of the wine. It was surprisingly full-bodied, with a hint of tannin and a lot of grape. "You sure you should be drinking?" I asked. "I doubt the nurse would approve."

"Nurse Beckett? Shoot, Cassidy, she wouldn't approve of a Diet Coke."

Jo's voice was low and melodic, with a twinge of southern in it. I wondered where she was from. And what she was doing at Camp Turnaround. "Gracie tells me you two are up here snooping around," she said, beating me to the punch.

"She tell you why?"

"Little Maddie Boone thinks something bad happened to Annie Sisson. That someone killed her."

"What do you think?" I asked.

"There was so much going on that night, anything's possible, I guess. It's usually pretty quiet here in the evenings, but the night before Annie disappeared Maddie took off running. Coach usually lets the kids stay gone a while, gives them a chance to find out that they can't get far. Also scares the hell out of them, spending a night in the woods. Personally, I think he ought to go right after them. One of these days, someone's going to run into a cougar out there. But no one argues with Coach. Ever since he became part of the staff, he's kind of taken over."

"You were here before Coach was on staff?" I asked,

wondering how old she was. When I'd thought she was a boy, she looked about seventeen. Now I realized she could be in her late twenties.

She leaned back in her swing and gave herself a little push, bringing her long legs up into her lap, Indian style, in one graceful motion. "Hell, Cass. I was here when Coach was a still a student."

This took both Gracie and me by such surprise that Gracie nearly choked on her wine.

"Coach was a student here?" I managed.

"Yep. Same time I was. Though I was just a kid and he was eighteen. Word was, he'd been here quite a few years. Doc sort of adopted him, let him stay beyond his normal graduation date. He was a House Leader, back then. I guess he never left. I was as surprised to find him working here as you are to find out he was once a student."

The truth was, I was just as shocked to find out that she had been a student.

"How long were you here?" Gracie asked.

"Long enough to get straightened out. Doc's worth his weight in gold. I'd been to a few child psychologists before and I've been to a few shrinks since. Never had one as good as Doc. He uses hypnotherapy. Does regressions. He got me to remember some things I'd stored away — completely blocked out. Anyway, once I figured out why I was so angry, I learned to channel the anger. The anger didn't go away, but I quit taking it out on the wrong people."

She seemed unselfconscious about revealing all this and I admired her frankness. "So how long have you been back? As an employee, I mean?"

"The last couple of years I've hired on during spring foaling and stayed a few months to help Clutch with the colts. He saves this little cabin for me because he knows I like to garden a little. Summers, I move around the tourist spots, trying to sell my work. I winter in Seattle, which is crazy because it rains there most of the winter, but if I were somewhere warmer, I might be outside playing instead of painting."

"The watercolors inside are yours?" I asked. Now, I was really impressed.

"You noticed them?"

"Are you kidding? They're really good. Really."

Jo blushed. Gracie stood up to pace the porch, anxious to get back on topic.

"So you said Coach didn't go after Maddie until the night Annie Sisson left?" I prompted.

"Right. So Maddie was out there about twenty-four hours on her own, plenty of time to get lost or in trouble. I kept my porch light on that night and kept my ears and eyes open, hoping she'd come back on her own. Sometimes they do. But the next day, she was still AWOL. Coach waited until just after sundown the next night, then took off on his horse, trailing a pony for the kid. It was a couple of hours later that everything else started happening."

"Like what?" I asked.

"First off, Doc and Ben went by on their ATVs and I thought they might've gotten word from Coach that something had happened to Maddie but I was relieved when they headed in the other direction, off toward the mine. A few minutes later, one of those big-rigs roared into camp for a load from the machine shop. The truckers don't seem to care that half the camp's asleep. I guess they're on a tight schedule and roll into camp whenever they're good and ready. Anyway, they kick up a ton of dirt and scare the horses half to death. Luckily, they don't come that often — every couple of months is all. Still, it scares the horses, especially the new-borns."

"I can't see why it would affect the horses way down here. The machine shop's a mile away."

"Yeah, but they always make their pick-ups down by the mine where the merchandise is stored. Ben uses the boxcar to transport the finished products to the mine. It's about the only thing the place is good for. A hundred years ago, I guess it gave up some gold. Now it's just a great big, air-tight, waterproof storage shed."

"Hmm. So the truck came through camp a couple hours after dark? What time was that, more or less?"

"Around ten, I'd say. I was out on the porch, keeping my eye out for Maddie when they came through. I was just thinking that it sure was a busy night when it got busier. Next thing I knew, I saw a light on back at the stables and I used my binoculars to see who was there. It's not completely unheard of for some of the staff to take an evening ride, but I wanted to make sure it wasn't one of the kids trying to sneak a horse. It was just Clutch, though. Probably remembered something, like forgetting to turn off one of the sprinklers, I figured. I was gonna offer to go do it for him but he didn't come this way after all. He headed back toward the camp on his horse."

"Why would he do that?" Gracie asked.

"Don't know. Maybe someone radioed him to help out with the gates or something. Since Coach was off looking for Maddie while Ben and Doc were down at the mine supervising the loading, the staff was probably short-handed. I know one thing. Clutch's usually in bed by ten. He's an early riser. So it musta been something important. Anyway, it was about a half-hour after that that Annie Sisson showed up."

"Showed up where?" I asked. Jo got up and went into the cabin, emerging with the bottle of Pinot Noir. As she refilled our glasses, she went on.

"She was at the stables, saddling up Apples, her favorite horse. I figured she'd decided to go for an evening ride, though it was kind of late. She headed off into the pasture and I watched her for a while. Then I went in to get a glass of wine and when I came out, I'd lost her. After that, all sorts of stuff happened. The truck left. Next thing I knew, Clutch was back at the stables, so he was finished with whatever he'd been doing. Pretty soon Doc came by on his ATV. Quite a bit later, Ben came by on his. As far as I knew, Annie was still off riding, though I might have missed her come back when I went inside a couple of times. Finally, I decided to call it a night, and went inside for good. Just before I fell asleep, I heard some of the horses whinnying and got up to look. It was Coach, coming back empty-handed. It was the first time, as far as I knew, that he hadn't been able to track a run-away, and it scared me. I was afraid something bad had happened to Maddie out there and I made up my mind to help look for her in the morning, whether Coach liked it or not.

"But sometime in the middle of the night, Maddie must have returned on her own. I guess Coach was so relieved to see her at roll-call, he went easy on her for once. Clutch confided to me that Coach thought he'd finally lost one. Said it was one of the few times he's ever seen Coach sweat something. He even seemed jittery to me, the next few days. But by then, we realized that Annie Sisson had taken off in the middle of the night and the whole camp was upset."

"You tell anyone about seeing Annie ride off?"

"Sure. As soon as I heard she'd left, I mentioned it to Clutch. I thought maybe something had happened to her in the woods. But he said Annie had cleaned out her whole cabin, taken her car and driven away some time before dawn. Her horse was back in the stable, so I didn't give it another thought. Just another weird thing happening on a totally weird night."

"And if Maddie Boone hadn't written a message about Miss Sisson being murdered, I might agree with you," I said.

"Don't like coincidences," Gracie said.

"Me neither," I said. "Did you know Annie Sisson and Coach were having an affair?" I asked Jo.

"Not for sure," she said. "But you see things from here,

you know? Like they'd take rides together sometimes. I wondered if once they got out in the woods, they maybe did more than ride."

"You think maybe Annie was going off to catch up with Coach that night? Maybe help him look for Maddie?"

"If so, it's a sure bet he didn't invite her. Coach doesn't like company when he's tracking. Won't even let Clutch tag along. Says other people make too much noise."

"But maybe Annie went after him anyway," Gracie said. "Maybe to help find Maddie, or maybe just to be alone with him."

"Lacy Godfrey told me that Annie thought Coach was seeing someone else," I said. "Maybe she went to confront him. Maybe she didn't really believe he was off looking for Maddie. You ever see Coach ride off with anyone else?"

"Seen him flirt, a little. Nothing serious."

"How about with the students?" I told them what I'd heard Dean Dobberteen mutter under his breath about Coach after Belinda Pitt had bitten his lip.

"I know the one you mean. Hell, I've seen her come on to Clutch, even. She's given me the eye a time or two, too." She giggled. "Probably die if she could've seen me earlier today. My camouflage works both ways, I guess. Keeps the cowhands and hard-ass boys away, but sometimes attracts the Belindas." Jo laughed, and I got the feeling it was as liberating as it was embarrassing. Gracie and I joined her. We weren't just thinking of Belinda Pitt's surprise, though. We were thinking of our own and I was pretty sure Jo knew it. Somehow, being able to laugh about it, made us all relax a little more. Or maybe it was the wine. "Anyway," she said, "I wouldn't put it past Coach, but I haven't actually seen them together."

"Lacy says there's no way Coach would mess with a student, that Doc would fire him on the spot."

"Yeah, I'd say generally that would be true. But like I said, Coach gets away with things here that no one else would even think of doing. Like that stupid cattle prod he carries with him. Doc and Clutch just put up with that. And the whole Isolation thing. That was Coach's idea from the start. Back when I was here as a student, Isolation didn't exist."

"What exactly is Isolation?" I asked.

Jo frowned, twirling her fruit glass between her palms.

"Best way to describe it, I guess, is mental torture. Coach's way of breaking a kid down. I don't agree with it at all, but I guess you can't argue with the results. Once a kid's been inside, he pretty much does whatever it takes to make sure he doesn't go again."

"Where is Isolation?" I asked.

Jo frowned again. "I guess that's the other thing the old mine is good for. From what I understand, Isolation's deep down in the belly of the mine."

Chapter Twelve — Madeline

Maddie was trying not to tremble, but on top of being afraid, she was cold. Though she'd tried to wipe it off, bits of Jello still clung to her face and hair.

"You ain't gonna cry, are you?" Coach said. "I hate crybabies. 'Specially when they think they're tough enough to go around bloodying other people's noses."

He'd driven the ATV right past the boxcar and Danger signs, through an electronic gate into the mine opening which looked to Maddie like a gaping, toothless mouth in the side of the mountain. The dank smell assaulted her nostrils the moment they entered. Coach's voice echoed off the walls.

"Careful, now. Watch your step. We've got a ways to go,

yet." He helped her out of the wagon and led her across the cold rock floor of the cavernous vault.

She blinked at the sudden darkness. It was as if the light had been sucked out of the air, and she wheeled around to assure herself that there was daylight behind her. Coach chuckled and used the cattle prod to nudge her forward. She knew with one touch of a switch, that prod could send an electric current through her that would knock her out cold. Just feeling the tip of the thing against her back made her skin go clammy.

"Where are you taking me?" she asked in a tiny voice. Her words echoed mockingly back at her.

"Someplace where you'll have plenty of time to think things over, Madeline. Sometimes a person just needs a little peace and quiet to get her thinking straight."

"I know what I did was wrong but she was being mean to the new girl," Maddie stammered. Coach wasn't even listening. He'd walked on ahead of her into an even larger, darker room. Maddie could see wooden beams running along the rock walls. Some of them were bowed and she wondered how long they could be expected to hold up the weight of the ceiling, if that was what they were there for. Coach was leaning over a coffin-shaped wooden chest against one wall, fumbling with a latch. "What are you doing?" she asked, starting to cry. Terror ripped through her chest at the thought that Coach might lock her inside the chest. He opened the lid and reached inside, pulling out a green wool blanket. "Catch," he said, tossing the blanket to her. She nearly tumbled backwards with relief. Coach reached into the chest and pulled out a few other items that Maddie couldn't quite make out in the dark.

"You won't starve to death or die of dehydration," he said, strapping a plastic miner's helmet onto his head. He dropped a plastic bottle of water, a roll of toilet paper, and a package of peanut butter crackers on top of her blanket. Then he urged her into a narrow tunnel with the prod.

"Follow the tracks," he said. Maddie looked down at the metal rails grooved into the rock leading into the mine. She looked back at Coach, her eyes wide with fear.

"Do it!" he said. She knew his finger was on the trigger of the cattle prod and she stepped forward into the growing darkness, barely able to see her own feet over the bundle in her arms. Suddenly, the tunnel before her was ablaze with light, startling her so badly she leaped backwards and stumbled. It took a moment to realize that Coach had turned on the light atop his miner's hat.

"Better?" he asked. Maddie nodded, though she wasn't at all sure that seeing was preferable to the darkness. The walls of the cave were steep, and the tunnel before her seemed to go on forever, far beyond the light emitted from the beam. Suddenly, a terrible moan rumbled up from the darkness ahead. Maddie stood stock still, frozen with fear.

"Don't worry kid. This old mine hasn't collapsed yet. Just tread lightly."

He nudged her again and she inched forward on wobbly legs, dreading each step as if it were her last.

"Oh, come on! We'll never get anywhere at this pace." Coach pushed past her and took the lead. Maddie glanced back the way they'd come and stared into pitch blackness. If she thought she'd survive a run for it, she'd have tried. But the entrance was too far away. She turned and saw that Coach was already ten paces ahead of her, taking his light with him. She hurried forward, more afraid to be left behind in the dark than to follow.

The slope grew steeper as they made their way deeper into the mine. Suddenly, the tunnel forked, one opening veering off to the left, the other curving to the right. The metal tracks took the right path and Coach followed them. Soon there were other openings, each one as dark and uninviting as the previous. Each time, Coach veered to the right, staying with the tracks, his beam bouncing along the dark, dank sides of the mine's tunnel.

Once again, a rumbling moan rolled through the tunnel, coming from somewhere below them, shaking Maddie to the bone.

"What is that?" she managed in a weak voice.

Coach turned around and faced her, the beam on his hard hat blinding her. "Any time you get to thinking you're pretty hot shit, Madeline, I want you to remember that sound. This mountain could swallow you up in one second. You're nothing to this mountain. Less than a gnat. Less than the shit of a gnat. You understand?"

She nodded, shutting her eyes to the light.

"You think you've had it rough, I know. You feel misunderstood. Get over it, Madeline. Until you do, you're nothing but a pathetic crybaby. This experience is gonna help you get over yourself. Understand?"

She didn't, but she nodded anyway, tears starting to slide down her cheeks. Coach turned away, leaving her to blink at the sudden darkness and she followed after him blindly, using the scratchy blanket to rub at her tears.

Finally, just as the slope seemed to level out, Coach stepped away from the tracks and entered a side tunnel. What differentiated this one from all the others, Maddie noticed, was that the opening had been framed for a door. Her heart pounded. On the knob of the door was a chain about ten feet in length. At the end of the chain, was a handcuff. Maddie backed away and nearly tripped over the track in the main tunnel.

"Might as well get it over with," Coach said. He'd taken off the cap and set it on the floor so that the light illuminated the small cave. The room was about ten feet wide and fifteen feet deep. The rock ceiling was low and in one corner she could hear the sound of dripping water. It wasn't so bad with the light on, though. If he'd leave her the light, she might be okay.

"You can set your stuff there," he said, pointing to the floor on the far side of the room. "Toilet's on the other side there. Go look now while you can see. It'll make it easier in the dark."

Maddie looked at him, wide-eyed. "You're not going to leave me the light?" Her voice boomed off the walls, mocking her again.

Coach laughed. "No, Madeline. Now check out the hole so you'll know where to go. There's a wooden lid."

Maddie moved cautiously across the cold floor toward the pit toilet. Even with the lid closed, she could smell the rank odor. She felt the edge of the toilet lid with her hands, but did not lift it up. She did not want to see inside. She did not want to breathe the foul odor. She'd just hold it as long as she could. She wiped her palms on her pants and backed away bumping smack into Coach.

"Okay, now here we go." Before she knew what was happening, he'd slapped the metal cuff over her left wrist and clicked it shut.

"That's so you don't get any ideas and try to break out of here. You'll be safe enough inside. You get out into the mine, you could get lost forever. You got everything you need?"

Like she had a choice. Like he would bring her milk and cookies if she requested them. "How long?" she asked, her voice breaking. She couldn't bring herself to finish the sentence.

"We'll see," he said. "I'll check on you in a couple of days and we'll talk about it then. Watch that corner back there. Could be bats."

With that, he picked up his miner's cap and took the light with him as he walked to the door.

"I'm not gonna lock this, okay? But keep it shut. Sometimes whole colonies of bats fly through the mine. You don't want them coming in."

He pulled the door closed and disappeared completely. Maddie stood in the center of the room, huge tears rolling down her cheeks.

"No!!!" she wailed in the utter darkness.

"Noooooo!!!" her echo wailed back, rolling around the rocky walls, surrounding her with the sounds of her own desolate terror. Maddie got down on her knees and crawled to the mound of scratchy blanket, threw herself on top of it and began to sob.

Chapter Thirteen

This time there was no doubt about it. I was dying. There was no light, little air and less hope. And this time, I knew exactly where I was. Down inside the mine at Camp Turnaround. I was suffocating. I knew I had to get out, to do something, to move! But my feet were plastered in place, it seemed, and all I could do was wait for death to take me.

I awoke with a start, my heart racing, feeling the now-familiar fear grip me. I gulped air, trying to clear my head. Was this some kind of premoniton? Or had something happened to make me suddenly vulnerable to long-suppressed fears?

I got up and paced the tiny cabin, trying to understand.

Even before Diane had died, I'd spent a fair amount of

time contemplating life after death. After she died, I thought of little else. I read everything I could get my hands on, devouring volumes of information on religion, reincarnation, angels, spirit guides, souls and eternity. In the end, I wasn't sure what I believed. I only knew that Diane was no longer in this life, and I was. And from that point on, I decided to put all thoughts of death aside and live my life while I could.

And it had worked for a long time. I'd lived with reckless abandon at times, developing a reputation for, if not bravery, at least risk-taking. But now, for no reason that I could ascertain, fear and doubt were rearing their ugly heads and I found myself questioning everything I thought I knew about myself.

I pulled on a pair of sweats and made a cup of coffee, trying to bolster my confidence. I couldn't afford this identity-crisis right now. I didn't have time to dwell on my own problems. If I could just focus on Maddie, maybe I'd be able to get back home unscathed. Then I could work on my sudden, unwanted vulnerabilities in private.

So I sipped coffee and thought about what to do next. One thing I knew for sure was that I wanted to check out the machine shop. That late-night transaction in the mine really bothered me and I didn't think it was just because of the dream. Why did the trucker wait until dark to pick up the merchandise? Was it really a matter of being on a tight schedule? Or was there some reason for not wanting to make the exchange in daylight?

Determined to stay focused, I made myself rehash the facts. Maddie Boone had run away on a Thursday night. Coach waited until Friday night to go after her — a fact that chilled me as much as his using a cattle prod on the kids. The more I learned about Coach, the less I liked him, and the more I thought I understood why Ida and Doc didn't push to make Camp Turnaround an accredited institution. The less outsiders knew about his behavior modification methods, the better. At any rate, soon after Coach took off on horseback, Ben and Doc drove their ATVs to the mine and a while later the semi met them there for a pick-up. A little later, Clutch showed up at the stables, saddled his horse and headed back toward the camp. Then Annie Sisson showed up, saddled her horse and headed off into the meadows, presumably never to be seen again. A little later the truck left, Clutch returned from wherever he'd gone, Doc rode his ATV back to the camp, and finally Ben followed on his. Not too long after that, Coach came back empty-handed and called it quits for the night. Some time in the night, Maddie Boone sneaked back into the camp, unseen, and returned to her bunk. Only the next morning at roll-call did they discover that Maddie had returned on her own.

Also, I'd learned something else while reading the students' essays. A girl named Tanya Payne had chosen to compare her weaknesses with another girl's strengths, an odd twist on the assignment I'd given. The girl to whom she chose to compare herself was none other than Belinda Pitt. It was the third paragraph, I found most interesting.

> *Whereas I'm pretty cowardly and chicken, Belinda's brave and daring. She's never afraid to stand up for herself or to try something new or do something dangerous, even if it means taking a chance at getting herself in trouble. For instance, one night when one of the girls in our house ran off, Belinda took it on herself to help look for her, because she felt responsible that one of her charges had taken off. She snuck out herself and spent several hours helping look for the little jerk. She wouldn't have told anyone, either, except I was awake when she came in, so she confided in me. So you can see, she's not only brave, but also unselfish, which is another thing I'm not. I can be really selfish and self-centered, too.*

Belinda Pitt had some of these kids totally buffaloed. Unselfish? Brave? Try manipulative and conniving. But regardless of what Tanya Payne thought, the fact was, Belinda Pitt had been out on her own on the fateful night that Annie Sisson disappeared, supposedly looking for Maddie Boone. I didn't believe for a second that that's what she was really up to. My guess was that Belinda had sneaked out of the girls house for an entirely different reason. Given Dean Dobberteen's reference to Belinda's relationship with Coach, it was possible that she was off looking for Coach, not Maddie. Had she found him? Had they had a little tryst in the woods? Had Annie Sisson seen Belinda sneak off and followed her? Had Annie caught Belinda and Coach together?

I let my imagination run, picturing the scene as Annie confronted Coach and Belinda, threatening to report their affair to Doc. Would Coach have killed Annie to keep her quiet? Even for Coach, that was a bit extreme, I thought. But what if he had hurt her accidentally and Belinda had been there? Maybe the two of them had conspired to cover it up. Could Maddie Boone have witnessed the whole thing from her hiding place in the woods? Or had there even been a murder at all?

Before I got too carried away, I reminded myself that Jo hadn't seen Belinda at all that night. I wondered who else might have been out and about that Jo hadn't seen. If Belinda had followed Coach, she hadn't done so on horseback. Maybe they had a pre-arranged meeting spot that didn't require her traipsing across the meadows. There were lots of potential hiding places in the compound. For that matter, it was possible that Belinda had sneaked off to meet with someone other than Coach. But then what had prompted Annie Sisson to ride off into the woods? Of course, I didn't know that she had actually gone into the woods, Jo had only seen her cross the pasture, then lost track of her when she went inside. Could Annie have turned around and ridden back toward the stables without Jo knowing it? Or maybe Annie had seen all the activity in the mine and gone in that direction to investigate.

Which brought me back to the question of the night-time pick-up. It occurred to me that I didn't even know exactly what the machine shop manufactured, and decided it was time to educate myself. I could do that while waiting to talk to Maddie, which I had to do soon, trust or no trust. I was spending way too much time and energy entertaining possibilities. What I needed were facts. The sooner I got them, the sooner I could get out of Camp Turnaround.

Ben Biscane was eating alone in the cafeteria, sitting at a far table, away from the bustling noise of the kids. He was holding a copy of Time Magazine with his left hand, shoveling scrambled eggs into his mouth with his right.

"Mind if I join you?" I asked, pushing back a chair. In truth, he didn't look too delighted to see me, but he nodded and put down his magazine reluctantly.

"I didn't mean to interrupt," I said. "Everyone else seems to have disappeared."

"Discipline Committee meeting I think," he said. "They're in the back room, if you want to join them. I'm not much on committees myself."

"Me neither," I said. "Cassidy James. The sub for Miss Sisson." I extended a hand and he shook it. He had big brown eyes and pleasant, though unremarkable features. There was little resemblance to his older brother, I thought. Ben's hair was brown and bushy and his beard was a little unkempt, unlike Doc's neatly trimmed goatee and sideburns. He was large-framed, but soft around the middle. It wasn't difficult to imagine him in front of the television, a Budweiser in one hand, a bowl of popcorn in his lap.

"Glad to meet you," he said. "Ben Biscane. I run the machine shop."

"Oh, really? I'd love to see it sometime. Is it like the woodshops they have in high-schools where kids make those neat projects?"

He laughed. "Hardly. This is a real, bonafide computer-assisted machine shop. We manufacture and wholesale hardware."

"No kidding. Like, what kind of hardware? For computers?" I bit off a piece of bacon, wondering if the dumb blonde act was too convincing. He was starting to come to life, the way some men do when they find they have a captive audience. I thought about what Lacy had said about there not being too many eligible partners in camp, and inwardly cringed.

"Oh, no. Nothing that exciting. Mostly boring stuff like farming equipment, tools, large machine parts. Actually, we can pretty much design whatever someone can imagine. That's the real heart of the business. Once the design is entered into the computers, the machines are set to specifications, and then it's mostly a matter of operating an assembly-line-style manufacturing plant. That's where the kids come in. Some of them learn to input data and actually work as machinists. Most of the kids work as machine operators, though. They're both great skills to put on a résumé."

"I bet. You must be pretty proud. I mean, it sounds like the whole program's a success." I was pouring it on thick and Ben was lapping it up.

"It really is. I don't mind saying it, either. I know it sounds a little boastful, but business is booming. If I had a larger shop and more kids, I could probably double our output. But how much does one man need? A few more years and I'll be able to retire if I want. As for now, this place isn't all that bad, you know."

"Are you kidding? It's a paradise. I can't believe anyone ever wants to leave. I still don't understand why the woman I'm replacing left."

Ben shoveled another forkful of eggs into his mouth and shrugged, his gaze meeting mine briefly. "Your guess is as good as mine," he said. The thing was, his eyes sort of slid to the left as he said it. I'd been watching people — kids and adults — lie for years, even before I'd become a detective. One thing I'd learned was, except for the really serious sociopaths, people's eyes almost always slid one way or the other when they lied. If they were making things up off the top of their head, their eyes tended to roll up as if searching the top of their head for the story. A slide to the right usually meant they were stalling, trying to dredge up something they'd forgotten. A slide to the left could mean that they were hiding something. This wasn't exactly based on scientific proof. But I'd bet anything old Ben here was hiding something. I decided to push a little harder.

"So Miss Sisson didn't even tell you she was planning to leave when you saw her that night?"

Ben's eyes narrowed. "What are you talking about?"

"Oh, I just thought that since she rode out there to the mine during the delivery that night that maybe she was telling you all goodbye and that's why she'd ridden out there. To say goodbye."

Ben was staring at me, dumbfounded. "I don't have any idea what you're talking about. You must have your facts mixed up. The last time I saw Annie Sisson was at breakfast the day she left. What in the world made you think she was at the mine that night?"

"I guess someone said they saw her ride out there. It's no big deal. I just figured she was telling you all goodbye."

"Well, you figured wrong, and someone got their facts wrong too." He seemed to catch himself getting wound up, and sat back, chuckling at himself. "Forgive me. Being a stickler for details, I detest it when people get things fouled up. Who told you that?"

"Gosh, I can't really remember. It seems like since I got here, all anyone's talked about is what a neat person Annie

Sisson was and how much she'll be missed. I guess since I'm taking over for her, people just feel compelled to talk about it. Even the students are talking. But you know how it is. It's like that telephone game. Person A tells Person B something and he tells Person C and by the time Person X hears it, the original message is all garbled. That's probably what happened here." My dumb blonde act was starting to convince me.

Ben had pushed his plate away and was downing the rest of his coffee. "You're right," he said, regaining his good humor. "I've heard everything including one rumor that she left to hide the fact she was pregnant and another that she ran off with a new student to get married. Can you imagine?"

"She was pregnant?" I deadpanned. He laughed and pushed back his chair.

"See? That's exactly how these rumors get started. Stop by sometime and I'll give you a tour of the shop."

"I'd like that. Thanks. Maybe I'll swing by after breakfast."

I couldn't tell if he was pleased at the prospect or not. I watched him walk out of the cafeteria, wondering what to make of the eye slide and the fact that my wild assertion about Annie stopping by the mine might have hit a nerve. But then, maybe he was, as he said, just a stickler for details. And my sliding eye theory wasn't exactly fool-proof either. There were probably dozens of reasons people's eyes got shifty. I finished my breakfast, then headed toward the machine shop, deciding to take Ben Biscane up on his offer while it was still good.

Chapter Fourteen — Madeline

She couldn't believe she'd slept. It was another deep mournful moan of the mountain that brought her to her senses, and she was once again gripped by fear. She sat bolt upright in the darkness and waited, shivering in the cold, dank cave. How long had she slept, she wondered. There was no way to tell whether it had been an hour or four hours. Wistfully, she imagined that she'd slept the whole night through and that any minute Coach would be coming for her, telling her it was all over.

But he'd said a couple of days and then they'd see. She hadn't slept away two days. She probably hadn't slept much at all.

She stood and stretched, annoyed by the metal handcuff that had left a painful impression on her cheek where she'd rested against it. She rubbed at her cheek and then her wrist, wishing she could unhook the cuff. Then, for the first time since she'd been dragged off in the wagon, Maddie remembered the hidden treasures she'd confiscated that morning in the kitchen, safely tucked away inside her pants.

Hurriedly, she unpinned the plastic baggie and laid it on the blanket, using her hands to blindly sort her treasures in the dark. She had a knife! Better yet, she had matches! And a box of birthday candles! If only she could make a fire, the cave might not be so unbearable!

Quickly, she fumbled one of the matches out of the baggie and struck it against the rock floor. On the third try, the match caught, flickered in the blackness, and went out. Maddie nearly panicked, grabbing at another wooden match before she stopped herself.

Think, she commanded. Don't act like a scared little girl. Which was precisely what she was at the moment, but it didn't matter. She couldn't afford that weakness.

She calmly returned the match to the baggie and sat back on her heels, thinking. There was a draft in the cave, which was probably why her match had blown out so soon, but overall, that might be a good thing. If she could get a fire going, she'd need ventilation. But the draft might also mean that it would be more difficult to get a fire started. Not that she had anything to burn. Her tiny birthday candles wouldn't last long, she knew. She stood up and followed her instincts toward the back of the cave where Coach had said bats might be lingering. Holding her breath, she reached out and tentatively traced the cave wall until she felt the ledge. Slowly, she inched her hand inside, eyes wide-open in the dark. Sure enough, there was a draft coming down an open shaft. With her other hand, she felt the opposite side of the ledge and imagined a three foot cubbyhole maybe another foot deep. Big enough for something bigger than bats to hide in. Suddenly, she withdrew her hands and stepped back. What if there was an animal lurking inside? What if there were snakes?

Knock it off, she told herself. The important thing was, there was a draft, so a fire would have ventilation. All she needed was wood. And patience, she reminded herself. And then it hit her. Despite the dark, despite the fact that she was trapped inside this hideous mine, for a few minutes she'd been thinking of something other than her fear. She was planning, and that was a good thing. All Maddie needed was a plan, and she could get through this.

She worked her way back to the blanket in the darkness. If only she could see to check out the Swiss Army knife. Maybe there was something in there small enough to help her remove the handcuff. Because if she could get the damned cuff off, maybe she could somehow find wood. And if she found wood, she could try to build a fire.

Using her body to block the draft, Maddie risked another match, striking it against the rock floor. Once it caught, she held the flame to the tiny wick of a birthday candle and said a little prayer. The candle flickered, casting a dim glow in front of her. She let some of the wax drip onto the floor, then set the candle firmly into the melted wax to hold it in place. It wasn't much, but the faint light gave her hope and determination. Quickly, before the flame flickered out, she went to work.

Maddie's fingers were small but strong, and soon she had all the tools pulled free, testing each one with her fingertips, trying to figure out their use in the dim candle light. The screwdriver was easy, as was the little saw and the knifeblade. There was also a pair of scissors, a fingernail file, a rough-edged hasp, a bottle opener, and last but not least, something that seemed about the right size for a toothpick. That, she decided, might be the most valuable tool of the lot at the moment.

Her hands shaking more with excitement now than cold,

she closed the other tools and got a firm grip on the pick. The problem was, she couldn't see the handcuffs well enough to know where the pick should go. She felt along the smooth metal, and finally detected a small hole on the outside surface. Had to be the key hole. She'd seen people pick handcuff locks on television. She wished she'd paid more attention.

Luckily, Coach had cuffed her left hand, leaving her free to maneuver with her right. Gritting her teeth with determination, she worked the pick into the hole and gently turned. Nothing. She pulled it out and reinserted it, trying again with the same results. Damn! she thought. This has got to work. She pushed the pick in and pressed against first one side and then the other, careful not to push too hard, lest the pick break. She rotated the pick, then out of frustration, pushed it in as far as it would go. Suddenly, to her utter amazement, the little lock sprang free.

"I did it!" she shouted into the cave.

I did it! her words echoed back.

She slid the bracelet off her wrist and flung it to the ground. "Yes!" she yelled.

Yes! came the exuberant reply.

Maddie stood up and danced around her blanket, now free of both cuff and chain. The little candle went out and Maddie came back to reality. Before she got too carried away, she carefully looped the chain like a hose and carried it to the far wall of the cave, leaving the cuff unlocked. If Coach were to suddenly return, she wouldn't want him to know she'd freed herself.

Now that she was free, her single most intense desire was to find something to burn. She knew that the door was wooden, but even if she used the screwdriver to unhinge the latches, the door was a thousand times too big. She didn't want to smoke herself to death. She just wanted to warm herself and get some light.

If only she had a flashlight, she thought. As frightened as she'd been following Coach down the tunnel, she knew that with a light of her own, she could make her way back to the entrance. All she had to do was follow the train tracks. And then what? Once he found she'd escaped, he'd surely make sure she couldn't the next time. Her best bet was to do what she could to make her stay bearable and work on an escape plan for later.

First things first, she chided herself. Find something to burn! She carefully stowed everything back in the baggie, adding the peanut butter crackers, and repinned it to her waistband. If somehow she was unable to find her way back to this room, at least she wouldn't starve to death. She took a small sip of water from the bottle and tucked it under the blanket for safe keeping, then made her way to the door.

She was seized by a moment of panic, thinking that maybe Coach had tricked her and locked the door after all. But with one easy pull, the door opened inward and Maddie was back in the main tunnel.

She'd come from the northwest and she turned that way now, choosing the familiar over the unknown. She'd seen wooden beams along the way, supporting planks where the walls of the mine had started to crumble. Maybe she could whittle some shavings from one, get some kindling.

She was concentrating on her feet, picking her way through the darkness, straining to see the metal track while her left hand trailed the wall. She was starting to wonder if she'd ever come across any of the beams she'd seen, when suddenly the ground rose up in front of her, sending her sprawling.

Maddie lay on her stomach, her elbows and knees scuffed and probably bleeding. She'd tripped over something sticking up where she hadn't expected it. She pushed herself up and reached back to feel along the ground. To her surprise, a second pair of steel tracks veered off the main track, heading north. It seemed a railroad tie had worked itself loose from the secondary track and when her fingers grazed the misplaced splintered wood, she nearly laughed aloud. The steel tracks were all resting on wood! On her hands and knees, she followed the second track, feeling the wooden ties as she went. Whereas the main track's ties had seemed solid and secure, much of the wood along the second track was rotted and splintered. She didn't need to go in search of beams. There was wood everywhere!

She selected one of the rotting hunks of wood, tugging and pushing on it until it came free. It was only a few feet long and at its thickest section, half-a-foot wide. At its tip, it was no bigger than a pointed stick.

Smiling in the dark, Maddie turned and made her way carefully back toward the cave. This may not be enough for a bonfire, she thought, but it would be a start.

It didn't take long for Maddie to realize how fortunate it was that her cave had a door. Otherwise, she might not have recognized hers from all the other entrances that veered off the main tunnel. Without the door, she realized, it would be possible to become hopelessly lost in the depths of the mountain. She felt along the cold side of the tunnel until she came upon the wooden door marking her little cave and was surprised to find herself so relieved to be back. It wasn't exactly home, but it was better than being lost in the depths of the cold, dark mine.

She lugged the rotting log inside and sat down on her blanket to catch her breath. What next? She'd need to find a spot far enough away from the draft to get the fire started. Maybe over there by the wall, she thought. That should be protected. But wouldn't the cave smell like smoke? Coach would know there'd been a fire. Maybe that ledge could serve as a fireplace! Her grandparents' chimney at home sometimes had a downdraft, but that didn't stop it from working properly. She could start a small fire there to see if it worked. If nothing else, she'd be able to see inside, make sure there weren't any animals hiding there.

Closing her eyes to that thought, she lugged the railroad tie over to the ledge, then took out her knife again and began whittling rotted chips, shaving them into a pile on the ledge. The little knife was relatively sharp and easy to use. She nicked herself once, but not deeply. She sucked on the blood a few times, then continued her work until she had quite a handsome pile of kindling. Next she tried to chunk off some larger pieces to add to the fire once it was started. This was harder work but since the wood was partly rotten, she was able to make some headway. She left the largest piece intact. If she ever got the fire going, it would serve as her main log. She added a little tissue paper for good measure, arranged it beneath the kindling which she positioned in a miniature teepee toward the back of the ledge, making sure some air could get through the bottom, and stood back. All she needed was a match and a little luck.

Maddie solemnly selected a wooden match from her precious stockpile and brought it to the fireplace. She kneeled down, wishing she knew a prayer or some good luck oath. She sucked in her breath, crossed the fingers on her left hand and scratched the wooden match against the rock.

It caught on the first try and Maddie held the tiny flame to the toilet paper, blowing on it gently as it took hold. The flame burned blue for a second, started to flicker, then caught a draft, wavered dangerously, and finally licked the kindling above it. Maddie blew harder, willing the little flames to take off. As if on command, the kindling caught and she gingerly added a small chunk of the rotted wood and then another, careful not to crush the delicate fire, afraid that too big a fire would smoke her out. But the ventilation was good and the smoke obediently sought the drafty shaft above the cubby hole. She couldn't have designed a better fireplace if she'd wanted! With the fire burning, she began to see the little alcove clearly. There were no bats or snakes. The smoke drifted upward a few feet before being sucked through a two-foot crack on the back side of the wall. Not only would she have warmth and light, but there wouldn't be any telltale smoke lingering in the air when Coach returned.

Satisfied that she could sit back for a minute, Maddie allowed herself a minute of exhilaration. She'd done it! She looked around the little cave, realizing that the flickering glow from the fire made her cave far less frightening. She stood and walked the perimeter of the rock enclosure, no longer terrified by its confines. The pit toilet in the corner was not as menacing as it had seemed, which was a good thing, because now that she thought about it, she had to pee. She walked toward it bravely, lifted the lid and, holding her breath, relieved herself. No sooner had she shut the lid, than her fire started to dwindle.

She rushed to it and added another chunk of soft wood, then another, until the flames were practically roaring. Suddenly, she was famished. She smoothed her blanket in a neat square near the fire, gathered her precious belongings beside her and sat back for an eloquent repast of cold water and peanut butter cheese crackers. She thought long and hard about it, but in the end she couldn't remember having a more satisfying meal in her life.

When her eyes could barely stay open another minute, she placed the last and largest hunk of wood on the fire and took her blanket a safe distance away from the heat. The flickering light was comforting and the heat lulled her into a restful sleep she wouldn't have thought possible hours earlier. Even the moaning and groaning of the mountain didn't disturb her much. She wasn't sure how long she slept, but when she finally awoke, the fire was no more than low gleaming coals and as she stared at them, an idea began to blossom. She thought about it so long, her eyes grew heavy again, and this time when she slept, she dreamed of escape.

Chapter Fifteen — Madeline

She was sure it was morning, though there was no real way to tell. But she'd always awakened at dawn and she was counting on this day being no different. Which meant she'd survived a whole night in the mine! Her twenty-first day of captivity in the camp and her second day in Isolation. She stretched, wishing she'd brought a little more wood in the night before. Her cave was pretty dark, but it was still fairly warm. She treated herself to two peanut butter crackers and a good swig of water, then ventured over to the pit toilet to relieve herself, amazed that she wasn't more afraid. Fire and food did wonders for the human spirit, she decided. What she needed was to build up the fire, then work on her plan with a clear head.

She pried open the knife blade on her Swiss Army knife and carefully headed out the door, no longer as fearful of the bat colonies Coach had warned her about. But she'd grown accustomed to her firelight and the tunnel was startling dark. She turned west, back toward the mine entrance feeling her way along the tracks, searching for the secondary track that veered off the main one. Suddenly, she felt a vibration on the rails through the soles of her shoes. Before she could even react, she heard the gathering rumble of machinery coming toward her.

Maddie pressed her back to the cave wall, holding her breath. Coming around the bend she sensed something dark and ominous moving toward her along the track. It was the boxcar, chugging along its rail, oblivious to her presence. It moved slowly but steadily and she stood plastered to the wall, straining to make out the car as it rattled by. It was headed away from the mine entrance, probably back toward the machine shop for another load of refuse. She'd asked about the boxcar once, and understood that's what it was used for. Briefly, she fantasized about hopping aboard, hitching a ride into the machine shop, walking calmly through the surprised student workers and out into the light of day.

She abandoned this fantasy as quickly as it had appeared. For one thing, the boxcar was long gone. For another, she had much bigger plans than that. The idea that had taken root the night before now gave her hope and a renewed sense of purpose.

She reached the second track and edged along the rail, feeling the railroad ties for rotted sections she could easily pry loose. It didn't take her long to find a few suitable hunks of wood, and now that she knew the way, even in the dark, she was able to make good time as she groped her way back to the cave.

Once back, Maddie used the smouldering coals to build a fire and before long, her little cave was filled with warmth and light. Only then did she allow herself the luxury of sitting down in the mellow glow of the flames to go over her plan.

She'd known since that night back home when Ben and Coach had kidnapped her that she would escape. She didn't know how or when, only that she wasn't about to allow herself to be dominated like that any longer. She wouldn't return to her grandparents' house and she wasn't sure where she would go. All she knew was that she was going to get free.

She'd started an escape kit even before she had a plan. Everyone knew that Coach always caught the runaways within a day of their leaving. In fact, he generally let them get a day's headstart, just for fun. She wasn't cocky enough to think that she could accomplish what no one before her had. If Coach could track seventeen-year-old boys in the woods, he wouldn't have much trouble with a skinny, thirteen-year-old girl.

Still, she'd been watching and waiting for something to occur to her, and now something had. The plan was so bold, it was brilliant — so simple, no one would think of it. She wouldn't run away into the woods. She'd run to the mine. No one would dream of looking for her in Isolation. Coach would head off into the woods and exhaust himself searching. After a few days he'd give up. They'd think she'd done the impossible — escaped from Camp Turnaround. Maybe they'd think she'd been eaten by wolves. Maybe they'd even inform her father that she'd died in the woods. That would certainly serve him right. Not that he'd probably care that much. But whatever they did, they'd never think to look inside the mine. By the time they did look there, if they ever did, she'd be long gone.

The beautiful part was, once they quit looking in the woods, she was free to go there. If she had enough food, water and matches, she'd survive. And there were creeks everywhere so water wouldn't be a problem. But she'd need other things — a blanket maybe. And something to carry everything in, like a backpack.

Then another thought hit her. What if she didn't go into the woods at all? What if, after hiding in the mine for several days, she hopped onto the boxcar and rode it to the machine shop? It wasn't that far from there to the staff parking lot. What if she could sneak into the cook's purse again and take her keys? Maddie would have to find out which car was hers. And she'd need to figure out the code to the gate, not to mention learn how to drive!

She got up to stoke the fire, thinking. Maybe she wouldn't take a car after all. If she could get from the machine shop to the road, she could follow it on foot all the way to civilization. She'd have to investigate the machine shop, see exactly where the boxcar ended up. If she could ride the boxcar, then hide inside or near the machine shop until dark, she could probably get to the road without anyone seeing her. Once she was on the road, it would be easy traveling. If a car came along, she could duck into the woods until it passed. She wondered how much food she'd need if the walk took her three days or more. But if she could survive in Isolation for a few days, she could certainly survive out in the open, she told herself.

It was a good thing they got to choose their work stations, she thought. She'd had her heart set on working at the stables after her shift in the cafeteria was up, but now she knew it was more important to work in the shop. She could continue to see Shadow Dancer during her free time. That was the only thing that gave her pause about the whole plan. Once she escaped, she'd never see the shiny black colt again.

Even so, Maddie was so excited thinking about her escape, she could barely sit still. She wished she had paper and a pencil so she could start making a list of everything she'd need to survive — first in the cave and then on the road. Too bad she couldn't start stashing stuff now. She'd need to have quite a stockpile to make it work. At least enough for a week.

Suddenly, she had a thought. As long as no one was

looking for her right now, it was a perfect time to scavenge. She couldn't very well venture outside where she might be seen, but there was no reason she couldn't go back to the mine entrance where Coach stored the crackers and water. Even if she only took a few of each, it would be a start. She could hide them away in the cave until the day she escaped.

When she stepped back out into the tunnel, she was surprised at how quickly her eyes had become accustomed to the firelight. Now she was totally blind. She trailed her hand along the cold mine wall and let her feet pick their way carefully along the tracks, staring into the darkness ahead. Suddenly another low, terrifying moan rumbled up from beneath her, nearly causing her to lose her footing. But the mountain hadn't crumbled on any of the previous groans, so she fortified her courage with that thought and continued on her mission.

The long, terrifying trek with Coach through the blackened tunnel had seemed to last hours so she was surprised to suddenly see a shaft of light illuminating the tracks in front of her. She froze, realizing it might be Coach coming toward her with his miner's cap on, and she plastered herself against the mine wall, her heart pounding. But the light came no closer, and after a minute, she inched forward, until she reached another bend in the tunnel and found herself standing in the entrance of the cave. It hadn't taken more than fifteen minutes, she guessed. It was different, she supposed, when you knew where you were going more or less.

The sight of daylight outside made her heart soar and she longed to run headlong into the fields where the horses were grazing. But the electronic gate was shut tight and anyway, if she were seen it would ruin all the plans she'd made. Her tools would be discovered and taken away. She'd be put in Isolation without any way of making fire for who knew how long. And her chance for escape would be gone. If she could force herself to be patient now, it would pay off later.

She tore her gaze away from the daylight and searched for

the wooden trunk. She'd brought her knife with her, in case she needed to pick the lock, something she wasn't sure she'd be able to do as easily as she had the hand cuff. But the flimsy padlock on the trunk was unlocked.

Her heart racing, she lifted the heavy cedar lid and peeked inside. It still reminded her of a coffin, but the trunk was loaded with goods. There were three more blankets stacked on the left, two cases of bottled water, and several cardboard boxes of the cellophane-wrapped peanut butter crackers. Better yet, there were half a dozen miner's hats stacked one on top of the other, a couple of flashlights and a metal toolbox. Maddie had to caution herself, glancing over her shoulder to make sure no one was coming. She carefully took the top miner's hat off the stack and strapped it onto her head. It was too big but gave her a wonderful feeling of invincibility. She didn't dare take one of the flashlights — there were only two and might be noticed. She helped herself to six packages of crackers, which she doubted Coach would notice, and two bottles of water. She was afraid he'd notice a missing blanket when he returned hers to the trunk, and besides, it would be too bulky to carry. If only she had a back pack, she thought. She slowly opened the toolbox and looked inside. There were wrenches, pliars, links of chain, a hammer, some nuts and bolts and other things she supposed were used for the boxcar. Nothing she really needed at the moment. She closed the heavy cedar lid and stood up, looking around the rest of the room.

On the far side of the room, wooden crates were stacked against the wall. There was printing stamped on the outside of the crates and when she got closer she realized they held the merchandise made in the machine shop. She scanned the words, wondering if they contained anything she could use. It only took her a minute to realize there wasn't much she could do with axle rods, hydraulic pistons or pump encasements. She toured the large room, knowing she should get back to her cave, but lingering near the sunlight as long as she dared.

In one corner, she spied a stack of blue plastic tarps with bungee cords attached to the metal holes along the edges. Maybe these were used to cover the boxcar when it was raining, she thought. She started to turn away, then stopped. Maybe she could fashion a backpack out of one of the tarps. The bungee cords might come in handy too. She quickly bundled one of the tarps into her arms, wrapping her other pilfered goods inside, including an extra blanket after all, and hurried back the way she'd come. With the light from her miner's cap blazing the trail, the trek back to her cave was a piece of cake.

Long before Coach came for her, Maddie had put out the fire, moving the ashes into a far recess of the alcove so there'd be no trace of it. She'd also explored the crack that served as her air vent and discovered another room off the first, about half as big, but with an added bonus. There was water trickling down the face of the cave wall. She'd smelled the water carefully, taking a bit on her tongue to make sure it was fresh, then had stripped off her clothes and given herself an ice-cold spit bath. She'd even wet her hair, in case there was any lingering scent of smoke, then rubbed herself dry with the extra woolen blanket before dressing again. The second room was also a boon because it gave Maddie a place to stow her hidden treasures. She spent the last few hours sitting in the dark of the first cave, the handcuff back on her wrist, though not locked, the door to her cave open enough that she could see the beam of Coach's light bouncing along the tracks. When at last she saw it, she clicked the handcuff shut, rolled into a fetal position on her blanket, and began what she hoped seemed a pathetic, simpering moan.

Chapter Sixteen

An hour after breakfast, the machine shop was already in full-swing. I was surprised at the efficiency and professionalism of the kids working behind their plastic goggles, dressed in green jumpsuits. They looked every bit as competent as auto-plant workers in Detroit, I thought, though some of them were barely five feet tall and a couple sported braces on their teeth. Even Maddie, whose green jumpsuit was two sizes too big, looked deadly earnest as she concentrated on the levers in front of her. For someone who'd run away a week ago, then written a cryptic e-mail message to her father about a mysterious murder, she looked strangely serene working the machine, I thought. But no sooner had the thought crossed my mind, than Maddie glanced in my direction as if aware that I'd been watching her. I was determined to talk to her, but couldn't just march up to her in the machine shop. I'd try to catch her right after the morning session, before she reported to the mess hall for lunch. If I missed her then, I'd wait for her afternoon free time when she visited Shadow Dancer. It was the only time she seemed to be alone.

Ben was showing me around, obvious pride in his voice as he spoke over the roaring motors. "Today we're working on propeller blades," he said. "One of the power companies in California uses them on their windmills. They contract with us to design them to their specifications and manufacture the product."

"You just make one part at a time?"

He laughed. "Even the most complicated contraption imaginable is made one part at a time. Then it's just a matter of assembly. We manufacture the parts and ship them, complete with assembly instructions. It's much more cost-effective to ship parts than entirely assembled hardware. Especially with the bigger items. Of course, we do assemble some of the smaller stuff here on the premises."

The room was the size of a gymnasium, with lime green machinery stretching from one end to the other. It seemed every square inch of the room was being utilized. Bright yellow lines painted on the concrete floor separated the workstations, and overhead, florescent lights cast a sickly glow over the entire production area. Along one wall, sealed crates were stacked three-deep and twice that high, a yellow forklift poised for action beside them. I noticed a glass-enclosed loft above the north side of the shop with gray computer terminals and large drafting tables visible through the windows.

"And you personally do all the designing?"

"That's the fun part. Let me show you." He led the way past the kids working at their stations and stepped onto a lift, painted the same green as the machinery. I followed him onto the lift and soon we were rising above the noisy shop to the loft.

"A little quieter in here," he said, closing a dual-paned slider behind us. "I call this the think tank."

"Impressive," I said. And it was. Computers lined the walls, their screens glowing with geometric designs and three-dimensional views of mechanical parts. The hardwood tables in the center of the room held architectural drawings, slide rulers and other tools of his trade. I examined one of the drawings and Ben came over to explain.

"Right now, I'm working on a design for a self-loading staple gun. The guy who patented the idea has contracted me to manufacture it, but his design is faulty. We're still negotiating, but I figure by the time I've worked out the problem, he'll have come around."

"So you do more than just manufacture farm equipment," I said. I walked around the loft, which had glass windows on three sides, designed, no doubt, so that Ben could keep an eye on his charges. On the far northeast corner of the shop, I saw the same boxcar I'd seen at the entrance to the mine.

"What's the boxcar used for?" I asked.

"Hauling our refuse, mostly," he said, coming to stand beside me. "We load it here and the car takes it right through the mine to the sledge heap on the other side of the valley. We also use the mine to store some of the finished products awaiting pick-up if we get backed up in here. As you can see, I've already maximized the use of this facility. In the beginning, I thought this would be more than ample space. Not that I'm complaining, mind you. Growth is a good thing. But we've had to get creative."

"I'd like to see that mine sometime," I said, thinking about what Jo had said about Isolation.

"Oh, not me. You couldn't drag me into that bat-infested hellhole for anything. I go as far as the entrance where we store the crates, but that's it. I thought I'd ride the boxcar through the tunnel, one time, you know, just to see what it was like? That was the last time I ever did that! About scared me half to death." His eyes were wide and I believed him.

"So, if no one rides the boxcar, how does it get from the shop to the mine entrance and back?"

"Battery," he said, smiling. "Just like a golf-cart. We charge her up and put her in gear. She chugs right along the track like clock-work. We meet 'er on the other side of the mine to unload merchandise or down at the sledge heap to dump debris. The miners used the cars to haul out the tailings and dump them down the ravine where the tracks end and we use the same dump they did for our refuse loads. Turns out the mine wasn't a complete waste after all."

I looked out at the kids, genuinely impressed with their working demeanor. They were industrious and efficient. There wasn't the usual horseplay you'd expect with a bunch of teenagers.

"You train them, too?" I asked.

"Yep. I get them for four weeks at a stretch, just like the ranch and mess hall. The first week is nothing but safety instructions and dry runs. They don't get their hands on a machine until the second week, and then it's pretty elementary. By their third week, they're ready to roll. I work them for forty-five minutes and give them fifteen-minute breaks out back. I've got tetherball, racquetball, ping-pong, a trampoline, stuff kids like. They look forward to those breaks. It makes the machine shop one of the most sought-after shifts at the camp. That, plus they're really learning usable skills. By the end of the year, every kid has had a turn at most of the different machines here. Each time they come through, we're making totally different stuff, which keeps them from getting bored. The last thing I want is a bored teenager working heavy machinery."

"I'll bet," I said, thinking about all the child labor laws being broken here. It was probably another reason they didn't want Camp Turnaround to be accredited. The last thing they'd want was someone looking over their shoulders, breathing down their necks. Just then, the forty-five-minute bell clanged. Like automatons, the kids stepped back from their stations and even through the thick glass, I could hear the sudden quiet as the machines shut off. The kids removed their goggles and hung them on pegs next to their stations. Next, they shrugged out of their green jumpsuits and hung those on the pegs beside the goggles.

"I can't believe how efficient they are," I said.

"They've practiced a lot. And this is a particularly good group. They behave because they know I'm watching. Somebody deviates from the routine, they lose their break. How do you think I keep things so clean in here?" he said, chuckling. "I count on someone screwing up at least once a day. The screw-ups get clean-up duty on their breaks. Oops, there's one now."

Ben slid open a window and produced a whistle from his pocket which he stuck between his lips. The shrill sound caused the students to freeze and glance in his direction.

"Gonzalez! You just lost your break! Put your suit back on. The rest of you, you've got fifteen minutes!"

The kids bustled out to the rec. area behind the shop, with the exception of Gonzalez, a chunky Latino who was looking up at Ben with his arms outstretched in frustrated innocence.

"What? What'd I do this time?"

"You're sagging, man. How many times do I have to tell you to cinch up your pants?"

"But they slip down, man! I was wearing the jumpsuit. It wasn't hurting nobody!"

"You know the rules, Gonzalez. We don't allow that gang-banging crap here and you know it. You gonna give me a hard time about this?"

"No?" he said, more than a little whine in his voice. For a big tough kid, he looked ready to cry.

"Good. You can start with the broom. You do everything else right the rest of the day, I just might let you take the next break. "

Gonzalez said something under his breath and Ben let it slide.

"The other nice thing about a break every hour is that it gives me a chance to sneak a smoke. Care to join me?"

"No, thanks. I better get to class. I appreciate the tour, Ben. I'm really impressed."

"And I appreciate the company. Stop by any time."

Chapter Seventeen

So far, the day wasn't going very smoothly. After my morning class, I'd hurried to the machine shop to wait for Maddie only to find that Ben had sent the crew off to lunch early. After lunch, Ida escorted Maddie to Doc's office for a therapy session. I spent much of the afternoon class getting to know the students better, but still didn't have any reason to believe that one or more of them was involved in Miss Sisson's disappearance. The only remotely promising lead came when a tall rangy kid named Todd Timmins angrily etched Defy Authority, Anarchy Rules and Life Sucks! on his desk. He seemed surprised that I wasn't going to report the incident to Coach. After class, I asked him if he would've defaced the desk if Miss Sisson was still there and he shrugged. Then something happened that I least expected. Todd started to cry.

"You must miss her a lot," I said, wondering where all the emotion was coming from.

His green eyes looked tortured and he really started to blubber. "You don't understand," he stammered, still crying. "She was, she was nice to me. She believed in me. And she made a promise to me. Then she broke it."

"What kind of promise, Todd?"

"It was personal," he said, pulling himself together. "Between her and me." It was obvious he wasn't going to divulge the nature of the promise. Had the promise been broken because she left? Or had she broken the promise before she left? I didn't get the chance to ask because Todd Timmins turned and stormed from the room, but not before issuing a terse warning at the door. "You better not tell anyone," he said.

I didn't know if he was referring to the crying, defacing the desk, or the secret promise Annie Sisson had made and broken.

To top off an already frustrating day, I waited for Maddie at the stables, but she never showed up.

Now, the late afternoon breeze made the grass ripple across the meadow seductively and Gracie and I were surreptitiously watching Jo Bell as she tried to capture the motion on canvas from her front porch. She was an enigma, I thought. From the back, she looked every bit the boy I'd first thought her to be. She wore a sleeveless flannel showing off well-developed biceps and tanned, sinewy arms, though they were currently crisscrossed with cuts and welts from the barbed wire. Her worn jeans hugged her handsomely and her scuffed black cowboy boots and hat completed the picture. But her movements were graceful and she had an aura about her, I thought, that radiated both strength and sensuality.

"I can't concentrate if you watch," Jo finally said, gracing us with that boyish grin I found so appealing.

"Who said we were watching?" I asked.

"I can tell," she said. "You're supposed to be working, I thought."

Earlier that day, I'd written the names on note cards of people I thought had either had an opportunity or motive to kill Annie Sisson, if in fact she was really dead. Gracie and I were moving the cards around on the little table between the Adirondack chairs. Gracie picked up the card with Doc's name on it and flipped it in the air.

"Can't see the motive with Doc, Cass."

"No. But he was out and about that night. Anything could have happened."

"No way," Jo said, giving up on the painting. "Doc is not involved in whatever you think might've happened." Her tone was firm and it was clear she wasn't open to speculation on the issue.

Gracie sighed and picked up the next card. "The truckers? What possible motive could they have had?"

"Maybe a hit and run," Jo suggested, only halfway kidding. "Anyone want a beer?"

"I'll take one," Gracie said.

"I'll help," I said, getting up to follow Jo into the kitchen.

"Thanks," she said, giving me a quizzical look. I found myself blushing as she handed me two cans from the fridge.

"You do that a lot, you know?"

"Do what?" I asked.

"Blush. Like right now. I make you nervous, don't I?"

"No. Of course not. Not really."

Jo laughed. "Yeah, I do. You're not sure what to make of me. But you like me, huh?" She pushed back the brim of her cowboy hat and grinned.

I looked at her, feeling my cheeks grow even warmer. She was right. I liked her. And she made me nervous. Before I could muster an answer, Jo leaned forward and touched her lips to mine. It was so brief, I barely had time to feel it, yet the jolt that slammed through me was undeniable.

"I like you, too," she said, brushing past me on her way out to the porch. I was left holding two cans of beer, wondering what had just happened. The only thing I knew for sure was that my heart was thudding like an adolescent's. And as uneasy as it made me, the feeling was one I liked.

Gracie was holding the card with Clutch's name on it, twirling it between her two index fingers.

"No way Clutch had anything to do with it either," Jo asserted. "Him or Doc. Why don't you all just ask little Maddie what happened? It'd be a whole lot easier than trying to piece it together."

I told them about my failed attempts at getting Maddie alone so I could question her and Gracie nodded.

"It's almost like she's afraid to be alone," she said.

"Clutch says he thinks she's planning to run again," Jo said.

"When was this?" I asked.

"He mentioned it yesterday Said the way she's always looking off into the woods is a dead giveaway. That and the fact that she's pilfered beef jerky from his stash in the tack room several times now — he figures she's stockpiling supplies for another trek in the woods."

"Clutch mention this to Coach?"

"I kinda doubt it. They're not that close, really. I get the feeling Clutch doesn't always approve of the way Coach handles the kids. I know for a fact he doesn't like the whole Isolation thing. And that stupid cattle prod. I saw Clutch about blow a gasket the one time Coach used it in front of him."

"So how come they let Coach get away with it, if no one approves?"

"Beats me. He was always the golden boy of camp. I guess he still is. Hey, now. What's this?"

Jo stood and reached for the binoculars that hung on a peg near the door.

"Damn! Somebody lost their ride."

"Whaddaya mean?" Gracie asked.

"See that palomino tearing across the meadow? She's got a bridle but no saddle and no rider. Come on."

We followed Jo the short distance to the nearest stable and bridled three horses, not taking the time for saddles.

"You ride bareback okay?" she asked, leaping onto her black gelding.

"More or less," I said. My leap wasn't quite as graceful as either Jo's or Gracie's, but I managed not to fall off the other side as we shot out of the stable and across the meadow toward the palomino who had slowed to an agitated trot. Before we even came to a stop, Jo slid off her horse and took the palomino's reins, speaking into his ear in soothing tones.

"It's one the kids take." she said, looking out across the grassy meadows. "Clutch let them go on an outing today."

"By themselves?"

"We keep an eye out. Clutch was out mending fences during their ride so he wasn't ever too far away. And I know Ida took a ride this afternoon, which she does all the time, but I'm sure today she planned it because of the outing. The kids get a sense of freedom, but they're never too far away from staff. They shoulda all been back by now, though."

"Doesn't someone count?" I asked. "What if one of the kids decided to bolt?"

"You still don't get it, do you?" she said, gliding back onto her black horse. She pushed her cowboy hat back off her forehead and settled her blue-gray eyes on mine. "It's not worth it to screw up here. Ten minutes of freedom, or even twenty-four hours of it if Coach decides to let you stay gone that long, aren't worth the punishment. Only the real die-hards risk it. It's because they know they'll be punished if they do something wrong that they're allowed any freedom at all. Clutch can afford to give them the occasional outing because he knows they won't dare screw up."

She had already started off across the meadow, trailing the palomino behind her.

"You think someone fell off?" Gracie asked.

"There should be a saddle," Jo said. "The kids are never allowed to ride bareback. That's what bothers me." She used the binoculars still strung around her neck to scan the borders of the valley. "Oh, shit," she uttered. "Someone's down."

She set off at a gallop and we kept up beside her, kicking up dust as we flew across the grassy meadow. In the distance, I saw what Jo had seen with her binoculars. A form lay motionless on the ground, a smaller lump not far away, equally as still.

As we neared, I saw that the second lump was indeed the missing saddle. The saddle blanket lay in a crumpled heap beside it. A dozen feet away lay the inert form of Belinda Pitt.

"Holy shit," Jo said under her breath.

We leaped off our horses and rushed to the girl, who, at the sound of our footsteps, started to move. She mumbled something that sounded like "Coach," or maybe "Clutch."

"Belinda. Are you all right?" I asked, bending over her. Her face was deadly white and covered with perspiration.

"My leg," she said, her lip starting to tremble. From the odd angle, I could tell it was badly broken.

"Are you hurt anywhere else?"

She started to shake her head, then nodded, then started to cry.

"It's okay, girl," Jo said. "We'll get you outta here." She was leaning over Belinda and I noticed that the top two buttons of Jo's flannel had come undone. Her words were as soothing as they'd been with the trapped colt, but Belinda's eyes had opened wide. Even in her state of shock and agony, she was blatantly staring at Jo's breasts.

"We should keep her warm," I said. "I think she's in shock." I glanced pointedly at Jo's breasts and grinned, causing Jo to glance down and then turn bright red. "You do that a lot, you know," I whispered, brushing past her as I went for the horse blanket.

Gracie kneeled down beside Belinda and started pressing

her fingers along the back of her neck, gently probing. "I don't want to move her until we're sure it's just the leg," she said. I laid the blanket beside them and watched Gracie expertly assess the degree of Belinda's injuries.

"Hey, look at this," Jo said. Gracie and I turned around and saw Jo bent over the fallen saddle. She motioned for us to come closer, out of Belinda's hearing range.

"Someone cut the cinch," she whispered.

Sure enough it appeared to have been cut about two-thirds of the way across. The last part had torn on its own.

"Now what?" Jo asked.

"First, we figure out a way to get Belinda back to camp. Let's just keep this saddle business to ourselves for now," I said.

"Who do you think would've done this?" Gracie asked, her voice low.

"From what I've seen, she makes a habit of pissing people off. Dean Dobberteen comes to mind," I said.

Gracie nodded. "I don't think Ida Evans likes her much, either. I saw her watching Belinda earlier this afternoon while Clutch was helping Belinda adjust the stirrups. Ida didn't look amused. The truth is, Belinda should be able to adjust her own stirrups by now."

Jo said, "Come to think of it, Maddie's not real fond of Belinda either. Belinda's the one who got her sent to Isolation."

Gracie and I stared at her for what seemed a full minute, then suddenly both spoke at once. "Maddie was in Isolation?"

"I thought you knew that," Jo said, brow furrowed.

"Because of running away?" I asked. My heart had momentarily stopped. The thought of a little thirteen-year-old girl trapped alone in that mine made my blood boil. It was bad enough that he did that to eighteen-year-old thugs. But Maddie? It was all I could do to contain my anger at the asshole. But it was more than anger I felt. Once again I was gripped with an all-encompassing dread. And then it occurred to me for the first time. Maybe it wasn't my fear I was feeling. Maybe it was Maddie's. Maybe it wasn't my death I'd been dreaming about at all.

Jo's voice interrupted my thoughts. "No. This was before she ran away. That's what made it so odd. Usually, once a kid spends a couple of days in Isolation, they tow the line pretty good."

"Let's get her back," I said, fighting my own emotions. "We can use the blanket as a litter."

Chapter Eighteen — Madeline

Twenty Days Earlier

Once she was back in camp, Maddie could hardly contain her excitement. She had a plan! Every waking hour was spent either perfecting it or acting on it. She no longer thought of this as her twenty-fifth day in camp. She thought of it as just over a week before she could make her dream come true, and escape. But she knew there was a lot to accomplish before then. For one thing, she decided, she'd need a lot more baggies. She would keep stashing the goods in her mattress until she had enough stockpiled to make her escape.

Working in the cafeteria was a boon, though she only had a few more days before the shifts changed and she began her stint in the machine shop. She decided to take full advantage of it while she could. The kitchen was loaded with valuable goods. The danger was in getting too greedy. She couldn't afford to be caught, even once. So she became a master of patience, always watching for the windows of opportunity that inevitably presented themselves.

She couldn't count on always having access to the kitchen, but quite often Pat, the cook, would send her on errands. "Fetch me another spatula, would you, honey?" Pat would say, patting Maddie on the shoulder. When this happened, Maddie went to work quickly, helping herself to a few baggies, a few matches, a can of food — whatever she could easily get her hands on. Sometimes she took things she didn't really need, but couldn't resist. Like the time she'd nicked her finger washing knives and had been sent off to Nurse Beckett for a bandage. The nurse had left her alone in the infirmary and Maddie had swiped a rolled-up Ace bandage and a handful of plastic-wrapped antiseptic wipes just lying in the cupboard. It wasn't until later that she realized all the uses to which she could put that bandage. For one thing, it would make an excellent rope from which to crawl out of her dormitory window. She could use it to bundle her goods and then tie them around her waist, leaving her hands free when she travelled. She lay awake at night and thought about these things. And each night, her bed grew a little lumpier as she continued to stuff her pilfered goods inside the mattress.

Chapter Nineteen

By the time we got Belinda back to camp it was dark and she was writhing in pain, mumbling incoherently. I'd asked her a few times if she knew what had happened, but Belinda was in no shape to answer questions.

It seemed the ranch hands were all at dinner, so we were forced to heft Belinda all the way to the infirmary ourselves. Where was Coach's ATV with the wagon when you needed it? My arms ached with the effort of keeping from jarring Belinda's makeshift litter as we carried her. Despite the fact that she was utterly unlikable, with each painful step, I felt more and more sorry for the girl.

One look at Belinda's leg and Nurse Beckett summoned Doc who immediately radioed Coach to bring a van. The nurse gave Belinda something to calm her down and treated her for shock, but it was clear that setting the fractured leg was not something she cared to attempt.

"I'd go with her myself, but I shouldn't leave the camp," the nurse said looking at the three of us as Doc and Coach eased Belinda into the back of the van. "If one of the other children were to fall ill, I'd be negligent." Nurse Beckett was the only one who ever called the kids children.

"I'll go," Gracie said. Nurse Beckett looked at my friend dubiously.

"She's a trained E.M.T.," I said, realizing too late that I might have just blown my cover. But Nurse Beckett was still fussing over Belinda, and Doc and Coach were busy inside the van.

"That's perfect, then," Nurse Beckett said, obviously relieved.

Coach didn't look too happy about having to drive the van, I thought. Which was interesting. In fact, he didn't seem to be showing much concern at all for Belinda's condition. Was his apparent indifference an intentional cover up for their affair? Or was he just an asshole? Maybe there never had been an affair. Maybe it wasn't Coach whom Belinda had sneaked out to see that night, after all.

"Keep an eye on my, uh, horse, will you guys?" Gracie said, climbing into the back of the van. Jo and I both knew who she was really talking about.

"Sure thing," Jo said, folding her arms over her chest. The top button had come undone again and she seemed suddenly self-conscious.

"How'd this happen?" Doc asked Jo.

"No idea. I'm just glad we noticed her horse when we did."

Doc walked Nurse Beckett back to the infirmary, leaving Jo and me to watch the van until its taillights disappeared around the bend. Jo's arm brushed against mine and neither of us pulled away.

"Looks like we missed dinner," she said. "You hungry?"

Actually I was starved. But her arm against mine sent shivers through me that had nothing to do with the evening chill and all I could do was nod. Warnings were going off in my head but my damned body didn't seem to be paying the slightest attention.

"Maybe we can get Pat to let us fool around in her kitchen. I'm sure we can put something together."

She moved away and my skin tingled where she'd made contact. Goosebumps raised on my flesh as we walked side by side, our arms lightly touching, our legs keeping pace with each other.

We had to go to the back door to finally get Pat's attention. It was clear she was through cooking for the night. The dishes were already put away, though the aroma of lasagne lingered in the room. Pat had a legal-sized yellow pad in one hand, a calculator in the other.

"What happened to you?" she asked when she saw Jo's arms. Jo gave her a quick summary of the barbed wire incident, then recapped the last few hours, skipping over the cut cinch.

"You must be famished!"

"We are. I thought maybe if you let us look in the fridge, we could fix ourselves a quick bite."

"There's a tiny bit of lasagne left. I put it in the fridge already, but I could nuke it for you. Or we could make an omelette. There's some cheddar and onions, maybe some red bell peppers in the crisper." She'd moved to the commercial-sized refrigerator and begun rummaging through it. Jo stopped her.

"Pat, please. We didn't come here to make you work. Just let us help ourselves. We'll clean up, promise. I know you're dog-tired."

"Actually, I am working on my inventory. Are you sure you don't mind?"

"Positive. We like to cook."

Pat looked from Jo to me and back again, her kind brown

eyes seeming to assess the situation. She smiled. "Okay, then. Holler if you need anything." She turned on her heel and headed for the back office.

"You do like to cook, don't you?" she whispered, turning to face me. We were standing only a few feet apart but Jo stepped closer, backing me against the still warm oven.

"I do. How did you know?" I ignored the fluttering in my chest. I also ignored the voice in my head that told me to run.

"I caught you checking out my pots and pans the other day. When you thought I wasn't looking."

"Hmmm."

"That's not all you were checking out, was it, Cassidy James?" She took my hands in hers and brought them up between us. Her gaze was locked with mine as she drew my hands to her lips and kissed my fingers. I felt my insides tumble.

"I'd like to kiss you," she said, her voice going husky.

"I . . . I . . ." There was still time to get out of this gracefully, I thought. I cleared my throat, planned my words carefully. But despite these good intentions, different words altogether came tumbling out. "I'd like to kiss you, too," I said, not daring to move. Jo leaned forward and pulled me to her. Her lips were soft and yielding, then suddenly insistent. I felt those graceful hands slide up and brush against my breasts and I heard myself moan. My own hands moved across her stiffened nipples and the sound she made came from deep within her.

"You gals finding everything you need?" Pat called out, moments before her footsteps could be heard in the hallway.

Jo stepped back, her calm-sea eyes glistening, her cheeks flushed. We were both a little breathless.

"We sure are," Jo said, opening the refrigerator door and hurriedly pulling things out. I grabbed a skillet and turned on the burner, wondering if the feelings showed on my face as transparently as they did on Jo's.

"Decided you might enjoy a little vino with your meal. I keep a hidden stash in my desk drawer for emergencies. It ain't fancy, but it's cheap." She hefted out a half-empty jug of something called Table Red. "Tell you the truth, I think I'll join you, if you don't mind. Here, let me get that for you. You two just sit on down there at the counter and let me whomp this up. It won't take but a minute and I can see you two have hardly made any headway at all. Jo, you wanna pour us some wine, honey?"

"What happened to the inventory?" Jo asked, looking at me with a mixture of exasperation and longing.

"Oh, well. I can do paperwork any old time. It's not every day I get to sit down with adults and sip a little wine. So tell me, Cassidy. What do you think of our camp, so far?"

And so it went. Jo and I sat side by side on stools at the counter watching Pat cook. She pulled up a stool on the opposite side of the counter and occasionally came over to sip wine, but she couldn't sit still for more than a second before jumping up to check on things. Every time Pat jumped up for something, Jo's hand reached out and touched mine, sometimes resting on my thigh, sometimes brushing against the zipper of my jeans, sending electric jolts straight through me. Just before Pat served us, Jo leaned over and whispered in my ear.

"I want you so bad, it hurts." She gently bit my ear lobe and before I knew what was happening, her fingers deftly worked the zipper of my jeans open. I suppressed a gasp as she slid her hand in farther and pressed her fingers against the thin cotton fabric beneath my jeans. I'm afraid the moan I made got Pat's attention. My cheeks were burning, both with mortification and desire.

"Here it is," she said, setting two plates in front of us, looking at us closely for our reaction.

"Oh, God," I said. I wasn't talking about the food and Jo knew it. She stifled a sigh, easing her hand out of my pants so she could pick up a fork. My breath caught in my throat and my heart was beating so hard I was afraid it would explode.

"This looks delicious," Jo said, taking a bite of her omelette.

"Just leftovers, really," Pat said modestly. "Aren't you hungry, Cassidy?"

The truth was, my whole body was throbbing with desire and I was afraid if Jo so much as brushed her arm against me one more time, I was going to lose control completely.

"Famished," I said. With a trembling hand, I picked up my fork and dug into the golden omelette. "Delicious," I mumbled, my mouth full. It was. The eggs were light and fluffy, folded over spears of asparagus with a hint of tarragon and chopped ham and sharp cheddar.

"You are a genius," Jo said, her mouth full.

"A life-saver," I said.

Pat beamed and poured us all more wine.

As much as one part of me longed to leave with Jo, another part was scared to death. What in the world was I getting myself into? I'd barely gotten over the last disaster and here I was letting myself fall into another one. I wasn't ready for this and I knew it. I had no business even thinking about it. As tortured as I felt right then sexually, I was actually relieved when Pat settled in for a good long gossip. When I got the chance, I didn't hesitate to steer her toward the night Annie Sisson disappeared. A couple of times, Jo's hand slid over onto my leg, but I brushed it away and kept Pat talking. Once, Jo actually groaned and got up to do the dishes.

"So what's your theory for why she left?" I asked.

"Oh, honey, that poor child had more on her plate than people realized. She kept her social life private, but being right next door, I saw things. I think she was heart-broke, plain and simple."

"Because of Coach?" I asked.

Pat looked surprised. "You know about that?"

"I don't think it was as much of a secret as they thought. Word is, he was seeing someone else."

"Well, if he was, he was still seeing her plenty at the same time. He even came by that night."

"Coach came to see Annie the night she disappeared?"

"He sure did. Had to be two, maybe three in the morning. I got up to pee, like I always do about that time, and noticed the light on in her cabin. See, my window looks right out on hers, though I can't see much on account of the trees. But I can see when the light's on, and it was on that night. Which I thought was kind of odd, so I just stood there a minute and watched until the light went out. That's when I saw Coach step down off the porch. I couldn't really tell it was him in the dark, except he was wearing that baseball cap he always wears which I could see the shape of in the moonlight. I just figured they'd had a little midnight delight and I went back to bed. It wasn't until we found out Annie was gone that I wondered whether she'd left after Coach came to see her, or whether she was already gone when he got there. Guess it doesn't matter, either way."

Oh, but it did, I thought. "Was he carrying anything with him when you saw him on the porch?"

Pat put her glass down and peered at me with narrowed eyes. "What? You think he carried her off somewhere? You suspect foul play?"

"No, I was just curious, I guess. She left her grandmother's quilt out back. Seems a strange thing to leave behind."

"Humph," she intoned, taking another swallow of the cheap wine. Jo, who was standing at the sink, gave me a look over Pat's shoulder, like Come on!

"Does kinda make you ponder, doesn't it?" Pat said. "But to answer your question, I couldn't tell if he had anything in his hands or not. I just caught the back of his head for a second. If it weren't for the baseball cap, I wouldn't have even known who it was."

Jo made a huge show of yawning and Pat finally got the hint.

"My goodness, I've kept you gals here far too long. After your ordeal today, you're probably exhausted."

"Well, I do have to get up early," Jo said.

"And I've got papers to grade," I added. "But it sure was nice of you to share your food and wine with us."

"It was my pleasure," Pat said, walking us to the door. "Stop by again, anytime."

Outside, the night was dark and cool, the sky littered with sparkling dots of gold.

"Almost a full moon," Jo said, slipping her arm in mine as we walked toward the cabins. The camp was quiet. The bunkhouses were all dark, as were most of the staff cabins.

"This may surprise you, but I'd like you to come over," I said, surprising myself even as I said it. So much for inner strength and resolve.

She laughed — a lovely sound. "I was kinda hoping you'd say that."

"The problem is, there's something I think we need to do first."

Jo groaned. "Why am I afraid to ask?"

"It shouldn't take long. But we'll never have a better opportunity. With Coach gone, this is the perfect time to look through his cabin. You heard what Pat said. Maybe there's something there that could tie him to Annie's disappearance. You game for doing look-out?"

"If I told you what I was really game for, Cassidy, we wouldn't be going to someone else's cabin. But, yeah. I'm game."

I ignored the feelings that continued to well up as I led her past the darkened path toward Coach's cabin.

"Wait here. Just keep in the shadows. If someone

approaches, act like you're looking for Coach to see how Belinda's doing. Play dumb, do whatever you have to do."

"Cass. I can handle this. Go, already."

I tried the front door, which was locked, then walked around the perimeter of the cabin, hoping we wouldn't have to go back for my lock picks. There were four windows in all, and it wasn't until I reached the tiny bathroom window, that I caught a break. The little window was propped open. It would be a tight fit, and I'd have to figure out a way to boost myself up, but it was definitely doable.

I called for Jo to join me, then let her boost me up so that I could shimmy through the open window. Even though I knew Coach was gone, my heart was pounding. Something about breaking and entering, I supposed. I had probably been a burglar in my last life.

I dropped down into the cabin, a near-mirror image of my own, and set about searching, wishing I didn't have to turn on a light, but knowing that without it, I'd never see a thing.

The first thing I noticed was a wicker basket like the one in my cabin. I pulled off the lid, only to find an impressive pile of soiled underwear and socks. I already knew all of the potential hiding places, having scoped them out in my own cabin, but I took my time just the same, in case Coach was somehow more imaginative than I thought. I checked the drawers, to no avail, the closet, the shower, beneath the toilet tank lid, the pots and pans, the freezer and fridge. I peered inside the lamp shades and beneath the throw rugs. I went through his pockets, tapped the walls for secret hiding places covered by drywall or plaster, and finally, only because it was the only thing I hadn't checked, I slid my hand beneath the mattress.

Coach's gun was only two inches from the edge of the bed. This ticked me off. Any idiot would've checked there first, which was precisely why I hadn't looked there. For some reason, I'd given Coach more credit than he was due. But I wasn't sure which one of us that made the stupider.

I sighed and hefted the pistol — a Colt .45, not unlike my own. I thumbed open the chamber and checked to see if any bullets had been spent. The chamber was full. Which didn't mean squat, I knew. If Coach had recently fired the gun, he could've easily reloaded. But in my search of his cabin, I hadn't come across any ammunition. Of course, that didn't mean he didn't hide it somewhere else.

I slid the gun back where I'd found it and looked around the cabin one last time, wondering if I'd missed something. There was not a single trace of Annie Sisson. No love letter, no stray pair of panties, no lipstick-stained shirt collar, nothing. The only thing remotely interesting in Coach's cabin was the gun hidden beneath his mattress. That and the fact that he'd apparently taken his odious cattle prod with him.

I thought of Gracie, hoping that she wouldn't do anything to put herself in danger. But even with his prod, I'd put my money on Gracie anytime. I let myself out the front door and locked it behind me. Jo was standing on the front porch, shivering.

"Find anything?"

"Not what I hoped for. But your buddy, Coach, does keep a gun under his mattress."

"He probably needs it when he tracks the kids," she said. "I mean, there are cougars out there."

"I suppose you're right, " I said, privately thinking that a Colt .45 wouldn't be my weapon of choice for defense against a cougar. "You cold?" I slipped an arm across her shoulder and started toward the cabin. She was still sleeveless and her skin was cool to the touch. It seemed like ages since Gracie and I had watched her paint on her porch.

"Not anymore," she said. "I get next to you, I'm on fire."

"Hmmm."

"You don't believe me?" She moved her lips next to my ear, whispering, raising goosebumps on my neck. "You want to feel how hot I am for you?" She took my hand and moved it against the crotch of her Levis. "Can you feel that?" she whispered.

"Jo," I managed. We had stopped walking and now she reached out and held both hands on my shoulders, locking her blue-gray eyes on mine. Her voice was low and husky, her tone strangely moving. "You make me want to paint pictures, Cassidy James. You make me want to write songs. But right now, all I want to do is make love to you. Okay?"

My heart hammered and my knees, already weak, trembled. "Okay," I said. "But I'll expect at least a song by morning." I led the way up the path to my cabin, boldly ignoring the little voice that kept insisting I still had time to stop myself from making another colossal mistake.

Chapter Twenty

The morning sun poured through the window, bathing Jo's golden skin in light. When she opened them, her eyes were the color of still water, gazing at me as we lay face to face, silently drinking each other in. I reached out and traced her jawline with my finger, then suddenly pulled my hand away and sat up.

"What?" she asked, a line furrowing her brow.

"Nothing. I'm sorry. I . . ."

She sat up and took my hand in hers. "Don't do this. Not after last night."

"It's just that . . ."

"Cassidy. God I love to say your name. Cassidy James. Why are you suddenly so afraid?"

"I'm not," I said, though as soon as I said it, I knew it was a lie.

"Then what? What just happened? One minute you're looking at me like you think I'm something special, the next second you can't wait to get away from me."

Jo stood up and started to dress.

"You are, Jo. You are something special, okay?"

She stopped dressing and turned to look at me.

"There's someone else, isn't there?" she asked.

I wasn't sure how to answer. There was and there wasn't.

"Why didn't you just say so? Last night?"

"It's not that simple," I said.

"Yeah, it is, Cass. It's exactly that simple."

I got up and started throwing on my own clothes, suddenly angry. "Maybe your life is that simple. Mine happens to be fucking complicated at the moment." Not entirely true. I was making it complicated. It didn't have to be that way.

She stared at me for a minute. "What's her name?" she finally asked.

I sighed. "Erica. She left me, for what it's worth. And it isn't the first time, either. So, I guess that makes me a world class idiot."

"Actually, I think it probably makes me the world class idiot," she said. She slid into her boots and ran her hands through her tousled hair. She looked sexy as hell.

"Jo, please. I just need to think this through a little. Last night happened so fast."

She held up her hands. "Hey, my mistake. I obviously got the wrong impression. I could've sworn the way you looked at me, the way you touched me, you know . . ."

I moved across the room toward her but she backed away. "Just tell me this. Was it because you were curious? Wanted to know what it was like to be with a cowgirl? Someone who dresses like a guy?"

"Jo . . ."

"Cause a lot of women are intrigued by that, you know? I

mean, don't feel bad, or anything. I just wish I'd known that's all it was."

"Jo . . ."

But she was gone. In four strides she'd reached the door and slammed it on her way out. I stood, half-dressed and open-mouthed, wondering how in the world I had screwed that up so badly. It had been a perfect night, and a perfectly horrible morning.

I got undressed again and stepped into the shower letting the steaming water pound away as I tried to clear my mind. I couldn't let what had happened with Jo distract me from my purpose but I was having trouble concentrating. My own conflicting thoughts stormed and swirled until I could barely think straight. Why had I not listened to the voice of reason last night? Why had I allowed myself to tumble into bed with a relative stranger? A cowgirl, of all things! A woman who dressed like a cowboy, painted like De Grazia, spoke to horses like they were her lovers and played the guitar? And why did this woman move me so much? There was no denying the way she made me feel. So what was I so afraid of? It was more than just being gun-shy after my repeated failures with Erica Trinidad. And it was more than the fact that my feelings for Erica had never really gone away.

Maybe it wasn't fear at all. Maybe I was just being smart for once! But somehow I didn't quite believe it. It was as if that damned dream had given me an unwanted awareness of my own vulnerability and now that I was aware of it, I was afraid to make a single move.

I finished showering and dressed, forcing myself to think about the case. Had someone really tried to kill Belinda Pitt? I was anxious to talk to Gracie and get her take on the interaction between Coach and Belinda. If it wasn't Coach she'd gone after that night, who was it? I was even more anxious to talk to Maddie but until I could, there were a few things I could do on my own.

The more I thought about it, the more convinced I was that the heart of the matter somehow lay in the mine and the easiest way to find out more about the mine was through the machine shop. Ben no doubt kept records of the shop's transactions. If I could get a quick peek at his files, I might learn what the truckers had picked up that night which might or might not shed some light on what happened to Miss Sisson. Maybe I'd find a blueprint of the mine's layout. Maybe there'd be some reference to the location of Isolation. And maybe I wouldn't find anything at all. But nothing ventured, nothing gained, I thought. My best bet was to slip into the machine shop during lunch, which meant I didn't have much time to prepare.

While I waited for Ben to head for the cafeteria, I unrolled a long strip of duct tape and folded it with the adhesive side against itself, making a ten-foot length of rope, which I neatly rolled and stuffed into my pocket. When at last I saw Ben leave the machine shop, I walked straight for it, figuring I'd have at least a half-hour to snoop around. The way Ben dawdled over meals, I might even have longer, but I didn't want to chance it. I anticipated that the front doors would be locked but even if they weren't, I didn't want to be seen entering. I made my way around the back of the building to the recreation area without running into anyone, though I knew that if someone were watching from behind a cabin window, they might be able to see me. Once I reached the rear of the building, however, I was well-hidden. The recreation area was bordered by an eight-foot concrete wall, just tall enough to discourage the machine shop workers from traipsing off during their breaks. There was, however, a maple tree growing at the south east corner.

Looking around to make sure no one could see me, I

looped the tape over a low-hanging branch and hoisted myself up, climbed up to the next branch and swung over onto the wall. I perched there for a moment, scanning the recreation area to make sure I was totally alone. Not only was the place empty, but the door leading into the machine shop was propped open with a door stop. I wouldn't even have to use my picks, I thought, smiling at my good fortune. I moved my tape-rope to a branch that hung over the wall so that I would have a way to pull myself back up once inside, then let myself down.

Inside, the room was eerily silent, with only a few overhead fans churning the hot air. No wonder they kept the back door open, I thought. Without the cross-breeze from the front doors, the heat from the machines made the shop stifling.

I started toward the green lift leading to Ben's loft when I spotted an alternate route. There was a steel spiral staircase tucked near the rear door that I decided to take instead. If someone came in before I was done, at least it wouldn't be obvious that I was up there.

I took the stairs and walked along the two-foot balcony that rimmed the glass-enclosed loft, making sure the loft was empty before I entered. Once inside, I wasn't sure where to start. There were half a dozen computers, all of them glowing and humming. I sat down at the closest and hit the space key which stopped the geometric design that was flashing on-screen, showing me the desktop. I clicked on the hard-drive and scanned the contents. It only took a minute to realize that this computer was used to activate the machinery downstairs. I moved to the next computer and found the same thing. I checked my watch, then moved all the way to the last computer and brought up the menu, crossing my fingers.

"Bingo," I said. But my enthusiasm was short-lived. Ben had more files in the hard drive than I'd be able to read in a month. I opened one, then another, searching frantically for something that resembled delivery dates. I'd never find what I was looking for in the time I had. I pulled open a few drawers until I found a box of floppy disks. I chose a blank disk and inserted it into the computer, then began copying his files onto the disk. I wasn't sure what all I was getting. Some files were labeled by number only, others by name. I didn't have time to sort through them, so I copied them all. I was nearly finished, when the front door suddenly opened downstairs. Two men stood in the doorway. One was Ben. The other was Doc.

I froze, then ducked down, ejecting the disk from a crouched position and clicked out of the hard drive. My heart was thudding against my chest as I backed away from the glass overlook, searching for a way to escape. From the grinding sound of the loft, I knew they were headed my way. Maybe I could sneak down the staircase as they came up. But they'd be sure to see me, I thought. The lift and staircase were directly across from each other. I could hear the lift screech to a halt outside the door and knew I didn't have much time. But there was nowhere to hide! Then I noticed the curtained window along the north wall. I'd never seen the curtain open, but I assumed it covered an outside window. If there was room on the window ledge behind that vinyl curtain, I thought, I might have a chance. The window was six feet off the ground and about twelve feet wide. I moved the heavy curtain aside, and sighed with relief. The six-inch ledge was just wide enough for me to stand on. I stepped onto a chair and hoisted myself up onto the ledge, pressing my back against the glass and pulling the curtain closed in front of me. As I did, the loft door opened.

"So what is it that's so urgent I can't finish my lunch, Ben?"

"I told you, we need to talk."

"Yes, but why here?"

"Because we can't afford to be overheard. People have been talking. And that new teacher, Cassidy James? She's been asking a lot of questions about Sisson."

"What kinds of questions?"

The vinyl curtain had a number of vertical cracks along the folds, some of which were large enough to peer through. When I carefully shifted to the left, I could see Doc leaning back in one of Ben's office chairs. He didn't look overly concerned, but Ben was pacing.

"She said she'd heard that Annie was out at the mine that night, for one thing. Don't you think that's a little odd?"

Doc sat forward, suddenly more interested. "She say where she heard that?"

"No. But the only possibility is that dyke that works with Clutch. Who else could've seen her?"

"Yes, I've seen them together. I think our little Jo has a new girlfriend."

Ben cut him off. "Doc. I don't give a rat's ass what their relationship is. The point is, your new teacher and her have been talking. I don't like the way this is going."

"I think what you're suffering from, Ben, is a touch of good old fashioned paranoia."

"Don't patronize me, Doc. I think we should check her out. I know you all liked her in the interview, but something's not right."

"Ida already looked into it. Her story checked out."

"Yeah, I understand about her teaching job, but what's she been doing since then? There's a pretty big gap there in her employment record."

"What? You think she's some kind of law enforcement?" He laughed, shaking his head. "Look, I know this whole thing has got you nervous, but it couldn't be avoided. For someone in your line of work, you panic too easily. Just let it blow over. Another month or two and no one will even remember Annie Sisson was here."

"What about her family? Sooner or later, someone's going to come asking questions."

"And we'll answer them. All we know is she said there was a family emergency and she left. End of story."

"What if they find the car?"

"Coach took care of it. Forget about it."

"That's another thing. Coach should have never been brought into this. It's another thing he can hold over us."

"Ben, we've discussed this. We decided a long time ago it was better to have Coach inside the tent, pissing out, than the other way around." Doc pushed back his chair and stood up.

"She said she was interested in going inside the mine."

"What? What brought that up?" Doc suddenly sounded interested again.

"That's what I'm trying to tell you. She was grilling me, trying to get information. I don't know if she actually knows anything or not, but she's asking too many questions for my taste."

"What did you say?"

"Told her it was bat-infested and dangerous." For the first time, Ben allowed himself a small smile and Doc laughed.

"Good. Listen, I'll keep an eye on her. Frankly, I'm more concerned about what Maddie Boone might have seen that night. We never were able to verify her whereabouts. And she's been acting spooked ever since."

"Why don't you just do your hypnosis thing on her and find out?"

"Not that easy. She's resistant as hell, but time's on our side. You just keep the shop going and everything will be fine. How's production?"

"Good. Fine."

"Maybe we should stick to the basics for a while."

"There's a shipment due in August. I'll need to start soon."

"Hold off for a while, Ben. Just to be safe."

Ben walked Doc to the loft door and they both stepped

outside. My legs were shaking with the effort of standing in such an awkward position but I didn't dare move until I was sure they'd both gone down in the loft. If Ben came back in, God knew how long I might have to stay perched on the ledge. And if someone walked by outside the shop and looked up, no doubt they'd see me plastered against the window. I heard the lift grind into gear and counted. If he was coming back in, he'd do it soon. I waited, then unable to stand it another second, I eased the curtain aside and peeked out. No sign of Ben from that position. I climbed down from the ledge. Then I froze.

Ben was standing ten feet away from me on the other side of the glass. His back was to me as he watched Doc descend in the lift. Any minute, he'd turn around and come back in. My only hope was to make it to the stairs and hide there until he was distracted.

I threw myself to the floor and crawled toward the steel stairway. Even if Ben turned around, I didn't think he'd see me on the floor. But my mind was racing, thinking up excuses if I was caught. After what I'd just heard, though, I knew an excuse wouldn't matter.

I made it to the steel stairway and crouched on the second landing, holding my breath. From where I was positioned, I couldn't see Ben, which hopefully meant he couldn't see me either. I waited, willing him to go back into the room so I could make my way down the rest of the stairs without him hearing my footsteps on the steel steps. There was still a chance he might see me as I went, but he'd have to be looking out the window in that direction. I'd just have to take my chances.

Finally, I heard the door open to the loft and, keeping as low to the stairs as I could, I crept down them. When I reached the bottom, I ducked down and raced out the open back door into the recreation area. My heart was pounding as I dashed for the tree. Praying the tape would hold again, I hoisted myself, clambered over the wall, pulled the duct tape free and dropped to safety on the other side, the disk safely secured in my back pocket. Now all I needed to do was get to my computer. Then I needed to talk to Gracie and Jo and figure out a way to get Maddie Boone the hell out of Camp Turnaround. With any luck, we'd be right behind her.

Chapter Twenty-One — Madeline

Eleven Days Earlier

On the night of May fourth, Maddie was so excited, she couldn't lie still. She had to pee, but didn't dare get up for fear of waking someone. Everything was in place and now she just had to wait for the snoring to start up. The night before, she'd unscrewed the window latches, and in the morning, after everyone had made their mad dash for roll call, she'd practiced opening it, which was a good thing because the window was rusted shut. But after a few tries, the thing came loose, and though it still made a little noise, with all the snoring, she hoped no one would hear it.

Two nights earlier, in the dark, she'd fashioned a knapsack out of one of her tee shirts, pinning the sleeves and neck hole together, then stuffing the laden baggies inside. She could use the ace bandage to tie it closed and then loop it over her shoulder once she was free. Getting down was going to be the tricky part, not because she didn't know what to do, but because there was no way to practice ahead of time.

Now, as the snoring began to fill the room, Maddie reached into the side of her mattress and began pulling her hidden treasures out, careful not to make noise. Luckily her bed was on the top bunk and at the far end of the room, allowing her relative privacy. By now, she knew the objects by their shape, so often had she taken inventory in the dark. One by one, she stuffed them into her knapsack and was pleased with how heavy it felt in her lap. She listened in the dark, staring out her window, waiting.

After what seemed an impossible exercise in patience, she pulled out the clothes she'd hidden that night under her pillow and quietly slipped them on. She tied her shoe laces in the dark, her hands trembling.

When once again she was sure that no one was stirring, she sat up and silently slid the end of her ace bandage through a metal hoop on the wooden window frame. She didn't know what the hoop was for, probably used in the old days to open and close the window with a window pole. She only hoped it would be strong enough to bear her weight. She slid the ace bandage through until she had equal lengths on either side, then tied her knapsack to the bottom of one end. Then she lay back and rested, willing her heart to quit racing.

Finally, she reached up and gently pushed against the window frame. The scraping noise was much worse than she'd feared, and she stopped immediately, afraid it had wakened someone. But the snoring continued, and after what seemed an eternity, Maddie pushed the window wider, breathing the fresh air with excitement. She lifted the ace bandage from her lap and tossed it, knapsack and all, out the window. She held her breath, but it hardly made a thud as it swung against the wall outside.

The next part was even trickier. She knew the bunk would creak when she stood on it, but she had no choice. Grasping the top of the ace bandage in both hands, Maddie stepped onto the window sill, said a silent prayer, and testing her weight just once to make sure, she stepped off the ledge into nothingness.

There was nothing to it, though. In seconds, she'd shimmied down her homemade rope and plunked softly onto the ground. Now she hurriedly pulled the ace bandage through the window hoop and rolled it up as she made her way to the machine shop.

This was the best part of her plan, she knew. She'd worked in the shop long enough to know that Ben left the back windows open at closing time for ventilation. The big machines were hot and the place didn't have air conditioning.

Maddie kept in the shadows as she made her way to the back of the recreation area. There wasn't a light on anywhere, but that didn't mean someone wouldn't look out a window to gaze at the moon or something. She didn't want to take any chances. She'd come too far.

She'd already decided the best way over the wall was the big maple tree and when she reached it, she quickly tossed the heavy end of her ace bandage over a branch of the tree and hoisted herself up. She scrambled up to the next limb and peered across the dark playground. Sure enough, the windows were open. Every one of them. To her amazement, so was the back door. Obviously, Ben wasn't expecting anyone to break into the shop. He was probably more worried about kids escaping than breaking in.

Not believing her good luck, she hopped down from the wall, pulled the bandage down behind her, and tiptoed to the open door. Then it occurred to her. Maybe the door was still open because someone was inside.

She peeked inside, then looked up at the loft. Sure enough, a dim glow could be seen through the glass panes surrounding the loft. Did Ben sleep up there, she wondered? Or was he working late? Or maybe the lights came from the computers; maybe he left them on all night.

The problem was, she couldn't afford to take a chance. If he was up there, she'd have to junk her plan to take the boxcar. The sound would wake him for sure. Maddie stood in the doorway, wondering what she should do. She'd planned for so long and been so careful, and now her whole escape was jeopardized because of that stupid light!

Well, she wasn't going to let a minor setback stop her. She'd just have to walk the tracks, she said to herself bravely. But she didn't have a light. The miner's cap was in her cave. She didn't know if she had the courage to walk through the tunnel in the dark. What if she got lost? She'd never walked that particular stretch of the tunnel before. What if she never found her cave again?

Don't be ridiculous, she told herself. The tracks lead straight to the mine entrance. Follow the tracks, grab another miner's cap, and back track to the cave. How far could it be, anyway?

Before she could talk herself out of it, Maddie made a quick dash across the shop floor to where the boxcar was waiting. It would've been so much easier if she could just hop in and press the lever that made it go. She'd seen Ben do it a few times. But she didn't have that luxury. She stood at the ugly yawning mouth of the mine, took a deep breath, and stepped into the darkness.

It was worse than she remembered. She closed her eyes and couldn't tell the difference from when they were open. The tunnel was black and cold and smelled musty. She heard water trickling from hidden corners and something that sounded like the soft flapping of wings that terrified her more than the horrible groaning sound that rumbled beneath her. She was tempted to turn around and go back the way she'd come. But if she didn't do this now, she never would. Carefully placing one foot after the other on the metal track, Maddie trudged forward into the gathering cold and darkness.

Even in the pitch black, she could tell when the tunnel veered off in another direction, plunging deep into the mountain. She resolutely stayed on the tracks, knowing that without them she'd never make it out alive. Still, each time she came to an opening on her left, she turned to face it, and reached out to feel for the door that marked her cave. Each time she did so, she cringed, because the air felt different over the entrances, colder, like the bottom had dropped out of them.

She had no idea how far she'd come. She'd tried counting but kept losing count every time she stopped at a new sound. She'd tried humming, to keep herself brave, but that didn't last long either. Finally, she just plowed ahead, praying under her breath.

Once again, the tunnel veered and this time, when Maddie turned to examine the entrance, she let out a small cry of relief. Her door! She'd made it to her cave!

Unless there were other caves with doors on them, she thought, pushing the door gently ajar. What if something was in there? Fear gripped her as she stood on the threshold, listening in the dark. Finally, unable to stand it another second, she slipped off her knapsack and rummaged through the baggies until she found one of the wooden matches. She struck it against the rock floor and cupped her hand over the tiny flame, peering into the cave. Sure enough, off to the rear of the room, she made out the shape of the odious pit toilet. She'd done it! Now all she had to do was get to the stuff she'd stashed, get a light on, a fire going and she was in business. She'd never felt so proud of herself in her life.

Chapter Twenty-Two

I was still shaken when I settled down with my laptop and started perusing Ben's files. It wasn't as easy as it sounded, because I had to transfer the files from IBM to Mac, something my Powerbook was capable of, but which took time. After the first few, I began to understand his filing system. The numbers apparently represented specific manufactured goods. The titles referred to everything else, from billing information to inventory. He even had the student work schedules listed. There didn't seem to be any rhyme or reason for the order of his files, so I went to the file menu and asked it to sort the files by date.

And there it was! May 25 was right there, up front, big as day. A delivery to someone called CTA was scheduled for ten p.m. So it wasn't just a matter of the truck rolling in late, I thought.

But a few other files came up for that date as well. One was fairly innocuous — a note to change Ben's dental appointment. I wondered where he went for it. Not Portsmith Grove! And surely Nurse Beckett didn't include tooth cleaning in her résumé. The next entry caught my attention. It was just a meaningless number, but it had an asterisk in front of it and was dated May 25.

Unlike the previous files which were primarily word-processing — or simple data base-generated, this one was comprised of fairly sophisticated technological renderings of shapes, labeled alphabetically like sewing patterns. I scanned down, wondering what the unidentifiable shapes represented. Obviously, they were the design for parts manufactured in the shop. And given the date of delivery, I had to assume they were what was picked up the night Annie Sisson disappeared. But the parts themselves were unrecognizable.

Since there was nothing else on that date, I tried the dates just before or after, but didn't find anything illuminating. But that asterisk still intrigued me so I went to the find file and punched in an asterisk. I didn't have any idea if it would work, but I was rewarded with an immediate list of numbered files with asterisks in front of them. I clicked a few open, and found more patterns and labeled shapes. Again, they reminded me of sewing patterns, I thought. Or assembly packages without the instructions. With a little time and luck, I could probably figure out how the parts went together, but it would be easier with directions.

I need a printer, I thought. I checked my watch. Afternoon classes were due to be over. There were printers in my classroom. I didn't know whether they'd be compatible with my PowerBook so I banked on the disk being compatible with the IBM in the room. If I hurried, I could at least print the file for the night Annie disappeared, and still have time to catch Maddie at the stables.

Half-way to the classroom, I ran into Ida Evans. She was decked out in riding gear, complete with red cowboy boots, jeans and a denim shirt adorned with gold and red rhinestones. But despite the fancy get-up, she looked a little frazzled, I thought.

"There you are! Where on earth have you been hiding yourself?" she asked.

"I've been working on a lesson back at the cabin. I was just headed to my classroom to finish up."

"Tsk, tsk," she uttered, shaking her head. "All work and no play. I understand you helped rescue poor little Belinda Pitt yesterday. Poor thing has a terrible fracture. I'm afraid she won't be riding horseback for some time now."

"Is she back?"

"They just pulled in a while ago. She's resting in the infirmary. As long as she's on the pain medication, Nurse Beckett will keep her there. We'd have sent her home, but her parents are somewhere in Europe and no one seems to know where to reach them. It's just as well, I suppose. From what I understand, she'll get better care here than she would with them. You have any idea how she fell?"

Yeah, I thought. Someone cut her cinch. But I didn't share that with Ida. I shrugged. "Looked like the saddle slipped right out from under her. What I don't understand is why none of the other kids spotted her. She must've been off by herself." More likely off with someone else, I thought.

"We tell them not to wander off by themselves. They know the rules. Some people just have to learn the hard way, I guess."

And someone had helped Belinda learn this particular lesson. I looked at Ida closely, wondering if Doc or Ben had already talked to her about checking up on me. She seemed agitated.

"Other than Belinda, everything going okay?" I asked.

Ida's eyes narrowed for a second like she thought it was

strange of me to ask. "Everything's just hunky dory," she said. "I'm just on my way out for an afternoon ride. Want to join me?"

"Maybe I'll catch up with you later. I really want to work on this assignment idea while it's fresh in my mind."

"All righty, then. But do take time out to enjoy yourself, Cassidy. A little fresh air every day does a body good."

Off she strode, her red boots clicking on the pavement, her arms swinging out as she walked, whistling a tune from an old musical. It made me wonder if she'd forgotten to take her medication that morning.

Once inside my classroom, I went straight for the computer. I wasn't familiar with the model, but in a few minutes I had it up and running, the old dot matrix printer grinding noisily away, happily spitting out a continuous stream of shapes and figures. I not only wanted a printout of what was delivered on May 25, but of every file with an asterisk next to it. While it worked, I tried to organize my thoughts. There was no doubt that Ben, Doc and Coach were all involved in the disappearance of Annie Sisson. The problem was, I couldn't prove it. Coach had gotten rid of her car. Had he also gotten rid of her? No, I thought. Whatever had happened to Annie had happened before Coach was involved. Ben had said as much and he wasn't happy that Doc had involved Coach at all. It would give Coach something else to hold over their heads, he said.

And wasn't that interesting, I thought. What else was Coach holding over their heads? Is that why he got away with things no one else approved of? Like Isolation and the cattle prod? And what did Doc mean about sticking to the basics for a while? Ben said there was a shipment due in August and that he'd have to start soon. Start what? Something beyond the basics, obviously. Something they weren't supposed to be manufacturing in the shop.

The printer beeped, causing me to jump about a foot. I

tore off the last page and folded the considerable stack of papers, resisting the urge to go through them right then and there. I couldn't afford to have someone come in and find me with them. I ejected the disk, wondering where I could hide it. With Ben being suspicious of me, I didn't think my cabin was the best place. It had occurred to me that Ida had been looking for me and that perhaps Ben or Doc had instructed her to keep me busy for a while so that someone could check out my cabin. That would mean that Ida was in on it, too, which I didn't want to believe. But I knew if someone did search my cabin and found my PowerBook, they might be able to surmise from the files on my own hard drive that I was a private investigator. If they knew that, I was dead meat.

I selected a book from the row of dictionaries on the book shelf and slipped the disk between two pages. In the morning, I'd think of a more permanent hiding place, but for now, the disk should be safe. Next, I pulled out my shirt tail and pressed the sheath of papers flat against my back, then tucked the shirt in, holding the papers in place. I'd grab a jacket from my cabin to better conceal the bulge before I headed for the stables. Finally, I turned off the computer and printer and headed for the door. To my utter dismay, a figure was standing in the doorway watching me. It was Coach.

"Thought I might find you here," he said. "You trying to impress the brass by working on your day off?"

"Just finishing up some lesson plans. What's up?"

Coach had the silly cattle prod looped through a leather holster on his belt. I wanted to ask him if he slept with the thing, but didn't think now was the time to tick him off. I wondered how long he'd been standing there and what he'd seen.

"Nothing's up," he said, like it was perfectly natural for him to be standing in my classroom doorway. He folded his arms, showing off his biceps. His pale blue eyes regarded me closely.

"Well, it was nice of you to drop by," I said, walking toward the door he was essentially blocking.

"Now that's a brush-off if I ever heard one," he said, not budging.

"I told Ida I'd meet her for a ride," I said.

"Humph." He unfolded his arms and removed his ball cap, running his hand across his sandy crew cut. "Is it just me, or do you not like guys in general?" he asked.

I thought about it. "Both," I said. So much for not ticking him off. But to my surprise, he laughed.

"That's a good one. So you dig chicks, then?"

"Coach, or whatever your name really is, I am not about to stand here trapped inside this classroom and discuss my love life with you."

"You feel trapped? Hey, I'm sorry. I just came by to be friendly." He stepped a foot away from the doorway into the hall, raising his hands in the air to show how harmless he was.

"Thank you," I said.

"It's cool with me if you're a dyke," he said.

"You're too kind," I said.

"Damn, you're touchy. What did I do to make you hate me so much?"

"I guess I'm not impressed with your behavior-mod methods. The cattle prod seems a bit excessive."

"This thing?" He whipped out the prod like a gunslinger and twirled it in his right hand. "Shoot, Cassidy. This doesn't hardly hurt at all after a few seconds. It's just to get their attention. Keeps 'em in line. I don't even have to raise my voice with the kids."

"How nice for you." I walked through the door and locked it behind me. Coach was standing a foot away and I could feel his jolly demeanor slowly giving way to anger. I knew I should cool it, but I didn't.

"Tell me, Coach. Back in the days when you were just a student here, and no one had thought up Isolation or the behavior mod prod, how did they ever manage to turn kids around?"

Coach seemed genuinely surprised that I knew he'd been a student at the camp. It took him a minute to recover. Then he started to chuckle. "I like that. Behavior Mod Prod. That's what I'll call it from now on. Long after you're gone, Cassidy James, I'll remember you for that. But to answer your question, I guess they got kids turned around okay. We just do it better now. And quicker."

"So the ends justify the means?"

"Something like that." He was still essentially blocking my path, though the hallway was wider than the doorway had been. He still held the prod in his hand and I wondered if Ben and Doc had already talked to him about me. Maybe they'd already discovered that I was a private investigator. I tried to put these thoughts out of my head.

"So, other than me, you like it here okay?" he asked.

I didn't know if Coach was stalling to allow someone else time to search my cabin, or if he was really that interested in me but I decided it was in my best interest to placate him a little.

"I like it fine. Actually, what I said earlier about not liking guys in general wasn't really true. I like most of them fine. I just don't sleep with them. As for you, Coach, I don't know you well enough yet to know whether I like you or not. Maybe deep down, you're a sensitive, caring, all-around nice guy. So far, all I've seen you do is humiliate kids and threaten them with torture."

He seemed a little dumbfounded. He put the prod back in its holster and ran his hand through his hair again. "I guess when you put it that way, it does sound pretty gruesome. But I do a lot more than play the tough guy. You just saw the worst part first. I wouldn't be here if I didn't care about these kids."

It was obvious that I'd hurt his feelings, which was a good thing. It meant he had some.

"Why did you come back to work here?" I asked. "Most kids can't wait to leave."

"Oh, they say that at first. But for quite a few of them, this is the best thing that ever happened to them. It was that way for me." He paused, rubbing his lightly stubbled jaw. "Why did you come to work here? And don't give me any more bullshit about wanting to get past that incident where you decked a kid. I didn't buy that for a second. I think you liked hitting him, like you said. And I think you'd still like it. I think you wanted to slug me a few minutes ago. It was in your eyes."

I laughed. "Touché, Coach. You got me. I admit I had a brief fantasy of grabbing your cattle prod and giving you a chance to see what it felt like. Luckily, the urge passed."

"Lucky for you," he said. I wasn't sure if he was trying for macho bravado or menace.

"I really did tell Ida I'd meet her," I said.

"Okay, okay. I'm sorry I wasted so much of your time. If I'd known you were a dyke, I wouldn't have bothered. It was a waste of my time, too."

This made me smile. "Next time, I'll just paint a big L on my forehead."

Coach smiled. "That might help." He stepped aside and ushered me past him with a courtly wave. As I walked down the hallway, I could still feel his eyes on me. I wondered if he could see the bulge of papers through my shirt.

"You do have a nice ass, though!" he yelled, just as I reached the outside door. I ignored the comment and let myself outside, resisting the urge to run like hell.

Chapter Twenty-Three

"We need to talk," I said as soon as Jo opened the door. One look at her and the morning's events came rushing back at me, making my cheeks redden involuntarily. Gracie was already sprawled in Jo's easy chair and looked beat but she sat straight up at my words.

Jo gave me a look that told me she was more hurt than angry and that beneath the hurt the passion still burned. I realized that that was another thing I found attractive about her. There was no pretense about her. What she felt, she showed. And just being near her, seeing the emotion in her eyes, made whatever resolve I'd momentarily felt earlier, dissolve.

"I think we should get Maddie out of here," I said.

"What do you mean?" Gracie asked.

"I'll explain in a second." I shook out the papers and spread them on the table. "This is going to take a while. You got any scissors and tape?" Jo found some, then came to sit by me as Gracie started tearing the perforated computer paper into separate sheets, while I went to work with the scissors. "According to Ben's records, these parts were what was in the crates that the truck picked up that night in the mine. By themselves, they don't look like anything to me, but I've got a feeling these shapes mean more than meets the eye. If we think of it as sort of a 3-D jigsaw puzzle, maybe we can figure it out."

While we worked, I explained about my visit to Ben's loft and overhearing his conversation with Doc. I told them about Ida looking for me and Coach showing up at my classroom door.

"You think he saw you hiding the disk?" Gracie asked.

"I have no idea. He didn't act like he suspected anything. He was either genuinely trying to hit on me, or doing a good job of faking it. If he was faking it, I assume it was to give someone else time to search my cabin. But when I went back, everything looked in order."

Jo was shaking her head. "You've got to be wrong, Cass. There's no way Doc would be involved in something illegal. I mean, I could see him maybe covering up one of Coach's messes, out of loyalty or fatherly devotion or something, but not like what you're suggesting. Tell Gracie what Pat said about Coach being at Annie Sisson's cabin that night."

I recounted the story to Gracie. "Given what Doc said about Coach taking care of Annie's car, I've got to assume it was also Coach who cleaned out her cabin."

"Makes sense," Gracie said. "But if one of them did kill Annie, what did they do with her?"

"We've got to find out from Maddie. It's the only way. They're going to be on to me soon if they're not already. Ben's too suspicious. I can't go asking any more questions. The thing is, we don't have proof that a crime was even committed. Maddie's the only one who can help us find that proof."

"Okay," Gracie said, standing up. "I agree. Maybe we should just get her and go."

"The problem is, as soon as they find out we've taken her, they could destroy any evidence that might exist. It'll be her word against theirs. And she's a juvenile delinquent. We've got to find proof."

Jo was pacing, clearly having difficulty believing that Doc was involved.

"Jo, I know you don't want to believe all this. But we can't afford to trust any of them right now."

She took a deep breath and let it out slowly. Her eyes resembled those of a little kid who's been betrayed. She turned to Gracie. "How are you going to get her out? You know the code to the locked gate?" She looked from Gracie to me and we both shrugged. "Me neither. It's a security thing they've got here. Only a few people know the code."

"Shit," Gracie said. "We're fucked."

"We'll just have to get hold of one of those remote openers. I saw Coach use one the day I got here," I said. "Let me run a scenario by you, see what you think. Gracie, how did Coach and Belinda interact on your little trip into town and back?"

"Not like you'd expect if they were secret lovers. Coach hardly gave her the time of day."

"I've been thinking. What if it wasn't Coach that Belinda sneaked out to see that night. What if it was Clutch? Jo said she saw Clutch head into camp. And she also said Belinda flirted with Clutch. Maybe he and Belinda had a secret rendezvous that night."

Jo folded her arms and shook her head, but she kept silent.

"Okay. So it's Clutch and not Coach the girl's screwing. How does that help us?"

"Let's say Annie Sisson sees Belinda sneak past her cabin

and figures, like we did, that she was running off to meet with Coach. She already suspects Coach is seeing someone else, so she decides to follow them and confront them. Once she saddles up, she's not sure where to go. That's because Belinda didn't go to the stables at all. She's off somewhere with Clutch. Annie's confused and heads across the meadow, still not positive Coach isn't out there with someone. Then she sees the lights on at the mine and decides to investigate."

"That kind of rules out your theory of a confrontation in the woods," Gracie said.

"Exactly. I think whatever happened to Annie had to be where Maddie could see it. And Maddie wouldn't be hiding right in camp. I don't think she was in the woods, either. I think Maddie was hiding in the mine."

"There's an electronic gate baring the entrance," Jo said, obviously eager to prove my theory wrong.

"Not from the machine shop. The boxcar is sitting right there. All a person would have to do is get in and go."

"Why would someone run away to the mine? It doesn't make sense," Gracie said.

Jo sighed, rubbing her arms as if suddenly chilled. Gracie and I looked at her expectantly.

"I knew a kid who tried it once," Jo said. "Back when I was a student here. She was the bravest kid I ever met. Meaner than snot, too. I had a huge crush on her. Anyway, her plan was to hide in the mine, then make a run for it when everyone had quit looking. Problem was, she couldn't tough it out. About two hours in the mine and she came straight back to camp."

"Like Maddie did," I said. "She came back on her own, too. But maybe what scared her was what she saw happen in the mine, not the mine itself."

"What do you think happened?" Gracie asked.

"I think Ben or Doc killed Annie because she saw something she wasn't supposed to see. Then I think they got Coach to get rid of the body. We know he got rid of her car. Maybe he put her in it first."

"If it were me, and I'd killed someone in the mine, I'd just put the body in the boxcar and dump it in the sledge heap. That'd be safer than trying to cart her all the way back to camp," Gracie said.

I stared at Gracie. Even Jo nodded.

"Makes sense," she said. "If it actually happened at all, that is."

"It would be the easiest way," I said. "And it means we've got a chance at finding our proof. If Annie's body is buried in the sledge heap, we should be able to find it."

"Not easily," Jo said. "I've looked down that thing a time or two. It's a straight drop. You'd need ropes and probably some of those things you drive into the ground to keep the ropes in place."

"Pitons," I said. "Maybe we can get creative. Speaking of creative," I said. "I think I just figured out what Annie Sisson saw that she wasn't supposed to. Hand me that tape." The shapes had finally begun to make sense, and once I got the general idea, assembling the pieces became easier. "Check this out." I held up the assembled cutouts and Jo's face went pale.

"Looks like a semi-automatic," Gracie said, coming over to examine the shape. "See the magazine clip? Pretty ingenious the way they made the parts unrecognizable."

"Even the stock is made in six pieces," I said. "By themselves, they just look like harmless hardware. But they're probably simple to assemble."

"Maybe they're not what they look like," Jo said.

We both looked at her.

"I mean, they could be replicas, you know."

"Well, just assuming they're real," Gracie said, "I wonder who he sells them to?"

"Hell, Gracie. There's so many weirdo groups out there right now stockpiling weapons, he probably has a backlog of buyers. Making them here, they'd be untraceable. These kind of guns are illegal as hell on the market. Which means they're worth a lot. I'll bet you anything this is what Coach has over Ben and Doc. Somehow he must've found out about the guns, then talked them into letting him in on the action."

"I wonder if Ida and Clutch know?" Gracie asked.

"No way," Jo said. "Even if these are what you think they are, Ida would never allow anything to ruin the reputation of the camp. And Clutch feels the same way about the ranch. If these really are actual guns, Ben's got to be the one behind this. The others wouldn't stand for it."

"Even so, Jo, it would be safer if we didn't trust any of them for the time being," I said.

Jo shot me a pained expression. "You sure you trust me?" she asked.

The silence was awkward, even for Gracie who was watching us both intently.

"Jo, look. I know this must be hard for you." I reached out but she stepped back.

"No, you don't know, Cass. Doc saved my life. Clutch and Ida are like family to me. You just waltz in here with wild notions about murder and guns and expect me to believe that the people I love and trust are evil?"

"I didn't say anyone was evil, Jo. But I think something's going on and Maddie might be in danger. And right now, we need your help."

Jo's gaze held mine, her eyes fierce. Finally, she sighed.

"I'll go along, if for no other reason than to prove you wrong," she said.

"Fair enough." I looked at Gracie. "Maybe we should split up. You figure out a way to get Maddie out of here and Jo can help me get down the cliff to the sledge heap. That way, if we get caught, it won't leave Maddie without someone who knows what's going on. At this point, no one suspects you."

"Makes sense. Hell, maybe we'll just ride out. I'll tell the kid who I am and what we've been doing. I'll show her a picture of her mom. That ought to convince her. By the time Coach figures out she's gone AWOL, she and I will be out of the woods and up on that road. I'm pretty sure I can find a way to get there. Coach may think he's a good tracker, but I bet he's never tried to track a real live Indian before." She grinned.

"You have a camera?" I asked Jo.

"One of those throw-aways. Why?"

"If we do find Annie Sisson's body, we should take a picture for proof." I checked my watch. "You'd better hurry," I said to Gracie. "Free time's about over. Once that bell rings, you won't be able to get to her until tomorrow. I think we better make this happen tonight. Take the gun assembly with you, too, Gracie. Once you reach civilization, you might need it for proof. Especially if something happens to Jo and me."

"Maybe we should all ride out together," Gracie said.

"As soon as we find out if Annie Sisson's buried in that dump, we'll follow. Somehow, I'll figure out a way to get that remote control."

"I better go. You sure you don't want to come with me and Maddie right now? We can always send the police to look for the body."

"No. I think it's best if Jo and I act like everything's normal. We'll let people see us together at dinner, make it look like we're romatically involved so no one will think it odd that I'm spending the night in her cabin. Then, when it's dark enough, we'll head for the dump. If all goes well, we'll be back before dawn. You guys head for Portsmith Grove and hide out there until we arrive. We can meet at the hotel there."

"Okay, champ. But don't go playing hero, okay? Let the police do the arresting."

"Not to worry," I said. Gracie tucked the taped-together papers into her back pocket and opened the door. "Here goes. I only hope I can convince the little booger to come with me."

Jo and I watched through the window as Gracie took long, determined strides across the pasture toward the stables.

Jo's arm brushed against mine, sending a flurry of goosebumps down my body and I felt my insides respond. Despite my misgivings, against my better judgment, I knew I wanted her. But when I turned to face her, she pulled back.

"Jo, about this morning . . ."

She put a finger to my lips, but only briefly. "Not now, Cass. Let's just get this over with."

Chapter Twenty-Four — Madeline

Three Days Earlier

Maddie sat in the orange plastic chair outside Doc's office, tapping her foot nervously. She didn't want to meet with Doc anymore. She'd pretended to get sick the last time, and so avoided most of the session. She couldn't very well pull that one again. He was still harping on her about the stealing business, trying to get her to reveal the real reason behind the thievery. He'd been on her about letting him hypnotize her, but she didn't want any part of that. No telling what he might ask or what she might say. He might even ask her about the night she ran away. She couldn't let that happen.

She checked the clock on the wall, knowing she'd become obsessed with time lately. At first, she'd thought of her life as divided between the days Before Camp and those After Incarceration. Later, she thought of everything in terms of After Isolation and Before Her Escape. Now, her whole world had come down to the days since her first Escape Attempt. It had been five days. Time was running out.

"There you are, Madeline. Come in, please," he said, opening the office door and ushering her in like she was a special guest and not some captive prisoner in his Labor Camp. She was careful not to glare at him, though. It was important to keep playing along. In fact, today she'd decided she'd throw him a bone, reveal a few secrets, maybe break down and cry a little. That ought to get him off her back for a while.

"How are you, Madeline?"

"Okay, I guess."

"No more thoughts about running away, I hope?"

Maddie shrugged. Best to keep it real, she thought. "Not too many."

Doc leaned back in his chair and laughed. It was a good, genuine laugh, not the phony kind that adults usually gave. Maddie smiled at her own admission.

"But you're getting along better. I see you interacting now with some of the others. The new girl, Rebecca Patterson. You seem to get on with her pretty well."

"Yes," Maddie allowed. The truth was, ever since her failed escape attempt, she'd stuck to Rebecca like glue. There was strength and safety in numbers, she figured.

"And have you thought any more about your stealing? Hmm?"

Maddie took a deep breath and let it out slowly. Doc waited. He was a very patient waiter. He was also a good bullshit detector. To do this right, she'd have to tell some truth.

"I think the reason I used to steal was because I was mad." There! She'd said it. Now maybe he'd leave her alone.

"Mad at whom, Madeline?"

"Everyone!" she said, surprising herself. She pushed back her hair and wiggled around in her seat. For some reason, it felt more uncomfortable today than usual.

"Well, that's a lot of people to be mad at. Maybe we should focus on one or two today. Which one do you think you're the maddest at, Madeline?"

Oh, for God's sake, she thought. He's not going to let this go.

"How about your mother, Madeline. Are you mad at her?"

"I don't know my mother. She's in prison for murder." It was the first time she'd uttered the words aloud and they sounded ugly. Her mouth felt dry and dirty.

"And how do you feel about that?"

"I'm not even supposed to know it, okay? They told me she was gone. I guess they were too ashamed to tell me she was a . . . that she killed someone. They wanted me to think she was dead. But she isn't. She's in the state penitentiary. I heard my grandmother tell someone. Like everyone knows it except me!"

Despite herself, a fat tear trickled down her cheek. She didn't even have to fake it, she realized. She felt another tear slide down and she rubbed at it with her fist.

"It's okay to cry, Maddie." Doc leaned across his desk and offered her a box of Kleenex. She took one, but kept it wadded in her fist. She didn't plan on making a habit of blubbering.

"So, you're mad at your mother for deserting you?"

She shrugged. "Like I said, I don't even remember her. Besides, she gave me up. Who needs a mother who's a murderer, anyway?"

"Hmmm," Doc said, leaning back and swiveling a little in

his chair. "How about your father? Why are you so mad at him?"

"Because!" she said, sounding more hysterical than she'd intended. "He doesn't care about me. He doesn't know anything!"

"What doesn't he know, Madeline? Hmmm?"

"Nothing." She felt herself clamming shut. She'd revealed enough for one day. Let the doctor go probe someone else for awhile.

"What doesn't he know? Do you remember?"

Maddie shook her head, feeling the tears threaten again.

"You know we talked about hypnosis. It can help you remember the things you're blocking out. Once you remember things, it's easier to talk about them, easier to get through them. That's what we need to do here, I think."

Maddie was shaking her head. "I don't want to."

"To what? Remember?"

"To be hypnotized."

"There's nothing to be afraid of, Maddie. It's absolutely safe. You feel safe with me, don't you?"

No! she wanted to scream. But she couldn't. It was like having to choose between two horrible options. She didn't want to talk about the truth, but she couldn't afford to have Doc hypnotize her, either. She took a deep breath and let it out slowly.

"My grandfather," she whispered. It was so soft, she wasn't sure he heard her.

"Go on, Madeline."

For several moments, which felt to her like an hour, they sat in silence. But her mind wasn't silent. Terrible scenes replayed themselves and without knowing it, she started to cry again. She didn't attempt to wipe the tears away this time. She let them fall, giving into the sobs that came up from the depths of her being and racked her body. She buried her head in her lap and cried for what seemed like hours. Finally, she looked up, her tear-streaked face red and anguished.

"He abused me," she said, the words nearly choking her as she sobbed. "He abused me and they didn't stop him." This time, she felt herself crumple onto the ground, and buried her head in her arms, crying her heart out.

"There, there," she heard him say and was shocked to find that he'd come to sit beside her on the carpet. He patted her head like she was a dog and for a minute it was almost comforting, but then she remembered not to trust him and she pulled away. Doc nodded, like he understood how she might not want him to touch her and he got up and went back to his chair.

"That was a very brave thing you just did, you know that? It must have been very difficult for you."

She nodded, still hiccupping a little, so exhausted she could barely keep her eyes open.

"We'll talk about this some more, later. I'll bet you're tired, hmmm?"

Maddie nodded. She felt like she was half-asleep already.

"Sometimes, when a person's been holding things in for a long time, letting them go takes every ounce of strength they have. You're a very strong girl, Madeline. I know right now it's hard to believe, but you're going to feel better after you rest a little. Would you like to lie down in the nurse's office for a little while before dinner?"

She nodded, unable even to form words. He stood up and she followed him out of the office, blindly putting one foot in front of the other. She wasn't sure it was worth it, she thought, lying down on the hard plastic couch. It had cost a lot to avoid being hypnotized by Dr. Biscane.

Chapter Twenty-Five

Jo and I spent an hour making a list and rehashing our plan, carefully avoiding too much eye contact, let alone physical contact. Once we'd exhausted every detail, we decided to raid the tack room while the cowhands were at dinner. I opened the door and was surprised to find Gracie Apodaca walking up the path.

"What happened? Where's Maddie?"

"She didn't come to the stable today. Apparently she had a therapy session scheduled."

"Damn. Is she still there?"

"Nope. Safe and sound in the mess hall with the others. But I can't very well charge in there and kidnap her. I'm afraid we'll have to wait until tomorrow. At least that'll give me a chance to set things up a little better. And I can join you and Jo tonight."

It was tempting to take her along. But if something happened to us, who would watch out for Maddie? Before I could make this point, Gracie cut me off.

"I can cover your back," she said. "When you and Jo take off, I'll watch to make sure no one comes after. If someone does come along, I'll run interference. It'll be safer all around."

"It's a good idea," Jo said, standing in the doorway. "You never know when someone's going to go for an evening ride."

"Okay," I agreed. I'd have felt better knowing that Gracie and Maddie were halfway to Portsmith Grove by now, but as long as Maddie was in a group, she should be safe. Doc's concern about Maddie had not seemed unduly urgent. If she'd gone this long unquestioned, another night shouldn't matter.

"Maybe Jo and I should make ourselves seen in public while you find the stuff we'll need for the climb," I said. "It's probably best if you're not seen with us."

"Understood. Now's a good time. The ranch hands are all at dinner."

I told Gracie what equipment I thought we'd need and she and Jo discussed the best places to look. After Gracie walked off toward the stables, Jo and I headed for the mess hall.

At dinner, we put on just enough of a show to catch my colleagues' attention, without drawing the curiosity of the few students who still remained at their tables. The play-acting was almost painful. Just being near Jo made me want to take her in my arms. But she was still seething and I didn't know if it was because of the way I'd acted that morning, or because of her feelings about Doc and Clutch. Most of the teaching staff were dawdling over coffee and desert at a large table near the far wall, but Jo and I chose a private table on the other side of the room where the ranch hands were sitting. Our entrance appeared to be well noticed. Jo put her hand on my arm a few times, letting it linger and though I knew it was for show, the effect this had on me was disturbingly erotic. Coach folded his arms across his chest and smirked at me across the mess hall. Pat, who was supervising cleanup behind the counters, waved at us, then to my surprise, winked. I saw Doc say something to Ida who leaned over and whispered to Clutch. Clutch shrugged and continued shoveling pie into his mouth, though I did see him sneak a peek in our direction. When I brushed my own hand across Jo's cheek in a show of intimacy, Lacy Godfrey's curiosity got the better of her and she actually came across the room to sit down at our table. Only after Jo greeted her did Lacy seem to realize that Jo was a woman, and then her face turned pink and she openly stared.

"Lacy, you know Jo, don't you? Works with the horses."

"I'm not much of a horse enthusiast," she said. "I guess I've seen you around, though."

"Glad to meet you," Jo said, reaching across the table to shake Lacy's hand. Lacy seemed almost afraid to touch Jo's hand, finally offering a limp handshake.

"Jo's what they call a horse whisperer," I said.

"No kidding." Lacy must have thought this was an exotic term for a lesbian because she blushed again and moved back in her chair. I could tell she was having a hard time figuring out what I was doing with a woman who dressed like a cowboy. She kept looking from Jo to me, clearly confused. "I've been wondering where you've been hiding out," she finally managed, seeming to put two and two together at last.

"Jo's been showing me around. Aren't you eating?"

"Oh, I've finished. I just stopped by to say hello. It was nice meeting you, uh, Jo?"

"Nice meeting you, too." Jo graced Lacy with one of her enigmatic smiles and Lacy practically tripped over her chair standing up to leave.

"I believe we've accomplished our goal," Jo said, finally

breaking into a grin. We watched as most of the staff got up from their table and bussed their trays.

"I'd say the rumor mill will be buzzing tonight. Wonder if I'll get a lecture from Ida on appropriate decorum in front of the children," I said.

"I don't know. I couldn't tell if she looked more stunned or amused. Doc didn't seem surprised, though. He's known I was gay since I was fifteen. The first person I ever told, actually."

"I know how hard this must be for you, finding out he might not be the upstanding citizen you've always thought."

Jo leaned forward, resting her elbows on the table. Her eyes sparked with emotion. "First off, we don't know that for a fact."

"Okay, okay," I conceded, holding up my hands.

"But if you're right," she went on, "if those things really are what you say they are, then there must be a good explanation for it. Clutch and Ida talked back then about the value of doing a good, honest day's work and I bought into it. I still believe in it. This camp changed my life. If those really are guns, then I want to know what they're doing with them. And I want to know who's behind it."

"Even if it includes Doc?" I asked.

Jo shot me a warning glance. Her jaw was firmly clenched.

"Even if he's not involved," I said, "what we find out could change everything. You know that, right? I mean the camp could be shut down."

Slowly, Jo nodded. "I still hope you're wrong," she said. "But if you're not, I mean, if something bad is happening here, then I'll do what I have to."

I looked at her. Her eyes were as still as deep water and regarded me with conviction. I wanted to tell her then and there that I was sorry about my cowardice that morning. That I was sorry about running out on her when all I really wanted to do was wrap her in my arms. That even if I had reasons to be wary of love, one night with her was enough reason to throw caution to the wind. I wanted, more than anything, to take her in my arms and hold her. But before I could do any of that, Jo pushed back her chair and stood up.

"Come on. Let's do this before I change my mind."

We stopped at my cabin and right away, I knew someone had been inside. Before I'd left, I'd done the old something-on-the-door trick. I'd placed a pine needle on the top edge of the door, knowing that as soon as the door was opened, the needle would fall. The pine needle was sitting on the welcome mat.

"Wait here," I said, gently pushing open the door. The little cabin was empty, but not undisturbed. I walked the perimeter of the room, checking my rushed attempts at intruder detection. I'd placed a hair from my brush on top of the PowerBook before I'd gone to Jo's. Not only was the hair gone, the PowerBook was missing.

I rushed to the chest of drawers and checked behind them. My gun and cell phone were still securely taped to their respective drawers. It was clear that someone had riffled through my drawers and no doubt looked under the mattress and in the cupboards but I knew they hadn't found anything incriminating. Unless they knew how to retrieve the files I'd erased from my hard drive before I'd come to camp, I probably still had some time. If they did retrieve them, it wouldn't be difficult to figure out that I worked as a P.I.

I slipped on my shoulder holster and pulled on a jacket to conceal it, putting the cell phone into my pocket before joining Jo on the porch.

"Everything okay?" she asked.

"Someone borrowed my computer. I erased most of my files, so I should be okay."

"I thought Doc told Ben not to worry," she said, sounding suddenly worried herself.

"Yeah, well. Little brother didn't seem to listen. I'm

betting he sent Coach to check things out. Come on. I get the feeling we're being watched and it's not just idle curiosity about our romance."

Jo and I walked past the parade grounds where the evening's activities included a team-building game called Trust. Nurse Beckett was running the game and a few of the other staff members were on hand to supervise. We watched for a minute as blindfolded teens leaned back, allowing their bodies to fall backwards into the joined arms of two other students who kept them from hitting the ground. I spotted Ida watching us and before she could wave me over, I nudged Jo forward.

It was just as well that we'd been seen, I figured. As long as everyone thought I was preoccupied with Jo, they wouldn't worry about what else I might be up to. At least that's what I hoped.

Back inside Jo's cabin, we saw Gracie had been productive. She'd pulled a blanket over a suspicious-looking mound on Jo's bed, under which was piled the equipment we'd requested. She'd found flashlights, ropes, a short-handled axe, a box of metal stakes, leather gloves and a shovel. Best yet, she'd even brought a leather saddlebag and a nylon backpack.

Jo stood at the window and kept a lookout for visitors as I organized the equipment. I'd done a little rock climbing and knew what we had was hardly sufficient for a difficult climb. But it would have to do. When there was nothing left to do but wait, Jo and I went out on the porch and she brought her guitar.

"You haven't asked for your song, yet," she reminded me.

This caught me by surprise. I'd almost forgotten the comment I'd made in jest, just before I'd taken Jo into my cabin.

"Huh. So you want to hear it, or not?" She'd starting picking out notes, gently strumming.

"Please."

She cleared her throat, strummed a few more times, then

began to sing. Her voice was surprisingly good. Both husky and melodic. Her eyes were closed as she sang, her fingers deftly moving across the strings. The tune was a little melancholy, I thought, until she reached the refrain which was upbeat and strangely uplifting.

You reached right in and pulled me down
Now, I don't want to get up again
cause you reached right in and showed me how
to love again, to love again

You took me up so high, so fast
I'm a little afraid to look down again
afraid to fall so far, so fast
to fall, to fall in love again

She sang the song all the way through and when she finished, she opened her eyes. I wasn't surprised to see tears in them. I felt tears in my own.

"That's beautiful," I said. "It's perfect."

"You think?"

"I do." I felt myself starting to choke up. "I'm sorry I was such a jerk this morning. I was afraid."

She strummed her guitar a few times, then quit. "But not now?"

I could see her eyes in the moonlight and they were serious.

"Now I'm even more afraid."

"Of me?"

"Of the way I feel. I'm hoping it will pass."

"The way you feel?"

"No. The fear. I'm working on it."

She laughed and began strumming her guitar again, this time playing another song she'd written about riding in the wind.

I'd never known anyone like her, I realized. She was

completely guileless, unpretentious, and though intriguing, uncomplicated. What you saw was what you got. She had boyish charm and surprising grace, sophisticated taste and simple wants. She made love with unparalleled abandon, yet was shy and gentle, too. I had never been so taken with anyone so unexpectedly. She wasn't even my type, I told myself. But I didn't care. She wasn't like Diane, or like Erica or Maggie. I'd been drawn to more polished women — professors, psychologists and writers. Here I was, head over heels in love with a cowgirl. I couldn't help laughing at the image and Jo stopped playing.

"What?"

"Nothing. Keep playing, please. I just realized something, that's all."

"What?"

"I realized that right now I feel happier than I've felt in a long, long time."

"This is good, right?"

"This is good. Play."

She did, and the time rushed by as we waited for midnight to fall.

Chapter Twenty-Six — Madeline

It had been a full week since her escape and she was so nervous, she could hardly sit still. She had another session with Doc which cut right into her free time with Shadow Dancer — the only thing that seemed to relax her. He'd let her brush him yesterday and Clutch said they'd been breaking him in and he'd be ready for her to ride in no time. She thought about that sadly, knowing she'd never get the chance, while she waited for Doc to come get her.

"Good afternoon, Madeline. How are you today, hmmm?"

"Okay."

"How do you feel after what we discussed last time?"

"Okay."

He chuckled. “I think we need to discuss your feelings toward your mother, again.”

“My mother? Why? What’s she got to do with anything? I don’t even remember her.”

“You were how old when she was arrested? Four years old? I’m sure you have some memories of her. They’re just buried that’s all. I think it’s important we unbury them.”

“Why? I don’t want to remember her.” Which wasn’t entirely true. She’d tried many times to capture the image that sometimes drifted across her mind. The image of long black hair, loving eyes, a warm embrace. She’d dreamed the image off and on, but awake, it was nothing more than a shadow. Sometimes, she thought she caught a glimpse of that shadow in the mirror.

“What are you thinking, Madeline?”

“Why do you care about my mother all of the sudden?”

“We can talk of other things, then, if you’d rather. Sooner or later, we’ll get through it all. Your grandfather’s abuse, your father’s failure to recognize and stop what was happening, your mother’s abandonment. Sometimes, it helps to start at the beginning. But it’s your choice.”

She was not ready to trudge through the whole abuse thing right now. It was too painful. She looked at the clock on the wall. They still had a full forty minutes to go. Maddie squirmed in her seat.

“Okay. What about my mother?”

“Do you sometimes dream of her?” he asked.

She nodded, not sure where this was leading.

“Can you remember anything at all? A smell? A sound? The way her skin felt when she held you in her arms?”

Again, Maddie nodded, surprised at how, now that he mentioned it, she did remember a smell. Her mother’s hair held the fragrance of apples.

“Close your eyes, Maddie. Can you see her?”

She shook her head, keeping her eyes wide open.

"You don't have to close your eyes, but if you want to, it's okay. Sometimes, we can see more clearly with our eyes closed, but either way, is okay. Just listen to my voice and try to relax and pretty soon you'll see exactly what you want to see, but you don't have to see anything you don't want. Okay?"

Maddie nodded, struggling to keep her eyes open. She really did want to see a picture of her mother.

"Good. Once I help you relax, you'll be able to focus on whatever you want, but for now, while you're relaxing there in the chair, you can just be aware of your body, aware of how your hands are resting on the arms of the chair and you probably can notice how nice and heavy they feel, because you're relaxing now and not worrying about anything at all. You can hear everything, my voice, the clock, your own breathing as it becomes a little heavier because you're feeling more and more relaxed. You're breathing so nice and slow, evenly and steadily because there's nothing to worry about, everything is fine and even your heart is beating so slow and steady now, you can actually feel it slowing down and relaxing because you're aware of everything, even the way your muscles are relaxed, the way your hands and feet feel so heavy, like they're almost asleep, but in a good way, and it's almost like you're so comfortable now you couldn't even be bothered to move a muscle, though of course you could if you wanted, but you don't want to, you're so comfortable and relaxed that you feel wonderfully lazy, like every cell in your entire body has loosened and let go, letting you finally sink down to the most relaxed state imaginable. That's where you are. Do you feel it?"

Maddie heard Doc's voice but wasn't sure she could lift her head to acknowledge him.

"That's okay, Madeline. Now that you're relaxed, you won't be disturbed or upset or frightened and when I count to ten, you'll be able to answer my questions without any fear or pain. You'll remember everything I ask and it won't be scary at all. You'll feel perfectly in control and relaxed. Are you ready?"

Again, she thought of moving her head, but it was too heavy and she couldn't be bothered. Doc was counting slowly, telling her that with each count, she could allow herself to become more focussed so that when he reached ten, she'd be able to talk to him. It was like sinking to the bottom of a deep, cool pool, she thought. Not at all unpleasant. When he reached the last number, she took a deep breath and was surprised at how clearly and easily she could see and breathe.

"You can open your eyes, now. How do you feel?"

"Fine. Good."

"Good. Now, Madeline, I want you to continue to relax while I ask you to remember. You will be able to see everything very clearly and none of it will bother you. We'll start with something easy. Do you remember the last time you had ice cream?"

She scrunched up her brow, then nodded.

"Tell me about it."

"It was here at camp. Pat let me have two scoops because she said I was a good helper. It was chocolate."

"Very good, Maddie. Now, do you remember the last time you felt frightened?"

She furrowed her brow, started to answer, then shook her head.

"It's okay. There's no need to be frightened now. You're just remembering. You're perfectly safe and relaxed. You can remember anything I ask and it won't bother you at all. Do you remember the night you ran away? Were you frightened then?"

Maddie nodded, biting her lower lip.

"Tell me, Madeline. Tell me everything that happened when you ran away."

It wasn't difficult at all to recount the details. She'd relived them many times since she'd returned from her failed escape. She laughed as she told Doc how she hadn't really failed at all. She'd come back on purpose. She was just waiting for the right time and she would make her final escape.

"So nothing happened the night you returned to make you come running back to camp, Madeline? Think hard and try to remember. Even if you've blocked it out, it should be easy to remember now. You can tell me anything."

Maddie nodded. She felt so safe and relaxed. And it was nice to talk about it. She hadn't had a soul to confide in since it happened.

"I had a secret cave," she began. She closed her eyes and sat back, letting the story unfold as if it had happened yesterday instead of a whole week ago.

Maddie woke and for a minute couldn't remember where she was. The fire had burned down to a few glowering coals and the cave was chilly. Then she jumped up, her heart racing at the sound of a noise in the tunnel. It wasn't the deep, terrifying moan that she'd almost grown accustomed to. She listened again, straining to see through the crack in her door. Then she recognized the clattering sound of the boxcar as it made its noisy way along the track leading from the machine shop to the mine entrance. She rushed to the door and watched it chug by. She calculated its pace, knowing that if she had a running start, she could easily hitch a ride. And she had several days to practice jogging along the railroad ties, while she waited.

It must be morning, she suddenly thought, excitedly. Ben always loaded the boxcar at the end of the work session, then sent it on its way through the tunnel first thing the next morning. She'd made it through the first night! Soon, Coach would be out scouring the forest for her. She smiled, thinking about how she'd outsmarted all of them. They'd never think to look for her here. All she had to do was be patient. She had a week's worth of food. She had light. She had fire. She had fresh running water and a pit toilet. And she could use the time to figure out what she was going to do when she got free. One thing she knew for sure. She wasn't going back to her grandparents' house ever again.

One problem, she'd realized right away, was that without a watch and without daylight, there was no way to keep track of time. She'd made a scratch on the wall near her fire right before she'd collapsed in exhaustion onto the scratchy wool blanket the first night. That marked her first night in the cave. Now she carefully etched another larger mark beside it and sat back to think about how she'd spend her first day as a runaway.

The first thing she did was arrange her treasured goods in the back hidden cave where she'd spend most of her time. Just in case Coach did decide to come looking for her in Isolation, he wouldn't be able to see her. With the light from the miner's cap illuminating the oblong room in soft tones, she experimented with making a fire against the back wall near where the water trickled down from above. It seemed there was a draft there, similar to the one between the caves, and if it worked as a chimney, it would leave her currently-used mantle free for easy movement between the two caves. More important, the fire wouldn't be noticeable from the Isolation room. To her delight, the second fireplace worked almost as well as the first. Once she had a decent fire going, she cleaned out the old fireplace and set out into the tunnel to gather wood, using her tarp and bungee cords as a backpack.

After what seemed like hours of prying off chunks of rotting railroad ties from the secondary track and hauling the wood back to her cave, Maddie was both tired and hungry. She stacked the wood neatly in the corner and sat on her blanket by the fire to eat her breakfast. She'd deliberately waited until she was famished. She wanted to make sure her meager supply of food would really last. But the peanut butter crackers tasted wonderful, and she captured ice cold water in the empty tuna can that she'd brought along for that purpose. The bottled water, she'd save for her trek in the woods.

After breakfast, Maddie cleaned herself up, using the little bar of soap she'd swiped from the cook's private bathroom to rub at the creosote on her hands. Some of the railroad ties were sticky with the black sooty stuff and she'd already learned that they weren't good for burning because they smoked too much. She thought about using one of the antiseptic wipes she'd taken from the nurse's office, but she decided she should hold those in reserve for emergencies. She couldn't go using up all her goods in one day. Besides, she had more wood to gather. There was no point in getting too clean, then having to wash all over again. What she ought to do was spend the day getting as much wood as she'd need, then go to work on her hands.

With the miner's cap strapped onto her head, traveling in the tunnel was almost fun. No longer terrified by the moaning and groaning, Maddie dared herself to peek into the hidden corners that veered off the main tunnel, realizing that many of them dropped deep into darkness while others seemed to simply meander off in another direction. Sticking close to the tracks, she worked her way back toward the machine shop, using her knife to pry off chunks of wood, then leaving them where they were so that she could gather them on the way back. No point in carrying them farther than she had to. Even so, after what seemed several hours, she was exhausted again and decided to lie down for a little nap.

This time when she woke, she had no idea what time it was at all. She was hungry again, so maybe she'd slept right through lunch. She treated herself to a piece of beef jerky, gnawing on it slowly to make it last. Then, unable to stand not knowing, she decided to risk a trip to the mine entrance, just so she could peek out and see if it was day or night.

By now, the trip through the tunnel was old hat.

Occasionally she heard a soft flapping sound which frightened her, but she hadn't actually seen a bat yet. And she didn't want to. She kept her light on until she knew from the turn in the bend that she was almost to the entrance. Then she quickly shut it off and made her way toward it in the dark.

As much as she had hoped to see daylight, the dark entrance meant a victory of sorts. Maddie had survived her first full day. She looked out through the slats of the electronic gate barring the entrance, wondering what time it really was. She couldn't see the moon but there were stars twinkling over the trees in the distance and she sat and watched them, glad to be out of her cave for at least a while.

She knew it was dangerous, but she couldn't resist snooping around a little as long as she had come all this way. She walked around the perimeter of the large room, peering through the dark at the now-familiar objects. She didn't dare turn on her light, but the faint glow of the moon was enough to take inventory in the dark. She noticed that the stacked crates were higher than when she'd been there last, a green forklift like the one in the shop, poised beside them. The boxcar was there, too, ready to be dumped the next morning. She could see the mound of charcoal-colored shavings from where she stood. She went to the trunk where Coach stored the blankets and crackers. Like before, the latch was unlocked. She peered inside and wondered if she dared take another hat. What if the battery on hers wore out? It might be a good precaution. And it would be nice to have her whole cave lit up now and then. She lifted a hat from the bottom, figuring that it might have been used less often and therefore might have more life left in the battery. She helped herself to a couple more packages of crackers and then went to explore the tool box again, thinking there surely must be something inside she could find useful. She noticed the pile of blue tarps in the corner, just where they'd been the last time, and was thinking about what she might need another one for when suddenly her heart rose to her throat and she froze, thoroughly panicked. The sound of an ATV had pulled up right outside the entrance and clicked off.

Maddie was rooted to the spot, though her mind screamed at her to run. She could hear the electronic hum of the gate sliding open and still she stood, unable to think clearly. She'd have to run right past the entrance to get to the tunnel and there wasn't time. Not knowing what else to do, she dashed for the corner, pulled up the pile of tarps and burrowed herself beneath them, willing her heart to quit pounding, so she could hear what was happening.

To her surprise, it wasn't Coach coming to get her. It was Doc and his brother Ben. She recognized Doc's deep, commanding voice immediately. She held her breath and waited, sure that any moment one of them would rip the tarps off of her and yank her to her feet.

But they didn't seem to be aware of her at all. They were discussing a shipment, she realized after a few minutes. Even under the tarp, she could tell an overhead light had been switched on. And soon, the rumbling roar of a truck could be heard as it made its way to the mine.

Maddie listened as Ben directed the backing of the truck into the mouth of the mine. Soon there were two other voices and somebody started up the forklift. She could barely hear their voices over the grating sound as the crates were pushed across the truck bed.

"How do we know this is what we're buying?" she heard one of the drivers say. "All I see are pieces."

Ben's voice sounded angry. "Because I say so. If that's not good enough, we can stop delivery right now."

"Now, now, Ben," Doc said. "He didn't mean to insult anyone. He's just being cautious. Show him the assembly package. Ben will walk you through it. Come over here where the light's better."

Suddenly, one of them came right toward her and Maddie was sure she'd been spotted. But she heard the sound of the tool box being opened and shut again, then the footsteps faded. As the men moved off toward the other side of the room, Maddie dared to move the edge of the tarp a half an inch so she could peek out at them. Ben had climbed onto the boxcar and pulled out a long plastic case buried just beneath the mound of shavings. He set it on the trunk Maddie had just gone through.

"Just look at your directions and follow along," Ben said, still sounding miffed. The trucker, a burly, red-faced man with a bulbous nose, was holding several sheets of paper in his hand, looking doubtful.

Ben opened the plastic case and the man's eyes widened.

"Doesn't look like much unassembled, does it?" Ben said proudly. "See how they're labeled on your sheet? Start with the stock. You've got six sections just for that. 1A, 1B, and so on. Get it? Harmless little pieces of plastic and metal. Watch this."

Ben deftly shook out a handful of screws from a plastic packet and began connecting the pieces with sure, practiced movements. In a few moments, he held up what looked very much like the stock of a rifle.

"That's all there is to it, Bud. You start with the ones, then the twos, and work your way to the end. When you're done, this is what you've got." He closed the lid of the long container and flipped it over, opening another lid on the bottom side. From it, he pulled out a fully assembled semi-automatic.

"Here, what do you think?"

Ben tossed the gun to the trucker who hefted it once or twice, then raised it to his shoulder and peered over the site, taking aim at various objects around the room. He leveled the gun at the mound of blue tarps and Maddie let the corner fall again, holding her breath.

"Feels good," the man said at last. "What about ammo?"

"Takes .223 caliber, full metal jacket, but you're on your own for that, as we discussed."

"And they're completely untraceable?"

"They've never even existed," Ben said. "In fact, until you assemble them, they're just harmless parts. That's why that one stays here." Ben reached up and retrieved the gun from the trucker.

"Satisfied?" Doc asked. He'd been sorting through a box the trucker had left on the ground.

"Yeah. You count it yet? All hundreds, totally clean."

"Good. I'll count later. I'm sure eveything's in order. Looks like you boys are in business."

The man operating the forklift had finally shut it off and was closing the back of the truck. He climbed into the driver's seat and the other man shook Ben's hand, then Doc's.

"Pleasure doing business with you fellows," he said, smirking.

"Likewise," Doc said. "I'll radio ahead for someone to let you out. Drive carefully."

The truck roared to life and rumbled away back toward camp.

Ben and Doc were tidying up, making jokes about the truckers and Maddie had almost allowed herself to relax a little when suddenly she heard a gunshot right outside the mine. Her heart nearly stopped. Ben and Doc both froze, staring past the mine entrance into the dark night.

"Good God, what have you done?" Doc asked, his face stricken.

"She heard everything," a gravelly voice said. "I caught her spying on you. She saw the gun." Maddie wasn't sure she recognized the voice but it sounded familiar.

"You killed her?" Ben asked, walking forward in disbelief. He was out of Maddie's line of vision, but she could hear his words clearly. "Jesus, one shot did all this?"

"She hit her head on the track when she went down. I didn't exactly have a choice, Ben. What did you want me to do? Sit her down and explain why you two are manufacturing illegal weapons?"

"Shut up, both of you!" Doc's voice reverberated off the mine walls and he pinched the bridge of his nose with his thumb and forefinger as if too tired to deal with another problem tonight. Then he raised his head.

"Go back to bed. Ben and I will take care of this."

Maddie heard the footsteps retreat. Doc let out a sigh. "Ben, grab one of those tarps. We'll wrap the body in it and dump it in the sledge heap." Maddie's whole body went rigid and she held her breath.

"Not tonight," Ben said. "After the truck went through, half the camp's probably awake. Someone will wonder why we're dumping at night instead of in the morning as usual."

"You're right. Damn it. Help me get the body in the boxcar."

Maddie closed her eyes and prayed as Ben walked right for the pile of tarps and pulled one off the top. She didn't dare peek out as the two men wrapped the fallen body and hefted it into the boxcar.

"Dump it first thing in the morning, before the cowboys are up," Doc ordered. "You better clean up, make sure there's no trace of blood. And clean off those tracks. She bled like a stuck pig."

"Where are you going?" Ben asked.

"There's a hell of a lot to be done before morning," he said. A minute later he was on his ATV motoring down the road toward camp.

It wasn't long after that the lights went out, leaving the mine pitch-black. Maddie heard the electronic gate hum shut and Ben's ATV start up. Even so, she stayed under the tarp a while longer, too petrified to make herself move. There was a dead body in the boxcar, not thirty feet from where she hid and she had no idea who it was.

Maddie forced herself toward the boxcar, her legs trembling. Maybe it was better if she didn't know, she thought. Maybe she could just run back to her cave and forget it ever happened. But something urged her forward and she found herself climbing onto the boxcar, peering over the top at the blue bundle. In the dark, the shape looked ominous. Maddie fumbled with the light on her cap and suddenly the tarp was in full view. She tentatively reached out and tugged at the top of the tarp, careful not to touch the blood that had leaked onto it. She heard herself gasp as she uncovered the blood-matted hair, daring herself to pull the tarp down past the bloodied face. In disbelief, she stared at the open eyes of her favorite teacher, Miss Sisson. And then she stifled a scream. The very eyes she was staring into, blinked.

Chapter Twenty-Seven

Jo fetched the horses just after midnight when the last light had twinkled off in the ranch hands' cabins. I was nervous, waiting, watching the dark for movement of any kind. But it seemed we were the only two still up. Except I knew Gracie was somewhere watching in the dark, ready to intervene if someone spotted us and tried to follow.

I handed Jo the leather saddle bag, which we'd rigged for her to wear like a backpack, then climbed onto my horse, my own rope-filled nylon pack heavy on my back. We took off at a leisurely pace, hoping that to anyone watching, we appeared as two new lovers, off for a midnight ride.

It wasn't until we let ourselves through the outer gate that we picked up the pace. We were traveling without the aid of the flashlight but the moon was bright and the stars filled the night sky with a dazzling display. For some reason, the horses seemed nervous. Perhaps they sensed danger. Jo talked to them, soothing their fears, but I had to admit, I was nervous, too. The bulge of the .45 nestling against my rib cage was some comfort.

As we neared the gorge, the sound of waterfalls grew louder and the horses grew even more skittish. Jo explained that we were almost there. The sledge heap was straight down a ravine at the edge of the forest where the tracks ended. I could see the gleam of the tracks in the moonlight, cutting a straight path along the base of the mountain toward the ravine. It was down that ravine that we needed to climb.

"We can tether the horses, here," Jo said, sliding out of her saddle. We hefted our bags to the edge of the ravine and I aimed a flashlight down the steep embankment. Gnarled tree roots jutted out of the cliff face here and there, which would give us something to tie onto and help our footing, but there were also nasty chunks of debris from the mine and machine shop that had caught on some of them when they'd been dumped from the boxcar into the gorge a hundred feet below.

"Maybe you should wait here," I said. "I think I can get down on my own. With the tree roots, I may not even need the stakes."

"I'm coming with you, Cass."

It was clear she wasn't budging on the issue, so while we adjusted the backpacks and pulled on our leather gloves, we talked over our strategy.

I tied the first rope around a stump along the ledge and eased myself over the cliff while Jo shined her light from above so that I could locate foot holds as I climbed down. Once I reached a good landing spot, I shined my light up for her and she followed. Then we repeated the maneuver, using a second rope, then a third and fourth as we painstakingly let ourselves down into the giant refuse pile.

The descent became more difficult as we went because there were more obstacles in our way, some of them razor sharp and rusted. On the last leg, Jo bounced against the metal edge of something jutting out from behind a twisted branch and sliced open her arm. By the time she joined me, a red blotch had soaked through her shirt sleeve.

"Let me look at that," I said.

"It's nothing. We'll look at it when we get back up. Let's just find what we came for." I noticed she couldn't quite bring herself to say the body.

We stood at the foot of the gorge and shined our lights at the heap of twisted metal and greasy debris. "How often do they dump?" I asked.

"I've never really paid that much attention. Seems like just about every morning. Whenever the boxcar gets full, I guess."

"Then it shouldn't take too long, if she's here. Let's start over here where the mound's the highest."

We cautiously climbed onto the highest pile where most of the junk had come to rest and slowly cast our lights over the area. Jo bent over and carefully hefted a large chunk of metal, setting it to the side. I followed suit and soon we were both sweating with the effort.

"Hey," Jo said. "Check this out, Cass."

I aimed my light in the direction she indicated and saw the corner of a blue plastic tarp.

"Kinda out of place," she said.

I picked my way over to her and together we uncovered the tarp, one heavy chunk at a time. We were both breathing heavily, and it wasn't just from the exertion. I felt sure the tarp had something to do with Annie Sisson. We finally pulled the tarp free, half-expecting to find a body beneath it, but there was just more junk and metal. And a couple of green woolen blankets which immediately seemed out of place.

"Look at this," I said, pointing my flashlight at a dark stain on the tarp.

"What do you think?" she asked.

I sniffed at the stain, then took off my leather glove and used my fingernail to scratch off a fleck.

"It's definitely blood. But is it hers? Damn it! She's got to be here somewhere. She couldn't have fallen too far from the tarp if she was wrapped in it." I checked the blankets but neither appeared to be stained or even soiled.

We both began to dig again but soon had to stop to catch our breath. I looked at Jo's arm and noticed it was still bleeding steadily. I stared at the massive heap surrounding us, knowing that our chances of finding a body beneath the rubble in the dark were not getting any better. We should've found her by now if she'd been wrapped in the tarp, I thought. And Jo and I still had to get back up the cliff.

"Let's take the tarp, at least," I said. "Maybe with this and the printout of the gun assembly, we can get the police out here. Maybe in the daylight, they'll find her."

Jo didn't argue. We'd done the best we could under the circumstances. We'd used all but one of the ropes and my backpack was nearly empty. Jo helped me stow the tarp inside it, careful not to smudge the stain, then followed me to the bottom rope. Neither of us was looking forward to the long climb up.

When I reached the top of the cliff and hauled myself over, I saw a horse galloping toward us at full speed in the dark. By the time Jo pulled herself up, the horse was nearly upon us. I held the Colt .45 at my side, my pulse racing.

"It's Gracie," Jo said, catching her breath beside me.

"You sure?"

"It's her horse."

Sure enough, Gracie Apodaca swung down off the horse as it came to a halt in front of us. "Maddie's run again," she said, breathless herself.

"What?" I asked. "How do you know?"

"I've been waiting in the shadows, watching out. About a half-hour ago, I saw Coach come around the bend on his ATV. He woke Clutch who came out to see what the problem was and I got closer so I could hear them talking. Coach told Clutch that he was off after Maddie again. She's run off.

"Ah, shit," I said.

"That's not all," Gracie said. "After Clutch went back inside, I heard Coach's walkie-talkie. I think it was Doc's voice but I haven't heard him that much. He said Ben had the shop entrance covered and he was going to bed unless Coach thought he'd need help handling them."

"Them?"

"Exactly. What do you think?"

"I think Annie Sisson may still be alive," I said. I told Gracie about the bloody tarp but no body.

"If she is alive, she may not be for long," Gracie said. "But I'm not sure what we can do about it. I came by the mine entrance just now and the gate's shut. Coach's ATV is parked right outside."

Whatever hope I'd been holding onto dissolved completely. One way or the other, we were going to have to go inside the mine.

Chapter Twenty-Eight — Madeline

"You're doing fine, Maddie. When you saw her blink, you must have been terribly upset. What happened next?" Doc's voice was soothing. Maddie's eyes were still closed but she could see it like it was happening right then and there. She took a deep breath and continued her story.

Miss Sisson was alive! Maddie could tell she was badly hurt and her eyes were glazed over but she was breathing! She rushed over to the wooden chest and pulled out a bottle of water, then held it to Miss Sisson's lips, begging her to drink a little. The water dribbled down Miss Sisson's face, but her eyes became a little more focussed which gave Maddie hope. Maddie pulled the tarp off of her teacher's body and her eyes grew wide at the spreading blood stain near her midsection.

"You've got to get up so I can help you get to safety," she said over and over. Finally, Annie Sisson seemed to hear her, and struggled to a sitting position.

"What happened?" she asked.

There was no time to explain. "You're hurt. We've got to get you out of here. Can you stand?"

Annie looked down at the blood on her shirt and her eyes glazed over again. She swayed, but Maddie held her up. "You've got to try," she pleaded. Something in her voice must have gotten through to Annie because she suddenly focussed her eyes and forced herself to a kneeling position. Maddie helped her over the side of the boxcar. Annie collapsed on the ground.

"We need to make it look like you're still in there," Maddie said, though she wasn't sure Annie could hear her. She ran to the trunk and grabbed two green woolen blankets, rolling them into tight cylinders. She wrapped the bloody tarp around the blankets and tried to arrange it the way it had looked wrapped around Annie. She gave a last hurried look around the room, then bent and struggled to pull Annie to her feet, draping Annie's arm around her shoulder, practically dragging her into the tunnel toward her cave.

It had taken forever to get there. Annie had needed to rest, sometimes crumpling onto the tracks, unable to get up. But Maddie had been persistent and now as Annie lay on the blanket in a deep sleep in the back cave, Maddie tended her wounds.

The head wound, it seemed, was much worse than the gunshot in the side which had cut right through a layer of fat and bled a lot, but didn't seem to have hit any organs as it passed through. But her head, which she'd hit on the tracks when she fell, was bleeding profusely and Maddie gingerly poked at the matted hair thinking she should clean the wound before it got infected. She used the little scissors on her Army knife and snipped away at Miss Sisson's pretty blond hair so that she could get to the wound. Then, using the antiseptic hand wipes, she dabbed at the open gash, causing it to bleed anew.

There was nothing to stitch her up with, but she carefully folded a thick wad of toilet paper into a square and held it to the open gash, then fetched her ace bandage and cut off a strip large enough to wrap around Annie's head, holding the bandage in place.

That Miss Sisson could sleep through this, worried Maddie, and she frequently checked to make sure her teacher was still breathing. Once she'd done what she could for the head wound, she tended her fire, stoking it up so that it would burn for several hours, then retrieved the tuna can and filled it with clean, bottled water. This she set on two rocks right on top of the fire and waited for the water to boil.

The wound in Annie's side made Maddie nervous because she'd never seen a bullet hole except in the movies. But she knew wounds should be kept clean and so, once the boiled water had cooled enough, she poured some right into the open wound. Annie Sisson sat straight up and screamed.

"Sorry," Maddie mumbled, trying to dab at the wound with an antiseptic hand-wipe.

Annie looked around her, utterly confused. She seemed to be seeing the little cave for the first time, as if she hadn't seen it at all when Maddie had half-carried her in. Her eyes were more focussed now, Maddie noticed. She did her best to explain while Annie Sisson listened. She told how she'd found the cave when Coach had put her in Isolation and how she'd used the Army knife to uncuff herself. She told how she'd stockpiled goods and hidden them in her mattress. She showed Annie the provisions, explaining how she could make them last for a week if she was careful, and how she could save matches by keeping the coals going. She explained where the toilet was and about the boxcar that came by every morning on its way to the dump before going back to the machine shop. She told of her plan to wait in the mine for three or four days, if she could stand it that long, until they'd given up looking for her, then sneak back into camp through the tunnel and somehow make it through the woods to the road.

Annie was looking at her, dumbstruck, as Maddie described her escape and subsequent trip to the mine entrance. In a voice as calm as she could muster, she told Annie what she'd heard and seen and what Doc and Ben had planned to do with Annie.

Annie nodded slowly as if the motion hurt her, and took another small sip of water from the bottle. She began to speak in an almost trance-like whisper. "A boy in my class told me he was afraid that the girl he liked was seeing Coach. He said he thought she was going to meet Coach tonight. I promised him I'd do what I could and when I saw the girl leave her cabin, I decided to intervene." She paused and caught her breath. Talking was clearly wearing her out, but she seemed determined to go on.

"I thought if I could talk to Coach first, I could talk some sense into him. When I saw the light on in the mine I thought he'd gone there. I tied my horse and walked the last on foot, afraid that it was too late — that somehow the girl had beat me there." She took another sip of water, her eyes focused now on Maddie's.

"Then I saw the ATVs and realized it wasn't Coach after all, and then the truck came." She closed her eyes for a moment and Maddie was afraid that the talking had worn her out completely, but Annie grimaced and continued.

"I stepped into the shadows and watched from a distance. Pretty soon, I'd crept right up to the entrance and could see Ben putting something together. Then I saw what it was. I started to leave, but was afraid they'd see me, so I ducked back down and hid. I never even heard anyone come up behind me. The next thing I knew, you were pulling me down a tunnel."

She tentatively touched her bandaged head, then leaned back against the cave wall, her brow furrowed, what little strength she'd had, depleted.

"We've got to get you out of here," Maddie said.

Annie shook her head. "Not strong enough. You go." Her face had gone pale and her voice weak.

Maddie shook her head. "I can help you!"

Annie forced herself to sit up again and opened her eyes, speaking with great care. "You've done a good job patching me up, Maddie, but I've lost a lot of blood. I need to rest." She took another swallow of water, mustering her strength. "But you need to get back to camp tonight. If you're back in camp, this place should be safe for a while."

Maddie's heart sank, but she knew Miss Sisson was right. This was no longer about Maddie running away. This was about someone trying to murder her teacher. Maybe things happened for a reason, she thought, trying to look brave. If she hadn't found this cave and stockpiled enough food for a week, and run away and been in the mine entrance when she was, then Miss Sisson might be dead by now. Or if not now, by tomorrow morning when they dumped the boxcar. As it was, Miss Sisson could rest here until she got her strength back, and then they could both make their get-away together. In the meantime, Maddie had to act as if nothing had happened. She would tell them she got scared in the woods and came back, her lesson learned once and for all. She wouldn't tell a soul what she'd seen. She explained all this to Miss Sisson, who nodded, though her eyes were closed and Maddie wasn't sure she was getting everything.

"Can't trust anyone," Miss Sisson mumbled.

"What if I e-mail my dad, tell him we need help?"

Annie shook her head once, wincing at the pain. "They

monitor the e-mail. It isn't safe. We'll just have to wait until I'm strong enough."

"But how will I know? How will I know you're all right?"

Annie tried to look around the small cave, thinking. It was obvious her head throbbed by the way she moved it. She closed her eyes again, unable to concentrate. Maddie felt the panic rise in her throat, but she hid it, trying to sound calm and authoritative for her teacher.

"Listen. I'm working in the machine shop now. Ben loads the boxcar at the end of the workday and sends it off every morning. It comes back empty during the morning shift. It wouldn't be that hard for me to peek inside the boxcar each day. All I have to do is get clean-up duty during the breaks. The kids all go outside and Ben sneaks off for a cigarette. I could look then."

Annie looked confused.

"See those reddish rocks in the corner?" Maddie asked, waiting until her teacher looked. "If you toss one into the boxcar each day I'll know everything's okay. If I don't see one, I'll know you're in trouble. You just have to stand at the door and toss them in. It moves pretty slow. Are you following this?" Miss Sisson was looking at her with big eyes. She nodded, though, and Maddie felt better.

"See the big rock? The speckled one? When you're ready to travel, throw that one. I'll come for you that night."

"How'd you get so smart?" Annie asked, a weak smile gracing her face. Maddie felt her chest fill with pride, but it was short lived.

"There's only enough food for a week," she said.

"I understand. If you haven't seen the big rock by then, go without me."

"No," Maddie said firmly. "If you haven't signaled me by the eighth day, I'm coming for you anyway." Her voice was as strong as she could make it. She didn't want Miss Sisson talking her out of it. "Okay?" she finally had to ask.

"Okay, Maddie. If you don't see the big rock before, come for me on the eighth day." She leaned back against the wall and closed her eyes. Maddie spent a few more minutes arranging the cave, making sure Miss Sisson had everything she needed within easy reach. Finally, she forced herself out of the cave, into the black depths of the mine, and headed back to camp.

"And you haven't seen her since?" Doc asked.

"No. I'm still waiting for the big rock." She furrowed her brow.

"What's wrong, Madeline. You seem concerned. I told you that everything is fine and you have nothing to worry about."

"The week was up today."

"That's okay, Madeline. I want you to take a deep breath and relax. We're going to talk about something else for a minute and then I'm going to take you back slowly to a complete state of well-being. You will not remember anything we've just talked about and you won't feel the least bit worried at all. Do you understand?"

"Yes."

"Are you worried at all right now? You don't need to be. Everything is perfectly fine and in a minute you won't even remember talking about any of this, isn't that fine?"

"Yes."

"Would you like to remember your mother's face, before we finish?"

"Yes."

"Okay, Maddie, close your eyes again and reach way back. Can you see her yet? She's right there if you want her to be."

For an instant, the image appeared and Maddie was filled with a sense of longing, wanting to reach out for her.

"Do you see her?" Doc prompted.

"Yes!"

"Good, Madeline. And you can take that image with you. It will be the only thing you remember from this session. Do you understand?"

"Yes."

"Very good. Now I'm going to slowly count backwards from ten, and with each number, you'll grow more and more awake until I reach one, at which point you'll feel totally refreshed and relaxed, not remembering anything but the image of your mother. Are you ready? Ten . . . nine . . . eight . . ."

When Maddie looked at the clock, she couldn't believe it. It felt as though she'd only been there a few minutes, but here Doc was ushering her out. She felt pretty good though. And for the first time in years, she could remember what her mother had looked like. It wasn't until later, after dinner, that she started to wonder what else she might have told Doc while hypnotized. But there was no time to dwell on it. Midnight marked the beginning of the eighth day.

Chapter Twenty-Nine

The second Gracie told us that Maddie had run off again, Jo and I leaped onto our horses.

"The machine shop," I said. "Come on! We need to hurry!"

The three of us raced across the meadows, startling a few sleeping horses as we tore through the darkness, past the stables and down the road toward the camp. When we got close enough to the cabins that someone might hear us, we pulled up and slipped out of the saddles. Our horses were winded and sweating and we left them to find their own way back to the stables, while we went the rest of the way on foot.

I led the way as we stealthily slipped past the cabins, then made a headlong dash for the wall surrounding the recreation area behind the machine shop. I still had the rolled up duct tape in my jacket pocket and I used it again to hoist myself up onto the tree. Gracie and Jo followed suit, and the three of us plunked silently into the recreation courtyard. I scanned the darkness for a sign of Ben. To my surprise, I could make out the single glowing tip of a cigarette about fifty feet away, just inside the open rear door of the shop. His back was to us. He was facing the mine entrance, smoking while he waited.

I motioned for Gracie and Jo to stay low, pointing to where Ben stood. Then I crept along the wall until I was out of his line of sight before dropping as quietly as I could to the ground. Gracie and Jo followed suit and we huddled in the dark, listening. Finally, taking a deep breath, I tiptoed across the recreation area grounds, keeping close to the building. I pressed my back to the open door, counted to three, and stepped around, into the open doorway, my gun drawn. Ben never heard me coming.

"Drop it," I said. He whirled around, his eyes huge. He had the semi-automatic held loosely at his side and for a brief second I could see he was thinking about bringing it up, but I cocked the hammer on my gun which was pointed directly at his forehead and Ben carefully set his weapon on the ground.

"Good choice, Ben. Where's Coach?"

"How should I know? What are you doing here?" His gaze darted over my shoulder as Gracie and Jo stepped into the doorway. Gracie came forward and retrieved the fallen semi-automatic.

"Is Coach supposed to flush them out this way?" I asked.

"I don't know what you're talking about."

"Sure you do, Ben. Doc told you to cover this entrance. Coach went through the other one. I just want to know whether you're part of the action or just a safety valve."

"Look. All I know is a kid ran away and Doc thinks they might've gone into the mine. I'm keeping a lookout, is all."

"With this?" Gracie asked, aiming the semi-automatic at him. "Kind of heavy artillery for a thirteen-year-old girl."

"I told you, I don't even know who the kid is."

"You're a lousy liar, Ben. I knew that the first time I talked to you. Your eyes go shifty and start sliding all over the place. It'll be interesting to see what they do when the police start asking you about where that gun came from. Especially when they see the blueprints on the disk I copied from your computer."

This time, his eyes practically bulged.

"So you gonna help us out voluntarily here, or does Gracie have to get tough?"

"I told you, I don't know what Coach is planning to do with them."

"Ah, so now you suddenly remember there's two of them. How long have you known she's alive, Ben?"

His face had turned ashen. "I don't know who you mean."

I turned to Gracie. "I don't have time for this bullshit. Do you?"

"Nope," she said. Faster than lightening, Gracie grabbed Ben's arm and yanked it behind him, practically lifting him off his toes. From her own jacket pocket, she produced the duct tape we'd used to climb the tree, and in a few graceful moves, she had gagged and bound Ben like a cowgirl trussing a calf in the rodeo. Ben struggled and mumbled incoherently to no avail. She liberated the walkie-talkie that was clipped to his belt and tossed it to Jo. She dug inside his pockets and came up with a thick wad of keys which she stuffed into her own pocket. From the other, she pulled out one of the remote controls for the electronic gates.

"This open the gate out front?" she asked.

He closed his eyes, refusing to acknowledge the question, lest he give away the answer.

"He's all yours," she said.

"Move," I said, waving the gun toward the tunnel entrance. Ben's eyes widened.

"Maybe your memory will get better after a few hours in the mine." I prodded him and he stumbled forward, clearly afraid of the darkness. But the minute we stepped into the mouth of the mine, I realized it was I who was petrified. The dream came rushing back at me and I could almost feel the air being sucked out of me.

"Faster," I said, disguising my fear. I was glad I still had the flashlight. Even with it, footing on the tracks was treacherous. Ben mumbled something unintelligible. He was not only pissing me off, but he was slowing us down.

"Ben, I'm going to give you a choice." I sounded much braver than I felt. "We're going to leave you tied up in here until the police arrive in the morning. The thing is, what I've read about bats is that while they can't see too well, they have a very acute sense of smell and are attracted by blood. Your first choice is, we leave you unbloodied. The second choice includes lots of blood. All you've got to do is tell me where Coach is and what he's planning."

He mumbled something and Gracie partially removed the gag.

"They're hiding in Isolation. That's all I know. What Coach does with them is his business."

"Where is Isolation?" I asked.

"Fuck if I know. Just follow the tracks."

"Put the gag back in, Gracie, and tie him to the tracks. Then catch up, okay?"

"Go," she said. Gracie's voice sounded funny and I suddenly remembered what she'd said about being claustrophobic. Consumed by my own worries, I'd forgotten about hers. But Gracie was nothing if not brave and this gave me strength.

Jo and I took off, moving through the dark mine as fast as we dared, the small beam from the flashlight bouncing along the tracks in front of us. We stopped every few feet and listened, then went forward again. Every time the tunnel curved, we slowed down, listening before rounding the bend. It was at one such juncture that Gracie caught up with us, barely winded.

With each minute that passed, my fear for Maddie grew. Coach had had too much of a head start. We reached a bend in the tunnel and slowed to catch our breaths. Just then, we heard a voice echoing off the wall ahead of us.

"I can't believe you're still here. I thought you'd run off! Put the stick down, for God's sake, Annie. I'm not going to hurt you. I was just looking for the kid."

"Stand back, Coach. Don't come any closer."

"Annie, what's happened to you? Don't tell me you've been down here in the mine all this time?"

We inched nearer, daring to get as close to them as possible without Coach seeing us. He was still around the bend from us, but I could see the light from his miner's cap ricocheting off the walls, illuminating the tracks in front of us in haphazard patterns.

"I said, back away. If you care about me so much, just go the other way and leave us alone." Annie Sisson's voice sounded strained.

"I don't understand. Don't you trust me?" Coach's voice sounded strangely convincing. "After everything we've been through, you think I'd come here to hurt you? If you're in some kind of trouble, I can help."

"I don't know what to think or who to trust." Annie sounded like her resolve was weakening.

I stepped around the bend and into plain sight. I had the gun trained on Coach.

"Drop the prod on the ground, Coach, and kick it over here," I said.

Coach looked up and his eyes narrowed with pure hatred.

"Get the fuck out of here," he snarled.

"Who are you?" Annie asked. She wasn't sure which of us posed the most danger. She was standing at the door of a cave just off the train tracks, protecting Maddie Boone behind her. Coach was a few feet away from them.

"You can't trust him, Annie. He's the one who cleaned out

your cabin and got rid of your car so it would look like you'd run off in the night. Only he forgot your grandmother's quilt hanging out back and the birth control pills taped under the top drawer."

I didn't know who looked more shocked, Annie or Coach. Gracie stepped up behind me and Jo followed. To Coach, it must have looked like there was no end to the number of us who might be waiting around the bend.

"She's lying," Coach said. "If there's some kind of plot going on, they must be in on it."

"How do I know you're telling the truth?" Annie said, looking from me to Coach.

"Maddie wrote a letter to her father. There was a hidden message in it. Her father didn't get it but her mother did."

"You're lying!" Maddie shouted. "My mother's in prison."

"Not anymore," Gracie said, stepping forward. "Your mother is my cousin. She got out a few weeks ago. She wants to see you, Maddie. Your father let her read your letter and she figured it out. That's why we're here. To help."

"Don't believe them, Maddie," Coach said. "They know about the letter because Doc monitors all the e-mail before it's sent. Now come with me while there's still time. I can help you get out of here."

"You gonna trust a guy who uses a cattle prod on kids?" I asked.

"Shut up, dyke. Come on Annie, we're running out of time."

"Ask him to throw the prod away, Annie. What's he need it for if he doesn't mean you any harm?"

"For protection against you!" he shouted. "You're the one with the gun."

Annie was looking from Coach to me and back again, unsure who to trust. Coach was holding his hand out to her. Gracie started to walk forward and Coach held the cattle prod out, warning her to stay back. Then in a surprise move, he lunged for Annie, who involuntarily stepped back. Instead, Coach grabbed Maddie by the hair and pulled her out into the tunnel.

"Stay back or I'll toast her," he said.

"You do and I'll shoot you right through the balls," I said, my gun leveled at him.

"You shoot, you're gonna hit the kid," he said.

"But I'm not," Gracie said. "You may stun her once but if you do I'm going to break your neck with my own hands. And then Cass can shoot you as many times as she wants. It may take her a couple of shots to hit the right parts, but I'm positive she'll do it eventually."

Coach still had his arm around Maddie's neck, the prod resting against her stomach, but he was watching Gracie as she walked slowly closer. On the other side of the track, Jo was also approaching.

"I mean it, I'll zap her if you get any closer." Maddie's eyes were huge but she stood stock-still, barely breathing.

"Not if you value your life," Gracie said. Her voice was deadly calm and Maddie, whose eyes had looked terrified a moment earlier, now watched her mother's cousin with awe.

Gracie reached out and put her hand on Coach's arm. "Let me have it, Coach. Before you do something you'll regret the rest of your life."

Coach's gaze darted from Gracie to me to Jo and back to Gracie again, calculating his odds. He could zap the kid, but once she was down, I'd have a clear shot at him. He could zap Gracie and hang onto the kid as protection from me, but I didn't think he was sure that Gracie would go down. And Jo was less than a few feet away. He couldn't take us all. Besides, once he grabbed Maddie, he'd lost his credibility with Annie. He backed away, still holding onto Maddie and lifted the walkie-talkie to his lips.

"Ben. Come in. Ben." He was startled to hear his own

staticky voice boom a few feet away and Jo pulled Ben's walkie-talkie out of her pocket, smiling as she stepped forward.

"Don't think Ben's gonna be much help," she said, waving it at him. Then Coach did something that surprised all of us. He let go of Maddie, pushing her toward Gracie, and lunged for Jo. He wrenched her arm backwards until she dropped the walkie-talkie. Then, in one quick motion, he pulled a gun from his pocket and held it against Jo's temple, holding Jo in front of him as a shield.

"Go ahead and shoot, Lesbo."

I realized that Jo made a better shield for him than Maddie had. Jo's face was twisted in pain as Coach slowly backed away from us. Gracie, who'd been inching closer to him, stopped in her tracks.

"Go ahead and try it," Coach hissed at her. His laugh echoed menacingly against the walls of the mine and I watched helplessly as he backed around the corner, taking Jo and the light from his helmet with him.

Gracie whispered in the darkness. "Once he's out of sight, he'll probably let her go and take off."

We were frozen in indecision, still listening to their footsteps, not wanting to do anything that might jeopardize Jo. Suddenly, horribly, a gunshot reverberated through the tunnel, painfully sounding as if a cannon had been shot off a few feet away. Before any of us could move, another shot came blasting around the bend and we all dove, hitting the ground as the bullet ricocheted off the tunnel walls around us. Gracie had dived on top of Maddie and lay sprawled over her, protecting her from the flying bullets. Annie was the only one safely hidden inside the cave. I was in the direct line of fire.

I rolled to my left and looked up, straining to see the form that stood less than fifteen feet away with a shotgun pointed in our direction.

I aimed my .45 at the shape, struggling to see in the dark.

"Put it down, girl," a voice calmly commanded. It wasn't Coach's voice. Could whoever it was see my gun that clearly?

"I can't," a different voice said. "They'll ruin everything."

"It's all right, honey. Just give me the gun. Then we'll go back and get your medication. It will be all right." Suddenly, the tunnel was illuminated and I blinked against the sudden light as Clutch Evans walked toward his wife, a miner's cap lighting the way.

"You don't understand," she said, still aiming the shotgun at us, her hands visibly twitching. Slowly I lowered my own gun and set it on the ground, raising my hands so she could see I was harmless. But Ida didn't seem to notice.

"Everything's falling apart. Annie found out about the guns and I couldn't just let her get away." Her voice had a revved-up, choppy quality and she was chomping gum between syllables.

"What guns?" Clutch asked, his voice deadly calm. He had his hand outstretched for Ida's gun, but hadn't moved any closer to her.

"You weren't supposed to know," she said. "Doc said you wouldn't stand for it. Even if they did start out doing it for a good cause." She was rhythmically swinging the gun between Gracie and me. Her voice had taken on a sing-song tempo, matching her movements.

"What good cause? What are you talking about, Ida?" Clutch took a small step forward, his eyes trained on Ida's.

She looked exasperated, on the verge of hysteria. "The guns, Clutchie. Ben and Doc started supplying arms to some stupid freedom fighters back in the Seventies. They were trying to overthrow a corrupt dictator or something. Doc thought he was saving the world. That's all I know and that's more than I ever wanted to know. They said it was for a good cause and I believed them. But then word got out to the wrong people and the next thing you know they're being blackmailed into supplying others. Everything got out of hand after that.

And now it's all falling apart! After everything I've done to hold things together!" Her eyes were glassy, the pupils non-existent.

"And you knew this? Oh, Lord, Ida. Why didn't you say something?" Clutch was struggling to keep his voice calm, and failing. Ida looked at him as if he'd slapped her.

"We needed the money, Clutch! The camp was barely holding its own. Until recently, I couldn't figure out why, but it was true. Month after month, the money didn't add up. Then I finally figured it out! Doc's been skimming the profits all along. To make me go along with their scheme, don't you see? They wanted me to think that without the guns, the camp would fail." Her voice was staccato now, and she smacked her gum between sentences, lending finality to each statement. She'd also started to bounce as she spoke, swinging the gun between Gracie and me as rhythmically as a cuckoo clock.

"Doc kept saying that this would be the last time. And then the next time would come along and he said that would be the last time. But it never was. Where was all that money, I wondered. Why, with the camp doing so well and the extra income from the guns, why weren't we rich by now?" She smacked her gum. "Wanna know why?" Her eyes, though unfocussed, seemed to demand an answer.

"Why?" Clutch obliged.

"Because Doc's been robbing us blind! He and Ben! There never was any inheritance. All those trips to Europe? That vacation home in the Bahamas? Every penny they've got was made right here. And Coach was in on it with them. Once he found out what they were doing, he made them cut him in, just to keep quiet. He had it coming, Clutch. He deserved what he got. He was going to ruin everything we've worked so hard for!"

"Okay, Ida. Let's just go back and rest a bit. We'll sort this all out. I'll talk to Doc. We'll get the money back."

"Don't you see?" she cried. "Doc's gone! He took the

money and ran! He left us to clean up his mess!" Ida had started to shake and the gun jerked about dangerously as her arms convulsed. "It's all falling apart, Clutchie! That's why we have to kill them all! It's the only way we can still save the camp."

"You don't mean that, Ida," he said, casting a worried glance at us. His eyes held less conviction than his words but his voice never wavered. "That's just your bad side talking. Let me just get you your pills and you'll feel better."

She was shaking her head. "It's to protect you!" she wailed, her voice finally giving way to hysteria. "You and the horse ranch!" Her eyes darted about as if unable to focus and Clutch seemed to notice for the first time that the front of her denim shirt was blood-splattered. Either Coach or Jo hadn't made it out of the tunnel. Maybe neither one. Clutch stepped back involuntarily but he managed to keep his voice low and soothing.

"And Belinda Pitt? Did you cut the cinch on her saddle to protect me, too?"

Ida slid a wild-eyed glance his way, then swung the gun back in our direction, still rocking, her head bobbing as she spoke. "She deserved what she got, Clutch. I know it wasn't your fault. A man has his needs. I understand that. But she had no right to take what was mine."

"You think I was screwing a sixteen-year-old? Oh God, Ida. I was trying to stop her from throwing herself at Coach, that's all."

"You met her that night!" she said, a surge of new strength in her voice as she turned the gun on Clutch.

"To make her go back to her cabin. She was bound and determined to go after Coach. I stopped her. That's all. Now give me that gun before you make things worse than they already are." He took three long strides toward her and held out his hand as if to take the gun but Ida had it trained on him, nearly pressing the barrel against his chest, her finger twitching on the trigger.

"If you're not with me, Clutchie, you're against me."

"That's not true, Ida. Please put down the gun."

But Ida's eyes had gone completely mad. Though my pulse was racing, my feet seemed rooted to the ground. It was just like the dream, I realized. The feeling of helpless paralysis. I was trapped by my own fear. If I didn't move, she might kill us all. If I did move, I might force her into it. I felt my throat clamp shut as the indecision turned to panic. Then I saw the look in her eyes and knew Ida couldn't stop herself.

"Watch behind you!" I shouted. Ida swung the gun in a violent arc toward the rear of the mine and I rushed forward, diving into her as the gun went off. The reverberating blast was deafening as Ida fell to her knees. I threw myself on top of her and grabbed for the gun but her grip was fierce and she struggled beneath me, trying to bring the gun around again. It took all my strength to wrestle it from her and as I did, she began pummeling me with her fists and feet. Finally, with Clutch's help, I was able to break free. Clutch grabbed her arms and held her. Then she began to jerk and convulse, every muscle and nerve twitching as he held her in his arms.

"Soon as we get you back, we'll get you some medication," he said soothingly, though I doubted she could hear him through her tortured convulsions. Over her shoulder, I could see his eyes were tearing. "You all better go now," he whispered. "Check on them." He glanced back the way they'd come, and his eyes were tortured.

I realized I was trembling. In a voice almost inaudible, I asked what I was most afraid to find out.

"Jo, too?"

Clutch just closed his eyes.

I raced forward around the bend into the darkness. The light from Coach's helmet illuminated the tunnel before me and I saw his body sprawled across the track. Jo's bloody body was beneath his. Heart pounding, I crept closer. Jo was on her stomach, pressed against the track. I couldn't see her face, but there was blood everywhere.

"Jo?" I whispered.

Slowly, she turned her head and faced me.

"Cass? Thank God. I thought she was coming back to finish me off. Get him off me!"

I was so relieved, tears blurred my vision as I pulled Coach's body off Jo and helped her to her feet.

"You sure you're not hit?" I asked, amazed at the blood.

I barely heard the others come up behind us. Clutch looked almost as relieved as I did that Jo was okay.

"Jo, I didn't know," he said.

Their eyes locked and hers looked almost as sad as his.

"I never doubted you for a minute, Clutch."

Gracie dug in her pocket and pulled out the electronic door opener she'd taken from Ben. "This open the outside gate?" she asked Clutch.

"Opens them all," he said. "My truck's parked right outside. You can take that if you want."

We did. We'd be back for our own cars in the morning, after the police had a chance to do their part. Right now, all any of us wanted was to get the hell out of Dodge. Maddie led the way, a miner's helmet that looked three sizes too big for her little head, lighting the tunnel in front of her. When at last we reached the entrance, the starlit sky seemed almost bright compared to the blackness of the mine. I gulped at the air gratefully and was surprised at how light I felt, as if a huge weight had been lifted. It took me a minute to realize what was missing. It was the fear. The relief that washed over me could have knocked me over.

I heard Maddie tell Gracie as they climbed into the back of the pickup that she had no intention of going back to her grandfather's house as long as she lived.

"It sounds like we both have some stories to tell," Gracie said. "You want to see a picture of your mom?" She dug in her back pocket for her billfold and Maddie stared long and hard at the picture, though it was probably too dark to see much.

"Is she really a murderer?" she asked, her voice small.

"Your mom? She's one of the sweetest, bravest women who ever lived. She made a bad mistake, Mad. She drove a car when she shouldn't have and got in a car accident. But the people who prosecuted her made a mistake, too. And now the judge has over-ruled them. Your mom has paid for her wrong-doing, Maddie. And she wants to see you."

As I climbed into the driver's seat, I heard the soft sound of a little girl crying with relief.

"You want to ride up here?" I asked Annie Sisson.

"Are you kidding? After a week in that mine, the only thing I need worse than a hot bath is fresh air. I'll ride in back with them."

"Guess you want to ride in back, too?" I asked Jo.

"No way," she said, sliding in beside me. She'd retrieved a horse blanket from the back and wrapped it around her to cover the blood on her clothing. As I drove up the driveway that led out of Camp Turnaround, Jo put her hand in mine.

As tired as I was, a sense of contentment washed over me. Maddie was safe. Annie Sisson was alive. And Jo Bell was sitting beside me.

For a moment, it almost seemed that all was well with the world. But I knew that Doc was out there on the road somewhere, Clutch was still back in the tunnel with Ida, Coach was dead, Ben was tied up in the mine, and that come morning, eighty-some-odd kids would be wondering why their camp was crawling with police. I sighed. As much as I longed to check into the Portsmith Grove Inn and make things right with Jo, I knew we had a long night ahead of us.

Epilogue

Sheriff Tom Booker was backing the horse trailer down his steep drive, one hand on the wheel, the other across the back of the front seat as he craned his neck to see behind him.

"Watch the left side," I called through the open window.

"He gets mad when you tell him," Rosie said. "Doesn't matter if he's about to drive off the cliff. He'd rather wreck the trailer than have someone tell him." Booker's wife was shaking her head. "I don't think I can watch this. Come on, Maddie. Maybe you should help me with the tamales."

"No way!" Maddie said. She seemed to realize that this sounded impolite and corrected herself quickly. "I mean. I will, but I want to see this first. Sheriff Booker says it's not every day he gets a new horse."

Rosie smiled as if she knew the kid would answer that way.

"How about you?" she asked Connie, winking over Maddie's head.

"Sorry, Rosie. Like Maddie said, it's not every day the sheriff gets a new horse." Connie winked back, looking almost as excited as Maddie. I couldn't get over how much alike they looked, standing side by side. And Connie looked so much healthier than she had that morning in my living room. Working on Booker's ranch obviously agreed with her. So did having Maddie back.

"Ay carrumba. Can't get any help these days!" Rosie walked back toward the house, but I noticed she stopped to watch from a distance, a satisfied smile on her face.

"That oughta do it, Tom," Jo called. She and Gracie were walking backwards down the steep drive, guiding Booker with hand signals. When he brought the truck to a halt and climbed out, Jo was already lifting the bar on the horse trailer, talking soothingly to the beast inside.

"Good boy. What a fine, young colt you are. Here we go, boy. Nice and easy. Let's just back out one step at a time, nice and easy. Good boy."

I glanced up at Maddie whose eyes glistened as she watched the black colt back out of the trailer. First came the shiny black tail, followed by the quivering haunches, the muscular legs, the silky black mane and finally, the familiar black face with the crooked blaze on its nose.

"Shadow Dancer!" Maddie whispered, her eyes huge.

Jo grinned and Connie clapped her hands, unable to contain her excitement.

"Is it really him?" Maddie asked, though she knew it was. She'd already rushed forward, and though the colt was nervous, he let her run her fingers down the blaze of his nose.

"I . . . I . . ." she stammered. "I can't believe it."

"He's yours, if you want him," Booker said. "That is, provided you take good care of him. Your mother's already got her hands full around here. You'll have to look after this one yourself."

Maddie's eyes filled with tears. She looked from Booker to her mother, to her Aunt Gracie, to Jo, unable to decide who to thank. Finally, she threw her arms around the colt's neck and buried her face in his mane.

"I think we did it," Jo said, grinning.

"By George, I'd say we did," Booker agreed. "Connie, why don't you and Maddie show this colt his new digs. I'm half-dying for a cold cerveza. Anyone care to join me?"

I watched as Connie and Maddie led the frisky colt toward Booker's stables. Jo slipped her hand in mine and we followed Booker and Gracie to the veranda where Rosie was setting out cold drinks.

"I appreciate everything you're doing for them," Gracie said, tilting her bottle toward Booker.

"Hell, I can use the help. Besides, it'll be nice to have a kid around. And that old cottage out there was just going to waste. Connie's already turned it into a right homey place."

"Still, you ever need a free hand with something, you know who to call."

"I appreciate that, Gracie. How about you Jo. You given any more thought to my offer?"

Once Booker had seen how Jo handled horses, he'd gotten it in his head that they should partner up. He was looking to expand his stable of horses but didn't have the time yet to train them. He'd be retiring in a few years and hoped to raise horses full-time.

"I guess I can paint in Oregon as well as Washington," Jo said. "It rains about as often."

Booker laughed. "That it does."

"What do you think?" Jo asked me. If she took the job with Booker, it wouldn't be just for a chance to raise horses.

"Isn't anyone going to help me with these tamales?" Rosie yelled from the kitchen.

The four of us got up and marched obediently toward the house.

"Well?" Jo asked again.

I waited, listening for the little voice that would no doubt warn me to play it safe, go slow, be smart, keep my distance. But the only voice I heard was my own, whispering into Jo's ear.

"Let's drive north tomorrow and pack your bags."

About the Author

Kate Calloway was born in 1957. She has published several novels with Naiad including *First Impressions, Second Fiddle, Third Degree, Fourth Down, Fifth Wheel, Sixth Sense, and Seventh Heaven,* all in the Cassidy James Mystery Series. Her short stories appear in *Lady Be Good, Dancing in the Dark,* and *The Very Thought of You.* Her hobbies include cooking, wine-tasting, boating, song-writing, gardening, and spending time with Carol. They split their time between Southern California and the Pacific Northwest; setting for the Cassidy James novels.

Publications from

BELLA BOOKS, INC.

The best in contemporary lesbian fiction

P.O. Box 201007 Ferndale, MI 48220
Phone: 800-729-4992
www.bellabooks.com

DEATH BY THE RIVERSIDE: The First Micky Knight Mystery by J.M. Redmann. 320 pp. Finally back in print, the book that launched the Lambda Literary Award winning Micky Knight mystery series. ISBN 1-931513-05-8 $11.95

EIGHTH DAY: A Cassidy James Mystery by Kate Calloway. 272 pp. In the eighth installment of the Cassidy James mystery series Cassidy goes undercover at a camp for troubled teens. ISBN 1-931513-04-X $11.95

MIRRORS by Marianne K. Martin. 208 pp. Jean Carson and Shayna Bradley fight for a future together. ISBN 1-931513-02-3 $11.95

THE ULTIMATE EXIT STRATEGY: A Virginia Kelly Mystery. 240 pp. The long-awaited return of the wickedly observant Virginia Kelly. ISBN 1-931513-03-1 $11.95

FOREVER AND THE NIGHT by Laura DeHart Young. 224 pp. Desire and passion ignite the frozen Arctic in this exciting sequel to the classic romantic adventure *Love on the Line.* ISBN 0-931513-00-7 $11.95

WINGED ISIS by Jean Stewart. 240 pp. The long-awaited sequel to *Warriors of Isis* and the fourth in the exciting Isis series. ISBN 1-931513-01-5 $11.95

ROOM FOR LOVE by Frankie J. Jones. 192 pp. Jo and Beth must overcome the past in order to have a future together. ISBN 0-9677753-9-6 $11.95

THE QUESTION OF SABOTAGE by Bonnie J. Morris. 144 pp. A charming, sexy tale of romance, intrigue, and coming of age. ISBN 0-9677753-8-8 $11.95

SLEIGHT OF HAND by Karin Kallmaker writing as Laura Adams. 256 pp. A journey of passion, heartbreak and triumph that reunites two women for a final chance at their destiny. ISBN 0-9677753-7-X $11.95

MOVING TARGETS: A Helen Black Mystery by Pat Welch. 240 pp. Helen must decide if getting to the bottom of a mystery is worth hitting bottom. ISBN 0-9677753-6-1 $11.95

CALM BEFORE THE STORM by Peggy J. Herring. 208 pp. Colonel Robicheaux retires from the military and comes out of the closet.
ISBN 0-9677753-1-0 $11.95

OFF SEASON by Jackie Calhoun. 208 pp. Pam threatens Jenny and Rita's fledgling relationship. ISBN 0-9677753-0-2 $11.95

WHEN EVIL CHANGES FACE: A Motor City Thriller by Therese Szymanski. 240 pp. Brett Higgins is back in another heart-pounding thriller. ISBN 0-9677753-3-7 $11.95

BOLD COAST LOVE by Diana Tremain Braund. 208 pp. Jackie Claymont fights for her reputation and the right to love the woman she chooses. ISBN 0-9677753-2-9 $11.95

THE WILD ONE by Lyn Denison. 176 pp. Rachel never expected that Quinn's wild yearnings would change her life forever.
ISBN 0-9677753-4-5 $11.95

SWEET FIRE by Saxon Bennett. 224 pp. Welcome to Heroy — the town with the most lesbians per capita than any other place on the planet! ISBN 0-9677753-5-3 $11.95